Thomas Wright

The Town of Cowper

The Literary and Historical Associations of Olney and its Neighbourhood

Thomas Wright

The Town of Cowper
The Literary and Historical Associations of Olney and its Neighbourhood

ISBN/EAN: 9783337367206

Printed in Europe, USA, Canada, Australia, Japan

Cover: Foto ©Andreas Hilbeck / pixelio.de

More available books at **www.hansebooks.com**

THE

TOWN OF COWPER

OR

The Literary and Historical Associations of Olney and its Neighbourhood

BY

THOMAS WRIGHT

PRINCIPAL OF COWPER SCHOOL, OLNEY

AUTHOR OF

"THE LIFE OF WILLIAM COWPER," "THE MYSTERY OF ST. DUNSTAN'S," ETC.

WITH PHOTOGRAPHS AND WOOD ENGRAVINGS

Second Edition.

LONDON

SAMPSON LOW, MARSTON, AND COMPANY

LIMITED

St. Dunstan's House

FETTER LANE, FLEET STREET, E.C.

1893

TO

JAMES WILLIAM CARLILE, Esq.,

OF

GAYHURST HOUSE, IN THE COUNTY OF BUCKS.

DEAR SIR,

 When I asked leave to dedicate to you "THE TOWN OF COWPER," you with great kindness acceded to my request, but at the same time were pleased to express your feeling that "such an honour should not have been offered to a stranger."

It is true that your connection with this neighbourhood has not extended over many years. And it is equally true that only a few months have passed since you first accorded me the pleasure of an interview; but during those few months I have been so greatly indebted to your kindness in connection with the collecting of material concerning not merely the history of your noble mansion, but also many of the other subjects to which I have given attention, that I feel it my bounden duty to make the only return in my power, and inscribe this small work with your name.

Kindly, then, accept it as a mark of gratitude and respect, together with sincerest thanks for your numerous favours.

 I have the honour to be,

  Dear Sir,

   Your humble servant,

    THOMAS WRIGHT.

PREFACE TO CENTENARY EDITION.

This edition is simply the Second with pages 3 and 4 revised and not a new issue. Since publication the old bridge referred to on page 17 has given place to a structure of iron. The gravel walk referred to on page 7 was sixty yards long, not thirty. The present pastor of the Baptist Chapel is the Rev. J. Samuel, of the Congregational Church the Rev. Thomas Scott.

Cowper Centenary Day,
    25 April, 1900.

COWPER'S HOUSE, OLNEY.

PREFACE TO SECOND EDITION.

SINCE the first issue of the "Town of Cowper" (May 1886) a good deal of new material has come to hand concerning the poet and his surroundings; my chief care, therefore, in revising the work preparatory to a second edition has been to bring it up to date. A few chapters dealing with occurrences not immediately connected with Olney have been omitted, but on the other hand several illustrations have been added, and the work has been enriched with notes kindly furnished by my friend Mr. Henry Gough of Redhill. The work is also indebted for various notes and suggestions to Mr. Yates Thompson, late of the *Pall Mall Gazette*, and the Rev. G. F. W. Munby, Rector of Turvey.

It is interesting to be able to state that a copy of "The Town of Cowper" was in all probability the last book read by the late Lord Tennyson. It was sent to him on September 23rd, 1892, as a slight acknowledgment of his kindness in responding generously to an appeal for pecuniary help made in behalf of Mr. James William Defoe, descendant of the great novelist; and the letter of thanks for it arrived on the 25th. The Laureate was taken ill a few days later, and died on October 6th. The notes received from the poet bear interest from the fact that they are autograph; but there is a far greater interest in knowing that one of the last acts of England's great

singer was a step towards the discovery of the " Holy Grail "
by an act of charity, and a pleasant conceit in the idea that
one of the last works to interest him was a book dealing with
a singer as pure and gentle as himself.

COWPER SCHOOL, OLNEY,
   October 1, 1892.

PREFACE TO FIRST EDITION.

NOTHING can be more appropriate than to speak of Olney as the Town of Cowper, for in this neighbourhood the poet lived for twenty-nine years, and wrote, with scarcely an exception, everything that he produced of any merit at all whether in poetry or prose. Of these twenty-nine years, nineteen were spent in Olney, and ten in Weston Underwood, a village with which from earliest times Olney has been closely connected. The following pages, however, will deal not only with the town itself, but also with the villages within walking distance, or, in other words, those that were, or could have been, frequently visited by the poet; for, as he himself remarks, it was to his feet, and to his feet alone, that he was indebted for transportation from place to place.

But we do not restrict ourselves to Cowper: we shall speak also of the other distinguished literary and historical personages connected with the neighbourhood,—the Digbys, the Throckmortons, the second Earl of Dartmouth, Newton, Scott, Sutcliff, Carey, and others; nor in noticing sites and objects hereabout shall we confine ourselves to those mentioned in Cowper's works, but shall take the opportunity to enlarge upon whatever has struck us as of peculiar interest, whether a stately mansion, a picturesque church, a sculptured stone, or a venerable tree.

Surely no other town in the kingdom has hitherto been treated so unfairly as Olney. Almost every person who has written on Cowper has given it a bad name! Here is a specimen of the way we are spoken of, and I take it from the "Introductory Memoir" of an excellent and well-known work, the Globe Edition of Cowper (first published, I believe, in 1870, but my own copy bears the date 1879), though I could easily point to a dozen other books containing similar and equally erroneous statements about Olney :—

"It is not an attractive town, and the staple occupations of its inhabitants, and the whole neighbourhood, lace-making and straw-plaiting, were, and still are, very prejudicial to health, wealth, and godliness."

Whether Olney is attractive or not, the reader that is unacquainted with the town will be able to judge for himself when he gets to the end of this work; but it is very certain that its staple occupations are not, and have not been for many years, either lace-making or straw-plaiting. Moreover, to represent Olney at the present day, as it has so often been represented, as unhealthy, poverty-stricken, and wicked, is giving a wrong impression of the town.

In the first place, it is one of the healthiest towns in the kingdom, one proof being that just before Christmas 1884 no fewer than thirty of its inhabitants were over 80 years of age; in the second, it is quite as wealthy as a town of some 2300 inhabitants can reasonably be expected to be; and in the third, although as regards religion there is ample room for improvement, we are decidedly in this respect in advance of very many other towns,—but it would be astounding indeed if the labours of Newton, Scott, Sutcliff, Gauntlett, and other laborious and self-sacrificing divines all counted for nothing. and Olney were a byword for its depravity. As a matter of fact, whatever Olney may have been in Cowper's time, it is now a quiet, industrious, respectable, and progressive place.

Many of the inhabitants are engaged in the shoe-trade. What though it sometimes appears desolate! A short time ago a visitor, after facetiously observing that "You might fire a cannon down the street all day, without injuring even a cat," inquired of a shoemaker, the only person to be seen, where the people were. "Where they ought to be," was the prompt answer, "all at work, sir!" Never again let it be imputed to us as a fault that our street is often empty!

In conclusion, and this is to me the most agreeable part of the preface, I beg to offer warmest thanks to those ladies and gentlemen who have so generously assisted in this under-taking; whether by permitting me to go over their mansions, houses, and grounds; by lending books and engravings; or by furnishing information in other ways. To the kindness of J. W. Carlile, Esq., of Gayhurst, I have already referred. My particular thanks are also due to Rev. J. P. Langley, M.A., Olney Vicarage; Dr. Macaulay of the *Leisure Hour;* Rev. J. Allen, B.A., Olney; Rev. J. Tarver, M.A., Filgrave Rectory; J. Garrard, Esq.; Rev. W. Sutthery, M.A., Clifton Rectory; and Rev. G. W. Wilkinson, Wainsgate.

COWPER SCHOOL, OLNEY,
May 1, 1886.

CONTENTS.

LIST OF ILLUSTRATIONS.

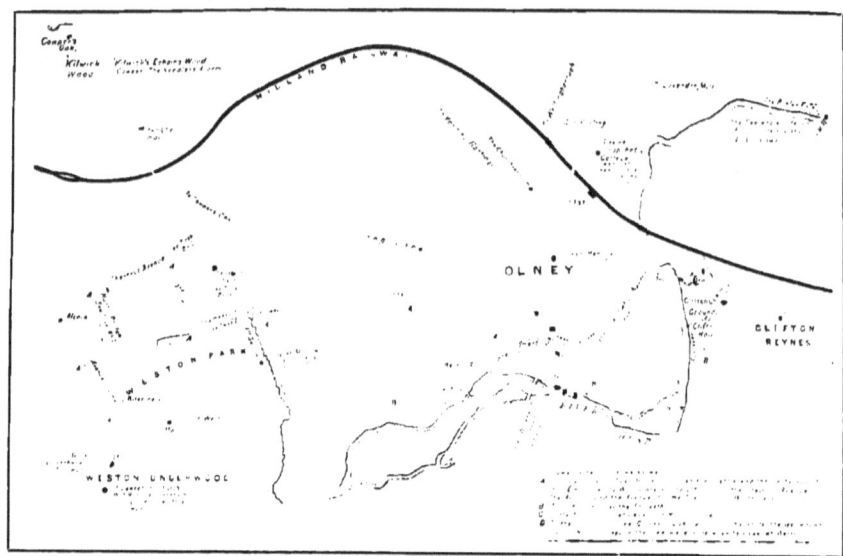

MAP OF OLNEY AND WESTON UNDERWOOD.

THE TOWN OF COWPER.

I.

COWPER'S HOUSE AND THE MARKET-PLACE.

I. Cowper's House.

The general appearance of Olney is probably familiar to all lovers of Cowper; even those who have never pilgrimaged hither have pictured to themselves its long broad street widening southwards into a spacious triangular market-place, the tall steeple with its bulging sides, and the silent river coiling half round the little town and winding tortuously through its meadows; and the fact, too, must be widely known that the large red-brick house, with stone dressings, sometimes called Orchard Side, that stands in the south side of the Market-place, was for nineteen years the residence of the poet Cowper. In his poetical epistle to Lady Austen, Cowper describes his house as

" Deep in the abyss of Silver End,"

an obscure part of the town, at the mouth of which stood two public-houses. Nothing, however, but poetical license justifies him in so describing it. We do not wish to give the idea that it was the most agreeably situated house in the town, for to live even on the verge of what was formerly the Alsatia of Olney must have been accompanied with certain disadvantages; but it faces the market-hill, its situation is far from unpleasant, and on the whole Cowper made himself very comfortable in it. It was by no means every day that the boys of Silver

A

End splashed his windows with mud, nor is it likely that the wailings of the infants of that locality were absolutely without intermission.   The accompanying engraving, which shows the house as it actually appeared in the time of Cowper, has never before been given to the public.   It is taken from a small etching (probably by Mr. James Storer) in my possession, which has written under it in neat lettering, "View in Olney,

COWPER'S HOUSE IN THE TIME OF COWPER.

(*The windows of the world-famous parlour are those between the two doors.*)

Bucks, Sept!. 1819," and, as the reader will see, represents the house with cornice and imitation battlements which hide the roof, and two doors instead of three.   The alteration to its present appearance is referred to in the following verse, taken from some clever lines by Mr. James Storer, that describe the various objects figuring in his large engraving entitled,

Photo by J. T. Newman, Berkhamsted.

MISS EVANS A' DRESSING THE CHILDREN.

By permission of the Editor of "The King."

THE DECORATIONS.

CENTENARY DAY AT OLNEY.

"A sketch from nature at Olney, Bucks, September 23, 1821:"—

> "That Mansion *late with mimic face*
> *Of architrave and frieze,*
> And kenn'd from many a distant place
> The Spire and Orchard trees,
> Departed times, impressive quote,
> When Newton preached and Cowper wrote."

To its castellated appearance Cowper himself refers in a letter of July 3, 1786. The first sight of the odd-looking place quite shocked Unwin. It seemed so like a prison, and he did not at all like the idea of his mother living in it.

The part of the house occupied by Cowper and Mrs. Unwin —for they never occupied the whole—was the western half, which is the farther of the two from Silver End. It should be borne in mind in reading this description that Cowper's house faces north. "You have not forgotten, perhaps," he writes to the Rev. W. Unwin (August 25, 1781), "that the building we inhabit consists of two mansions. And because you have only seen the inside of that part of it which is in our occupation, I therefore inform you that the other end of it is by far the most superb as well as the most commodious. Lady Austen has seen it, has set her heart upon it, is going to fit it up and furnish it, and if she can get rid of the remaining two years of the lease of her London house, will probably enter upon it in a twelvemonth."

On April 25th, 1900, the Centenary of the death of Cowper, Mr. W. H. Collingridge, of Enfield, generously presented the House to the Town and Nation, and in accordance with his wish Cowper's hall and the famous parlour adjoining have been fitted up as a Cowper and Newton Museum and Library. It contains a very rich collection of Cowper manuscripts, relics and other objects of interest connected with Cowper and Newton (including the original MS. of the Lines on Yardley Oak — eleven quarto pages in Cowper's handwriting), several original letters of Newton, a large number of books with manuscript notes by Newton, the famous Teedon's Diary, first editions of Cowper's works, and some valuable the oil paintings (all the gift of Mr. Collingridge); several original letters of Cowper including one to Lady Hesketh and one to Samuel Rose, portraits of Cowper, his father and mother and his friends, the warrant authorising the payment to Cowper of £300 a year, signed by King George III., and William Pitt, and hundreds of other interesting objects.

Other features of Centenary Day were an address on the Market Place to the children of Olney and Weston, delivered by Miss E. Evans; the singing by the children of Cowper's hymn, "God moves in a Mysterious Way"; a public Meeting in the Cowper Memorial Congregational Church, with addresses by Clement Shorter, Esq., Thomas Wright, Esq., and W. Ryland Adkins, Esq.; and an evening service in the church with sermon by Dean Farrar. The town was gaily decorated with buff and green, Cowper's favourite colours, and there was an enormous number of visitors.

At the back of the hall of Cowper's house may be seen the " port hole " through which Cowper's hares came leaping out to their evening gambols.

These hares were obtained in 1784, about seven years after Cowper came to Olney, and their names, it will be remembered, were Puss, Tiney, and Bess. Each had his peculiarities of character and temper. Puss at once grew familiar, allowed Cowper to carry him about in his arms, more than once fell asleep on his knee, and after recovering from a sickness of three days, signified his gratitude for the kindness shown him by licking Cowper's hand, "first the back of it, then the palm, then every finger separately, then between all the fingers, as if anxious to leave no part unsaluted."

Tiney was very differerent. " He too was sick, and in his sickness had an equal share of my attention; but if, after his recovery, I took the liberty to stroke him, he would grunt, strike with his fore-leg, spring forward, and bite. He was,

however, very entertaining in his way; even his surliness was
matter of mirth; and in his play he preserved such an air of
gravity, and performed his feats with such a solemnity of
manner, that in him too I had an agreeable companion."

> " Old Tiney, surliest of his kind,
>   Who, nursed with tender care,
> And to domestic bounds confined,
>   Was still a wild jack-hare.
>
> I kept him for his humour's sake,
>   For he would oft beguile
> My heart of thoughts that made it ache,
>   And force me to a smile." [1]

Bess, who was the largest and strongest of the three, died
soon after he was full-grown. "Puss was tamed by gentle
usage, Tiney was not to be tamed at all, and Bess had a courage
and confidence that made him tame from the beginning."

"These creatures," continues Cowper—for all along we have
been quoting from his charming paper in the *Gentleman's
Magazine* (June 1784)—"have a singular sagacity in discovering the minutest alteration that is made in the place to
which they are accustomed, and instantly apply their nose to
the examination of a new object. A small hole being burnt
in the carpet, it was mended with a patch, and that patch in
a moment underwent the strictest scrutiny. They seem, too,
to be very much directed by the smell in the choice of their
favourites! To some persons, though they saw them daily,
they could never be reconciled, and would even scream when
they attempted to touch them; but a miller coming in engaged
their affections at once; his powdered coat had charms that
were irresistible." Bess, as we noticed, died young; Tiney
lived to be nine years old; Puss to be eleven years eleven
months, dying of sheer old age. As the hall door opened
into the street, visitors, when the hares were out, were
"refused admittance at the grand entry, and referred to the
back door as the only possible way of approach."

"*Imprimis*," writes Cowper to Lady Hesketh (Feb. 9, 1786),

---

[1] Cowper: Epitaph on a Hare.

"as soon as you have entered the vestibule, if you cast a look on either side of you, you shall see on the right hand a box of my making. It is the box in which have been lodged all my hares, and in which lodges Puss at present. But he, poor fellow, is worn out with age, and promises to die before you can see him. On the right hand stands a cupboard, the work of the same author; it was once a dove-cage, but I transformed it. Opposite to you stands a table which I also made. But a merciless servant having scrubbed it until it became paralytic, it serves no purpose now but of ornament. On the left hand, at the farther end of this superb vestibule, you will find the door of the parlour, into which I will con-duct you, and where I will introduce you to Mrs. Unwin, unless we should meet her before, and where we will be happy as the day is long."

The parlour of world-wide fame, a room about thirteen feet square, has in front two windows (still retaining their shutters), and had formerly, besides the door opening into the hall, two other doors exactly opposite the windows, one opening on to a staircase, the other (now removed) belonging to a cupboard. The chimney is wainscoted, as are the walls for about a yard from the ground. As regards size, the parlour is now the same as it was in Cowper's time (when Hugh Miller visited Olney the parlour and Cowper's hall were one room, used as an infant school); but the door between the parlour and the hall was a couple of yards farther from the street than the present one.

The poet's favourite seat in the daytime was at the second window from the front door; but perhaps we like best to think of him in that room on a winter's evening, and to picture him giving expression to his well-known lines in the Fourth Book of "The Task :"—

" Now stir the fire, and close the shutters fast,
Let fall the curtains, wheel the sofa round,
And while the bubbling and loud-hissing urn
Throws up a steamy column, and the cups
That cheer but not inebriate, wait on each,
So let us welcome peaceful evening in."

The identical poker with which he used to stir the fire in this cosy parlour was presented in 1869 by a lady of Olney to the Bucks Archæological Society.

Working at his poems, writing letters to his friends, reading books of travels or his own productions to the ladies, or holding thread for them : in these pursuits the early part of the evening was spent. Then came supper, the most agreeable meal of the day ; and if Miss Catlett, Newton's niece, happened to be visiting at Orchard Side, Cowper of course could not resist having his little joke over about her name. "Now Miss Catlett," he would ask pleasantly, "shall I give you a piece of cutlet ?"

After supper the hares were admitted, when the Turkey carpet "affording their feet a firm hold, they would frisk and bound, and play a thousand gambols."

The poet's bedroom was the large one over the hall.

II. The Summer-House.

From Cowper's house a gravel walk of thirty yards extended to the summer-house, in which were written several of his minor poems and part of his translation of Homer. This tiny building, "not much bigger than a sedan-chair," which Cowper sometimes calls his boudoir, stands about half-way between his house and the Vicarage, but the garden containing it is now a separate property. It had formerly served an apothecary (Mr. Aspray) as a smoking-room, and in the floor is still a trap-door, "which," says Cowper, "covered a hole in the ground where he (the apothecary) kept his bottles ;" the same hole in which Mr. Bull, who visited Olney once a fortnight, used to keep his pipes and tobacco.

About half-way down the gravel walk which extended from the house to the summer-house stood until recently some cottages, the bottoms of whose lower windows were on a level with the garden ground, and it is said that the poet as he paced his walk could sometimes hear one of the cottagers, "an old breeches-maker," singing, as he worked, to the plaintive tune of Ludlow, the hymn beginning :

"O for a closer walk with God."

The tree of Ribstone pippins planted by Cowper, which stood near the cottages, has now disappeared. Of his garden

THE SUMMER-HOUSE.

he says, "The very stones in the wall are my intimate acquaintance—I should miss almost the minutest object."

Sir James Mackintosh, Hugh Miller, Elihu Burritt, and numbers of other distinguished personages have at different times visited the summer-house, and some of their autographs may be seen among the countless names that cover the walls and ceiling.

Cowper's greenhouse, in which he wrote "John Gilpin," and in all probability the greater portion of "The Task," has disappeared.[1] That it was quite distinct from the summer-house is stated by Cowper himself in a letter to Unwin dated June 12, 1785. To Newton (Aug. 16, 1781) he writes, "I might date my letter from the greenhouse, which we have converted into a summer parlour. The walls hung with garden mats, and the floor covered with a carpet, the sun too, in a great measure, excluded by an awning of mats, which forbids him to shine anywhere except upon the carpet, it affords us by far the pleasantest retreat in Olney. We eat, drink, and sleep where we always did; but here we spend all the rest of our time, and find that the sound of the wind in the trees and the singing of birds are much more agreeable to our ears than the incessant barking of dogs and screaming of children."

III. THE MARKET-PLACE.

To get an idea of the appearance of Olney in Cowper's day we must turn to our old sketches and lithographs. One view, taken, at the beginning of the century, from the end of Weston Road (or Dagnall Street, as it was then called), shows the old-fashioned shops with bow windows, the "Bull" with its sign-board and gilded grapes, then the "Saracen's Head" with its sign-post out in the road, and next, the narrow lane intervening, the shop of William Wilson, the poet's barber, showing bravely its parti-coloured pole. On the other side of the way we notice "the Swan"[2] (an inn in another part of the town is now so called), ornamented with a large wooden balcony— "the Swan," "where they are excessively careless," and "where letters are sometimes overlooked, and do not arrive at their destination, if no inquiry be made, till some days have passed

---

[1] In the first edition of this work the author erroneously treated the greenhouse and the summer-house as if they were one and the same.

[2] A private house now occupies its site, No. 6 High Street.

after their arrival in Olney." [1]   This was the inn to which the immortal postboy (" Task," iv.) used to consign his " important budget : "—

> " He comes, the herald of a noisy world,
>   With spattered boots, strapped waist, and frozen locks,
>   News from all nations lumbering at his back.
>   True to his charge, the close-packed load behind,
>   Yet careless what he brings, his one concern
>   Is to conduct it to the destined inn.
>   And having dropped the expected bag—pass on."

With Mr. Wilson the barber, who was one of the few persons to whom he would unbosom himself and talk with freedom, and whom he includes among " the men of best intelligence in the town," Cowper was exceedingly familiar. A very interesting relic that belonged to Mr. Wilson is a profile, on the back of which is inscribed, " Profile of Cowper the poet, taken from life by old James Andrews of Olney. It was done for Mr. Wilson, who well knew the poet all the years he resided at Olney—Sarah Wilson, 1858." Mrs. Wilson (who was thirty-two years younger than her husband) wrote these words a few years before her death, which occurred in 1869.

As the reader will see from our photograph of it in the frontispiece, this profile has a curious fault, the chin and lips being far too prominent.

Of Lady Austen and Mr. Wilson the following story is told. It was his custom to go out every Sunday morning to dress the hair of this lady. But about the middle of 1781, on account of religious compunctions (he was about to become a member of the Baptist Church), he sent word that although he should be only too happy to attend her other days, he could no longer do so on Sundays.[2]

At first thought the reader may not look upon this as a very great calamity to Lady Austen, but calling to mind the lofty and elaborate head-dresses of the last century, he will form

---

[1] Cowper.

[2] " The barber and hairdresser who officiates for me would not wait upon the King himself on a Sunday."—*Cowper to Rev. W. Unwin, June* 24, 1781.

some idea of the dilemma in which she found herself. Probably, too, whilst honouring the one, who sacrificed his interest
to his conscience, he will sympathise just a little with the other,
and think none the worse of her for being vexed and rating
Mr. Wilson roundly. All, however, to no effect; and as in
the small town of Olney there was only one barber (Cowper
adds, "one bellman, one poet"), she was obliged to have
her hair dressed on Saturday evenings. And we are told
that more than once she sat up all night to prevent its dis-
arrangement.

As every one will remember who has read Cowper's beautiful
lines about Voltaire and the cottager, the staple occupation of
the inhabitants used to be lacemaking. Let us take a peep
into one of the cottages. It is a winter's evening. A group
of three women are seated at their pillows, and a fourth is
turning her bobbin-wheel and filling the bobbins with thread.
In the midst of them is a three-legged wooden stool, upholding
a candle, in a wooden candlestick, surrounded by three flasks
of water with their necks inserted in sockets in the stool. Thus
with their pillows supported partly on their knees and partly by
a pillow-horse, also of three legs, and the candle-light reflected
by the flasks on to their work, they busily rattle their gaily-
spangled bobbins and marshal their regiments of pins. Their
expertness is amazing, and the work is done so regularly that
they can tell the hour by their pillows as easily as by the clock.
You can see, too, that the pillow no less than the lace is a subject of pride: some of the pins are large, and being furnished
with beaded or waxed heads, lord it magnificently over the
rank and file, and seem to act as colonels and lieutenants to
the Lilliputian army; the bobbins are particular objects of
emulation, for besides the plain and simple plebeians that
hang round in great profusion, there is a goodly sprinkling
of patricians, an æsthetic class, with carved initials or Christian
names on their elegant stems, or perforated with holes, and
exhibiting tiny columns (we have seen some beautifully carved)
—their spangles glittering with beads, shells, and coins. By
the fire are three pipkins, which a child is filling with hot
wood-ashes, and she will presently bring one to each of the

workers, who will draw it under her gown to keep her feet warm.

Then there were the lace schools, where some twenty or thirty children were tutored by old dames, who estimated their proficiency by the number of pins stuck in in an hour, and where to assist themselves in counting they chanted in a sing-song voice the amount of work to be got over :—

> " 20 miles have I to go.
> 19 miles have I to go.
> 18 miles have I to go."

These and the more elaborate songs sung at the pillow were called " Lace tellings."

At this time both men and boys as well as women and girls might have been seen at the pillow, but as the lace trade declined the former exchanged their bobbins and pins for the spade and flail.   Not a few old men, however, now living made lace early in the century; and some, curiously, after a life of rough labour, have turned to lacemaking again, in order to earn a few shillings at the pillow, since by reason of infirmities they are unable to work at anything else.

In the middle of the Market-place stood three fine elms, which overshadowed a curious old two-storeyed stone building called the Shiel Hall.   At the end facing north was a double flight of steps leading to the upper room, which answered for Olney the purpose of a town hall, and in which Samuel Teedon, the eccentric schoolmaster who had so much influence over Cowper, taught his pupils.   The word shiel, somewhat unusual in England, is used freely in Scotland for a place of shelter and a place where corn was winnowed when that operation was performed by the hand; moreover, it must be quite familiar to all readers of Burns, Scott,[1] and Hogg.

At its south end stood several houses and a blacksmith's forge.

To the north-east of the Shiel Hall was another conspicuous object, the Round House, Stone House, or town prison, a

---

[1] See last stanza of Burns's "Oh, leeze me on my spinning-wheel," and Scott's " Monastery," chap. xxix.

small hexagonal building; from which to the High Arch (the rise in the road near the Independent Meeting) and back again was the ancient whipping-distance for Olney.[1]   Thus in

THE SHIEL HALL (FEEDON'S SCHOOL) AND ROUND HOUSE.

(From an old drawing, the fault of which is that Cowper's House does not appear sufficiently distant from the Round House.)

the poet's time the Market-hill had four or five separate build-ings on it of one kind or another.   In his time, too, the main street of Olney was also singular in appearance.   A raised

<hr>

[1] See Cowper's amusing letter to Newton, Nov. 17, 1783.

pitched causeway with posts at regular distances ran down the
middle from the Swan Inn (in the Market-place) to "Simon
Johnston's" (where "the Queen" now stands, or thereabouts). [1]
It was kept in repair by a charity, called the Causeway Charity,
the origin of which is unknown, and was done away with in
1790 and 1791, when in lieu of it, and with the charity funds,
were made wide causeways or pitchings contiguous to the
houses. The necessity for such a causeway may not at first
thought be apparent; but in those days, it should be remembered, the roads were in a wretched state. Moreover, along
the west side of the High Street from Spout Lane (now Spring
Lane) to the High Arch ran a stream of clear water, which was
met by another stream which proceeded from the Yardley
Road. The combined waters poured through the High Arch,
and flowed thence into the river. The first mentioned was
the larger of the two, being generally about two yards in breadth,
but sometimes, of course, was much more formidable, and was
lined on one side by a row of willow trees. An old gentleman
of Olney remembers hunting for ducks' eggs along the stream.

The Shiel Hall was taken down about 1816, the Round
House about 1846. Of the three elms referred to, one seems
to have disappeared before the commencement of the present
century, another was blown down about 1832.

The third has at different times suffered cruel mutilation
from the winds; but the storm that broke over the town on
July 4, 1884, outdid all others in violence. After the pelting
rain and beating hail, accompanied by thunder and lightning,
had lasted about an hour, the wind increased in fury, and
another sudden and heavy downpour raised a dense mist.
About half-past three a crash was heard, and to the dismay of
the townsfolk, who ran out to see what was the matter, more
than half of the Market-hill tree was blown down, and the
ground covered with branches. "After receiving the shock,"
says a friend, "the part broken off, previous to falling, was
whirled round and round, and seemed for several moments
to hang suspended in mid-air." Then was witnessed one of

---

[1] For keeping the old causeway in trim, as the account books tell us, two
items were in constant requisition, namely, "besoms" and "bear."

COWPER'S FATHER.

COWPER'S MOTHER.

THE CENTENARY MEDAL.

MRS. UNWIN.

W. H. COLLINGRIDGE, ESQ.

the most curious scenes ever presented in Olney. The whole population, utterly regardless of the raging elements, poured into the street, and in a few minutes the Market-place was alive with people. Protected by an iron railing that has of late years surrounded it, the tree had been in a flourishing condition, and scores of starlings, sparrows, and bats had long held peaceful possession. The bats, thrown from their nooks and hollows, flew wildly overhead, and numbers of miserable fledgelings whose nests had been overturned fell helpless to the ground.

The poet himself had not infrequently to bewail the loss of his leafy favourites. "There was," he says in a letter to Lady Hesketh, dated May 1, 1786, "some time since, in a neighbouring parish called Lavendon, a field,[1] one side of which formed a terrace, and the other was planted with poplars, at whose foot ran the Ouse, that I used to account a little paradise. But the poplars have been felled, and the scene has suffered so much by the loss that, though still in point of prospect beautiful, it has not charms sufficient to attract me now." Thus in prose ; in poetry he mourns :—

> "The blackbird has fled to another retreat,
> Where the hazels afford him a screen from the heat,
> And the scene where his melody charmed me before
> Resounds with his sweet-flowing ditty no more."

In another letter we find him observing that the spinnie-trees "which screened me from the sun last summer would this winter be employed in roasting potatoes and boiling tea-kettles:"

> "Such various services can trees perform,
> Whom once they screened from heat, in time they warm ; "

and to-day we may apply his words to the tree he so often gazed upon from his parlour windows, for such doubtless has already been the fate of the greater number of its branches.

Its age is said to be about 280 years.[2] We use the present

---

[1] "Lynch Close," the field referred to, is near Lavendon Mill. Several poplars are still standing that have sprung up since the poet's day.

[2] During the reign of James I. Olney was holden by the Crown, and it is probable that the trees were planted to commemorate the union of the three kingdoms.

tense, for, notwithstanding the calamity just recorded, a very respectable portion is still standing, and not only standing but luxuriantly flourishing; and it will give pleasure to those who have not lately seen Olney to know that seven limes, planted a few years ago, now adorn the Market-place, standing each of them at a respectful distance, as is just and becoming, from the distinguished veteran in their midst.

II

OLNEY BRIDGE AT THE TIME OF COWPER.

"Hark! 'tis the twanging horn. O'er yonder bridge,
That, with its wearisome but needful length,
Bestrides the wintry flood."—*Task*, Book iv.

AMONG the curious relics of former days in the neighbourhood
of Olney, one of the most interesting is the narrow, irregular,
and comparatively ancient bridge that crosses the mill-stream
and unites the parishes of Olney and Emberton.   This structure
has altered but little of late years; but its continuation, the
famous bridge of twenty-four arches, referred to in the above
familiar passage about the post-boy with the welcome news-
sheet, has long since disappeared.

From an entry in the parish register we surmise that the
existing old bridge was erected in 1619.   The upper part is of
brick, the lower of stone.   It possesses three arches; the most
ancient arch, the one nearest the town, has conspicuous though
dilapidated dripstones, and, like other old bridges, its ascent
is rather steep.   On the left side of the road as you approach
the bridge from the town, where is now a shrubbery, there was
in Cowper's time a large shallow expansion of the river; and
opposite, on the other side of the road, stood the Anchor Inn,
the occupier of which was usually collector of what, from its
belonging to the Duchy of Lancaster, was called the Duchy
Toll.   There was no gate; but when sheep, pack-horses, and
other specified animals were driven up, a bar, attached at one
end to the bridge wall, was placed across the road, and the
animals being counted as they passed by singly, so many pence
were paid for each.

We come now to the bridge of "wearisome but needful

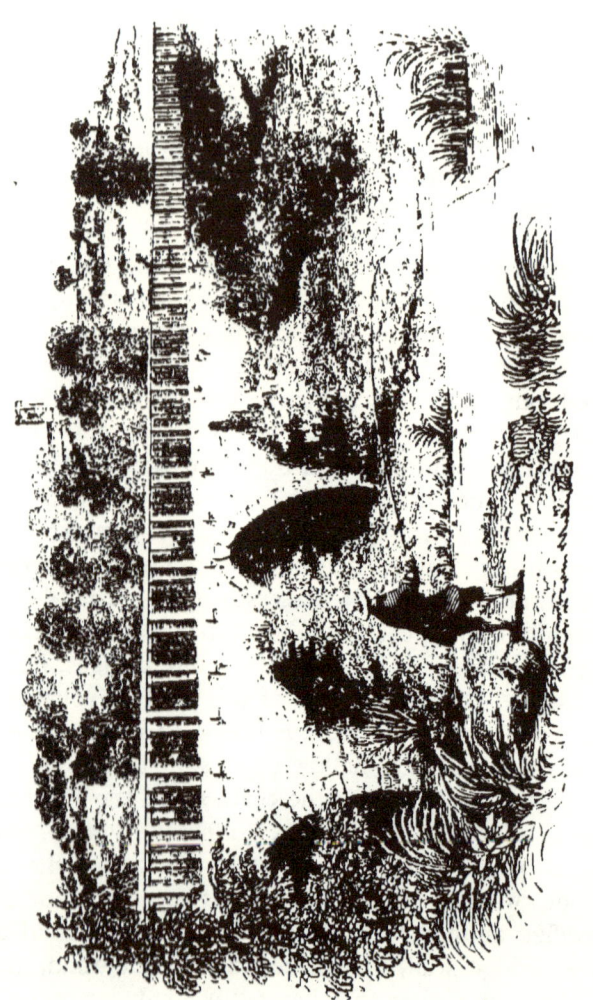

OLNEY BRIDGE AT THE TIME OF COWPER.

length ; " and concerning its origin the following story is told. In the reign of Queen Anne there existed between two of the most influential gentlemen in this neighbourhood a most cordial friendship : Sir Robert Throckmorton, of Weston Underwood, and William Lowndes, Esq., of Astwoodbury, Secretary to the Treasury, and for many years Chairman of Ways and Means in the House of Commons, hence commonly called " Ways and Means" Lowndes. These gentlemen were in the habit of visiting each other alternately and very frequently. There was at this time no bridge at Olney except the one just described ; and, consequently, those who would pass from Olney to Emberton were obliged, at the second arm of the river, to take the customary ford. But in consequence of the high floods, even this passage was often impassable ; so during much of the year all intercourse was suspended between the two friends. Sir Robert, to whom these isolations were especially distasteful, put up with the inconvenience for several years ; but at length, after a flood of inordinate duration, he declared that never again should the river prevent the meeting of him and his friend. So saying, he made for Astwood at his earliest opportunity, and proposed to Mr. Lowndes that they should build a bridge at Olney that should bestride the whole valley. " I will find the materials," said he, " if you will supply the labour." Mr Lowndes acquiesced in his proposal, and that very week was commenced the bridge that has since become so famous. Its appearance was most singular. The arches were at irregular distances ; the openings were of various shapes and sizes ; one was large and square, others were strikingly diminutive. Some had distinctive names, that, for instance, nearest the old bridge being called the Constable Arch. This causeway, which in the old engravings seems of interminable length, was lined on both sides by wooden railings, but in several places openings were left, so that, by means of stone steps, one could descend into the meadows. The two streams are now separated by a large plot of ground, but I am told by the gentleman to whom I am indebted for several of the particulars here mentioned, that in his childhood there was between them only a narrow strip, the Mill

Dam, which was strengthened on both sides by strong timbers that rose sheer from the water.

The whole length of this bridge, together with a view of the road at a distance, was, as Cowper observes, commanded by the chamber windows of the vicarage. Having become sadly dilapidated. it was in 1832 taken down, and the same year its successor, which still exists, was erected. Tedious as the road itself may have been, the prospect on either side embraced a hundred pleasant scenes. How beautiful, for instance, must the landscape have looked on that June morning in 1785 when the poet was on his way to Emberton to see the rector's tulips ! The meadow-land as well as the tulips could with correctness have been described as "a fine painting, and God the artist." On the right appear the steep of Weston Hill and the wooded slopes of Weston, whilst

> " Ouse, slow winding through a level plain
> Of spacious meads with cattle sprinkled o'er,
> Conducts the eye along its sinuous course
> Delighted ; "

on the left, the ancient mill, the aspens by the mill-stream, the great stone-steeple towering above them, and the embattled aisle peeping between; poplars, and willows, and hedges of hawthorn ; the Clifton uplands, the elmy fields of Emberton, and tips of far-away spinnies in Bedfordshire.

How fair in summer ! But how desolate in the dull days of winter, when the distant hills are wrapped in mist, and even the steeple is but faintly seen ; when the turbid streams sweep angrily and seethingly ; and the meadows are a monotonous lake with naked hedges and melancholy trees !

III.

THE ANCIENT CHURCH OF OLNEY AND THE LEGEND OF THE LORDSHIP CLOSE.

" It is not here, it is not here
That ye shall build the church of Deer."—*Old Rhyme.*

At the north end of Olney, near the commencement of the
road leading to the railway station, stands the ancient and
remarkable hollow-tree that time out of mind has been called
"The Churchyard Elm," a tree which, if for no other reason,
would deserve to be held in extreme veneration on account
of its great antiquity. It is supposed to be at least 600
years old. The Churchyard Elm it was called by our grandfathers and their grandfathers, and as every precaution, we
may be sure, will be taken for its preservation, the Churchyard
Elm it will continue to be called for many years to come ;
for the branches, which were too heavy for the trunk, having
recently been lopped off, it has sprouted again, and its venerable head is crowned with a rich profusion of vigorous green.
Its name, perhaps, to the casual visitor may cause some
surprise, seeing that Olney churchyard is half a mile away,
at the other end of the town. But the apparent mystery is
easily explained. In Saxon and Norman times this tree stood
on the boundary of the graveyard of an ancient church, the
first church of Olney, erected when Canute was king, and
possibly about the time he fought his famous duel with Edmund
Ironside, on the island of Olney, in the river Severn. It is not
because the island and the town have anything in common,
except the name, that we notice this little coincidence, which
after all may be mere conjecture, but because the island in
the Severn is one of the only two places in England, besides

our town, that are called Olney.[1]   The other is a moated field
ni Warwickshire, which Mr. Storer suggests may be the site of

THE CHURCHYARD ELM.   (*From a photograph.*)

a mansion belonging to the Olney family of Bucks, "a branch
of which was perhaps transferred to Warwickshire through the

---

[1] The origin of the first syllable of the word Olney is unknown ; the second,
the Saxon *ei* = water.

There is now a small town (population about 3000) called Olney in Illinois,
United States.

patronage of the Beauchamps, Earls of Warwick, of whose extensive domains the Buckinghamshire Olney so long formed a part."

That the ancient church previously alluded to was erected about the time of Canute has been inferred from an inscription discovered on a beam when the present church was repaired in 1800; and if such be the case, the diminutive island in Gloucestershire and the unpretending town in Bucks commenced their slender chronicles at one and the same time— slender, at any rate, as regards the latter, until the commencement of the eighteenth century. The ground near the tree, as we have already said, has long been called the old churchyard, and this designation occurs in the deeds of "the Castle," an adjoining public-house. On three or four different occasions human bones have here been discovered in great quantities. In 1881, at the time the foundations were being laid for the new cottages on the Feoffee Estate, several complete skeletons were unearthed.

Of the ancient church nothing is known; the building itself disappeared long ago, though its site probably continued to be used as a burying-ground until the Reformation, and the only name preserved that appears to have had any connection with it is that of the spring in the Home Close called "Christen Well." Probably, like most other Saxon churches, it was mean in appearance, and consisted of very little besides four thick walls; probably, too, it was dedicated with rejoicings out of all proportion to the magnitude of the building; and we have not the least doubt that, according to the inevitable custom of our ancestors, the incipient services were followed by substantial feasts and ales of extra strength.

About the year 1325, this old church having fallen out of repair, it was resolved by the inhabitants of Olney not only that a new church should be erected, but also that it should occupy a different site; and the one eventually decided upon was the field near the river, still called the Lordship Close. The foundations were laid accordingly; but imagine the surprise of the builders one morning on finding them not in the close where they had been placed, but in the adjacent field.

In spite, however, of their astonishment and fright, the workmen eventually summoned up sufficient courage to convey
them back to their original position ; and, this accomplished,
and night having drawn nigh, laid their foolish heads to sleep
again.   But in the morning the strange sight again met their
eyes ; not so much as a stone chip remained in the close, while
in the adjoining field their work was spread out with amazing
skill and precision.   Who had done it?   Certainly no human
being ! Angel or devil?   Some of the builders, comparing the
traditional activity of the latter with the pertinacity evinced by
the midnight toiler, were inclined to ascribe the deed to Satanic
agency, and in consequence strongly objected to have anything
more to do with the work.   It would be unpleasant, to say the
least of it, to have so disreputable a fellow-labourer.   Again,
it was not sufficiently clear what end was to be obtained by
conveying stones from one field to another by day when they
would be supernaturally removed by night; whilst were they
to build on the site preferred by the spirit, would they not be
acting in accordance with the will of the Evil One, and thereby
be consigning themselves to his keeping for ever?   Happily,
however, the more numerous party perceived, as did the priests,
that this occurrence could be none other than a message from
heaven, and, therefore, proposed to build the church on the
ground thus miraculously indicated.   Happily, too, the other
workmen, unable to refute the arguments of the majority,
honestly acknowledged the weakness of their own theory, and
once more resumed their chisels and hammers ; so, working
together with one heart, in due time the present church and
steeple of Olney were completed.

Similar traditions have attached themselves to at least two
other churches in this county, those of West Wycombe and
Quainton, and also to several churches of Northamptonshire.
At West Wycombe the edifice was originally intended to stand
at the foot of a hill, "but as fast as a portion of the building
was erected it was removed during the night by some invisible
agency, which deposited the materials at the top of the hill.
The nearest priest came with bell, book, and candle, and began
an exorcism, when a weird unearthly voice promised to abstain

from further annoyance if the church should be erected upon the spot to which the materials had been removed. This being done, the work proceeded without further interruption."[1] The people of Olney and Wycombe do not appear to have carried the stones back more than three or four times at the outside, but those at Stowe, or Stowe-Nine-Churches, as it is frequently called, a village near Northampton, had the pertinacity to replace them as many as nine times before they desisted and acquiesced in the desire of the night-fiend or goblin. From this occurrence the adjunct "nine-churches" is said to have been obtained. To the people of Stowe, moreover, an idea occurred that does not appear to have struck those at Olney: they set a man to watch at night; but they might have saved themselves the trouble, for his report was so vague and unsatisfactory that they could make neither head nor tail of it.

The origin of such traditions may sometimes be ascertained. That of West Wycombe seems to have been invented to explain the somewhat unusual fact that its church is built on a high hill.

As regards the adjunct "nine-churches" applied to Stowe, Baker, the Northamptonshire historian, asserts that it was received "because there were nine advowsons appendant to the manor." And perhaps the origin of the legend concerning Olney Church is to be found in the fact that many foundations, and these in all probability the remains of some religious house, are known to exist in the Lordship Close.

[1] A paper on West Wycombe by Mr. R. S. Downs.

IV.

OLNEY CHURCH.

In the Christian and literary world Olney Church is chiefly known as the sanctuary wherein Newton and Scott preached and Cowper worshipped, and as being the most conspicuous object in a district whose meadow and woodland beauties are stereotyped in "The Task;" but to all persons intimately acquainted with the neighbourhood, this ancient and noble structure, whose history is almost commensurate with that of the town itself, has naturally in numerous respects besides these a peculiar interest, not unmixed with love and veneration.

Olney Church, dedicated to SS. Peter and Paul, is almost entirely of the Decorated style of architecture, and was erected between 1325 and 1350; but by whom we cannot say. There is, however, in the north wall of the chancel an arched recess which is supposed by some to belong to the tomb of this unknown founder, but according to Mr. H. Gough it is the "Easter Sepulchre"—a usual appendage to a church of the Middle Ages. Olney Church in many respects resembles that of Emberton, and "there is much reason," thinks Mr. Storer, "to ascribe them both to the same masterly designer, one of the great though nameless architects of old, whose works—marred and disfigured though they be—still bear traces of an unearthly beauty." The nave, which had formerly a fine roof and a small clerestory of the Perpendicular era (destroyed about 1800), is divided from the aisles by five arches. At each end was originally a handsome latticed screen, one dividing it from the tower, the other from the chancel. Above the latter, called the rood-screen, was a gallery, the rood-loft, from which the Gospel was read at the morning service. On the rood-loft was raised the rood or figure of our Lord on the cross. Surprisingly beautiful were these screens of our ancient churches, for the artists and craftsmen of old spared neither time nor trouble so only they could produce a rich though cobweb-like appearance; and wrecks as most of them are of their former glory, those remaining in more favoured churches

OLNEY CHURCH. (*From a photograph.*)

than ours enable us to form an idea of their pristine wealth of splendid tracery and interlacing foliage, and their paintings of saints and confessors, kings and queens, bishops and apostles. The most interesting in this neighbourhood are perhaps the screens at North Crawley and Felmersham, the "Pride of Bedfordshire," as the latter beautiful church has admiringly been styled.

In former times there were doubtless in Olney Church at least two altars besides the high altar, and it is very possible that the image of the Trinity which was formerly in Olney Church, and before which Sir Thomas Digby willed to be buried in 1516, belonged to one of them. The small doorway through which the rood-loft was attained, which was in the wall northward of the chancel-arch, just under the tablet to John Thompson, was done away with at the beginning of the present century; and the last remains of the screen itself, some painted panels—representing probably, not, as was said, Elijah fed by ravens, but the legend of some saint—were destroyed in 1854.

The chancel, instead of being in a direct line with the nave, inclines considerably to the north, "a peculiarity mystically referring to our Lord's bowing down His head on the cross;" and the chancel-arch, like that at Emberton, dies into the side walls of the nave.

The two westernmost windows of the chancel, which are brought lower down than the others, are called Leper Windows or Lychnoscopes, because by means of them persons afflicted with leprosy could see the elevation of the host without entering the church; but, according to some, this peculiarity in the windows of churches has reference to the piercing of our Saviour's heart at the time of His crucifixion; hence they are also called Vulne windows.

On the epistle side of the altar, that is to say, in the south wall of the chancel, are, as is usual, the sedilia, or seats for the priests, and the piscina, or niche in Catholic churches, having a small hole at the bottom into which the priest emptied the water in which the chalice had been rinsed; and in the north wall is the ambry, or recess in which used to be kept the chalices, basins, cruets, and other sacred vessels.

There are now no brasses in Olney Church, but there were formerly at least two: one in the north aisle to the memory of "Elizabeth Parker, a woman whilst shee lived. lovinge to her husband, kinde to her children; Pittifull to the Poore, and a Pattern of a good Wife to all that knew her;" the other, which was on an ancient stone at the upper end of the south aisle, the portraitures in brass of a man and woman with a tablet at their feet.

The only gallery now existing—and this it is proposed to remove—is the one erected in the north aisle by John Newton, which contains the pew of the poet Cowper.

The earliest mention of a musical instrument in connection with the church is in 1520, when "Richard Cook, alius Squier, gave to a pair of organs here £6, 6s. 8d.," by which is meant, not that there were two separate instruments, but that the organ had more pipes than one, the word "organ," in those days, being used as synonymous with "pipe," and the word "pair" with "set."

The porch, above which is a small room with a fireplace used at the commencement of the century as a Sunday-school,[1] is of modern date, 1807, but occupies the site and incorporates the remains of a former porch, erected, as we should judge from the date on a square stone in front of the present one, in 1686. It is a somewhat unusual circumstance for a porch to be on the north side, but at one time there was a south porch as well. The tower has a fine west doorway, two light windows, and octagonal pinnacles at the angles; and the spire—the

> "Tall spire, from which the sound of cheerful bells
> Just undulates upon the listening ear"[2]—

is octagonal, rises from a cornice of masks and flowers, has four small lights with canopied heads, on the north, east, south, and west sides, each of which is surmounted with a cross, is 185 feet in height, and owes much of its nobleness of appearance to the *entasis*, or bulging of its sides.

Originally there were only four bells, of which the largest bore the inscription—

> "Ora pro nobis, virgo Maria."

[1] Before the Reformation the room over a church porch was called a parvise, and not infrequently a priest dwelt in it.   [2] Cowper: Task, I.

The present harmonious peal of six was recast out of the four in 1611.

The aisles are embattled, and the cornice to the chancel is rich in grotesque gargoyles,[1] masks, and flowers. Important restorations have gone on during the last few years : in 1870 the chancel was restored by the Earl of Dartmouth, when the stained glass window at the east end was given by Thomas Revis, Esq. ; and in 1873 a west window was given by Mrs. Welton of Olney, and a faculty was obtained for the removal of the west gallery, and for the restoration of the nave under the direction of Sir George Gilbert Scott,[2] who had also directed the restoration of the chancel. At the close of 1884 the top of the steeple was restored. At the same time the weathercock, which is 2 feet 9 inches from beak to end of tail, and 2 feet high, was taken down to be regilded ; and on it were found stamped the date 1829, the name of the Vicar, Rev. H. Gauntlett, the initials of the churchwardens at the time, B. C., J. H., W. L., and the following triplet, through which a bullet had pierced :—

> " I never crow ;
> But (sta)nd to show,
> Whence winds do blow."

The hamlet of Warrington is, and has always been, included in the parish of Olney : consequently in old books we frequently meet with the term Oulney-cum-Warrington ; but the inscription on the weathercock brought to our minds an old custom that had well nigh been forgotten, for on it are stamped the initials not merely of *two* churchwardens, as we should naturally have expected, but of *three*, an anomaly explained by the fact that the extra official represented Warrington. B. C., = Benjamin Coles ; W. L., William Lord ; and J. H., John Herring, the last of the race of Warrington churchwardens.

In the churchyard, at that corner formed by the mill garden and the Lordship Close, stood formerly a chantry or chapel to

[1] Projecting water-spouts. They are not infrequently figures of animals.

[2] Sir Gilbert Scott was born at Gawcott, near Buckingham, on July 13, 1811, and died in London on March 27, 1878. He was a grandson of the Rev. Thomas Scott the commentator.

the Virgin (erroneously styled the Earl of Warwick's chantry)
that originated with the last Lord Bassett of Drayton, and lord
of the manor of Olney, who endowed it that his soul might be
prayed for for ever. Most of the chantries belonging to our
ancient churches were destroyed by Henry VIII. at the dis-
solution of the monasteries (1536–1539); this one, however,
was standing as late as 1546; they were often lavishly enriched
with sculpture, beautiful tracery, and even with paintings. The
churchyard cross stood about midway between the north-west
angle of the tower and the wall of the Lordship Close. Its
base, for many years the only portion that remained of it, was
removed about 1800. Here pious worshippers would kneel
a moment and offer a short prayer preparatory to entering the
church; here, at times, services were held, and the officiating
priest would harangue his audience from the steps at its base;
and here, in those primitive times, when public buildings were
undreamt of, the town meetings were held; and the knight
or the farmer, the tradesman or the labourer, or anybody else
who had important business to transact, would be sure to
transact it at the churchyard cross.

Of the monuments in the churchyard, one of the most
interesting is that to the memory of Mrs. Newton's father, a
great invalid, who arrived in Olney in February 1776, and
remained here until his death in 1777. Only two of the
Vicars of Olney are known to be buried here, the Rev. Henry
Gauntlett and the Rev. Dr. Langley; a mural tablet, however,
to the memory of the Rev. Moses Browne is affixed to the
south wall of the chancel. Many of the well-carved gravestones, which are embellished with representations of angels,
skeletons, cherubs, and books, are the work of James Andrews,
the same who drew Cowper's profile; the best is that near the
porch, with a farmyard scene—a cut haystack, sheep, trough,
crook, shears, &c.; but unfortunately it has suffered much
from exposure to the weather. It is to the memory of William
Lambry, a pasture-keeper of Weston Underwood, who died
in 1779.

James Andrews taught Cowper drawing, and was called by
him "my Michael Angelo." "I draw mountains," says the

poet, "valleys, woods, and streams, and ducks and dabchicks; I admire them myself, and Mrs. Unwin admires them, and her praise and my praise put together are fame enough for me." In a letter to Mr. Newton he says, "James Andrews pays me many compliments on my success in the art of drawing, but I have not yet the vanity to think myself qualified to furnish your apartment."

On Andrews's stone to the memory of Charles Morgan, who died in 1795, aged seventeen, and Barbara Morgan, aged four, are the following lines, which are thought to have been written by Cowper:—

> " Let the gay youth review this solemn page,
> And see death certain here at every age;
> Not all the fondness that a mother knows,
> Nor all the sweet solicitude she shows,
> Can her loved offspring for a moment save,
> Nor snatch these objects from a greedy grave."

In the south aisle of the church is a mural tablet with a punning inscription to William Gaines, who died in 1657. The earliest gravestones in the churchyard whose inscriptions are legible are those of Robert Sharp (1667), Henry Belshare (1672), and Edmund Ball (1692).

The last is the coffin-shaped stone near the north-west corner of the tower; the inscription, which is difficult to read, being—

> " Edmund Ball, Died 11th Day of May 1692.
>
> My TIME is pass'd as you may see
> Prepare Thyselfe to Follow Me."

For the first fifty years or so after Olney Church was erected, Weston Underwood was merely a chapelry of Olney, and had not the right of sepulture; hence it is not improbable that the narrow way leading from the Weston Road to the churchyard, which bore the startling appellation of Dead Lane, now Lime Street, obtained its name from the fact that it was the lich-way or funeral-path along which bodies were brought from Weston.

V

THE VICARAGE.

" If pilgrimages formed part of the Evangelical course, the little town of Olney
should have attracted as many pilgrims as S. Thomas's shrine at Canterbury did five centuries before."—REV. J. H. OVERTON, *The English
Church in the Eighteenth Century.*

NUMEROUS and interesting are the associations that rise within
our minds at the mention of Olney Vicarage, the comfortable
and picturesque parsonage that was the residence at various
times of Newton, Cowper, Scott, and Gauntlett, of Lady Austen
and Lady Hesketh.

Until 1504 the benefice was a rectory, but the present
Vicarage occupies the spot on which stood the original parsonage.[1] The greater part of the ancient Rectory was rebuilt
by William Johnson, Esq., about 1642, at the time he enlarged[2] the " Great House," a spacious mansion that stood
between the church and the mill, of which we shall presently
have occasion to speak further ; but it was not until 1767 that
it assumed its present shape, being enlarged and almost rebuilt
by Lord Dartmouth for the Rev. John Newton ; "so that,"
says the latter, "from one of the most inconvenient, I have
now one of the best and most commodious houses in this
county."

Time has mellowed the appearance of the Vicarage, and the
newly built, "well-sashed" house of Cowper's letters is just
beginning to look venerable. The gates of entrance and

---

[1] The mistake of supposing that the " Great House " was the old parsonage
arose from the fact that the former was the residence of the Rev. H. Gauntlett
during the four years he was *curate* at Olney, and of some of the curates his
predecessors.

[2] The " Great House " was built previous to 1624, for there is a view of it in
the stuccos that were taken from the " John Brunt " house in Olney, and that is
their date.

egress for carriages are a comparatively recent institution, and what is now the carriage road once formed part of a dense shrubbery, to which belonged the acacias, laburnums, and lilacs that still partly screen the house from the street.

Of the rectors of Olney, Dr. Lipscomb mentions nineteen, beginning with Richard de Kenet, who died in 1263. Eight of them rose to high dignities in the Church, one, John de Buckingham (instituted in 1348), becoming Bishop of London. Concerning one of the early rectors, Master Nicholas Baching-denn, Mr. W. P. Storer relates the following curious circum-stance, which, as he observes, affords a strange contrast to the present condition of society: "It appears from the Hundred Rolls that in the fourth year of King Edward I. (1275-76), the Countess of Arundel, to whom the manor then belonged, with ten armed men, seized the men of Master Nicholas de Bach-ingdenn, rector of the Church of Olney, and imprisoned them, and forcibly took possession of three hundred measures of corn, two horses, two carts bound with iron, five cows, four sheep, two heifers, and ten swine, belonging to the rector—we need not be surprised that it is added 'to his no small loss.' We can hardly suppose that the Countess was *personally* concerned in such an act of violence, though very likely she was a party to it. Whether the reverend agriculturist obtained any com-pensation for this lawless deed does not appear."

The last rector was Henry Ainsworth, LL.D., who quitted Olney in 1504, when the living became a vicarage, and from that time to the present there have been twenty-five vicars.

In the time of Charles I., William Worcester, who had been inducted in 1624, was suspended, on account, in all proba-bility, of his Puritan practices and predilections, as appears from the following curious notice of the troubles of a towns-man of Olney, extracted from the "Lords' Journal" (February 9, 1640-41):—

" Petition of John James of Olney, but then of Earls Barton, against Samuel Clarke and Sir John Lambe (James being defamed went to Clarke as surrogate of the Supreme Court of Northampton): Clarke got defendants to turn witnesses against James, who could not get out of it, though there was

nothing against him. He was taken before the High Com-
mission Court, and had to pay £10 towards Paul's Church
(in London), pay the fees, a fine of £16, to the Court : he
gave Sir John a beaver, which cost the petitioner £4 more.
Afterwards the petitioner was cited to the Ecclesiastical Court
of Aylesbury in co. Bucks by the said Sir John Lambe and
Dr. Roane for going to hear a sermon from his own parish
church when William Woster the minister there was suspended : the petitioner was excommunicated unlawfully, and
when he was absolved they took the fees and £24 more for
fees, and forced him to subscribe, to stand up at *gloria patri*,
and to observe other ceremonies of the Church, and afterwards unjustly excommunicated the petitioner for being at
his own house with Mr. Woster and one other. All which
unjust proceedings of the said Doctor Clarke, Doctor Heath,
Sir John Lambe, and Dr. Roane have caused him to sell his
inheritance, and to spend above £100, and tended greatly to
his undoing." The Lords decided in James's favour, unless
cause could be shown to the contrary.

We come now to that succession of eminent evangelical
clergymen whose writings and other labours have made the
name of Olney so familiar throughout the Christian world.
The first of these was Moses Browne (born in 1703), who was
inducted into the living in 1753, and had originally been a
pen-cutter. He wrote several poetical works, and on the
institution of the *Gentleman's Magazine*, about the year 1730,
became a constant subscriber to it, and obtained some of
the prizes offered by Mr. Cave for the best poems. The
duty of deciding upon the respective merits of these composi-
tions devolved on Dr. Watts, and this led to the acquaintance
of Mr. Browne with that celebrated divine. It was not, however,
till he attended the services of some of the early evangelical
preachers that he began to view the things that concerned
his salvation in a clearer light, and that his sentiments and
conduct underwent complete revolution. Then it was that in
spite of the many difficulties that presented themselves he felt
a desire to enter the ministry ; and by the persistent efforts of
Lady Huntingdon, who began to interest herself in him, at

JOHN NEWTON'S STUDY IN OLNEY
VICARAGE.

length obtained ordination. Henceforward he gradually rose until he came to be regarded as one of the leading preachers of the Evangelical party. He commenced his ministry as curate to the celebrated Hervey of Weston Favell; from Weston Favell he removed to Olney, and after residing here ten years, was appointed chaplain of Morden College, Kent, and rector of Sutton, in Lincolnshire. Shortly after his appointment to the college chaplaincy he nominated as his curate at Olney that great and good man, John Newton. Mr. Browne died at Morden College in 1787, at the advanced age of eighty-four. His principal writings are poems on various subjects, "Sunday Thoughts" (1752), and a volume of sermons (1754).

Several of his sayings are preserved in the works of the Rev. A. Toplady.

On one occasion a friend said to him, " Mr. Browne, you have just as many children as the patriarch Jacob." "True," answered the divine: "and I have also Jacob's God to provide for them." At another time, in conversation with Toplady, he observed, "All the afflictions that a saint is exercised with are neither too numerous nor too sharp. A great deal of rust requires a rough file."

The Vicarage was occupied by Newton from May 1764 to January 1780, nearly sixteen years. The life and writings of this remarkable man will be dealt with in a subsequent sketch : but it must here be observed that the room used by him as a study is the one at the east end of the top of the house, with windows projecting from the roof. Over the mantelpiece may still be seen the wooden panel with the following texts in large lettering which he had painted on it :—

"Since thou wast precious in my sight, thou hast been honourable" (Isa. xliii. 4). " But thou shalt remember that thou wast a bondman in the land of Egypt, and the Lord thy God redeemed thee " (Deut. xv. 15).

In this room he wrote the Letters of Omicron and Vigil, the Olney Hymns, and that well-known volume of letters entitled "Cardiphonia, or the Utterance of the Heart." A few months after he left Olney, Newton thus humorously speaks of this room in a letter to his friend and spiritual son, the Rev. Thomas Scott—"Methinks I see you sitting in my old corner in the study. I will warn you of one thing. That room—(do not start)—used to be haunted. I cannot say I ever saw or heard anything with my bodily organs, but I have been sure there were evil spirits in it and very near me—a spirit of folly, a spirit of indolence, a spirit of unbelief, and many others—indeed their name is legion. But why should I say they are in your study when they followed me to London, and still pester me here?"

Twelve years after Newton left Olney, sitting in this same room as a visitor, he wrote to a correspondent in London the following words: "The texts over the fireplace are looking me in the face while I write. A thousand thoughts crowd upon me. What I have seen, what I have known of the Lord's goodness, and of my own evil heart, what sorrows and what comforts in this house! All is now past; the remembrance only remains, as of a dream when we awake. Ere long we shall have done with changes."

The poet Cowper, who had arrived at Olney on the 14th of September 1767, took up his abode for the nonce with Newton, and resided at the Vicarage from October 23 to December 7 of the same year; he was also at the Vicarage during the whole of that long derangement which lasted from April 1773 to the end of May 1774. The kindness of Newton to Cowper during this long and weary period exhibits a beautiful feature in his character. "Upon the whole," he says, "I have not been weary of my cross. Besides the submission I owe to the Lord, I think I can hardly do or suffer too much for such a friend, yet sometimes my heart has been impatient and rebellious."

About twelve months after Newton's departure, the Rev. Thomas Scott, famous afterwards on account of his Commentary, &c., became curate of Olney. Scott was at the Vicarage from spring 1781 to Christmas 1785, about four and a half years, during which period he published one of his chief works, "The Discourse on Repentance." This was written not in Newton's study, but in another room, where were his wife and family, for a separate fire was more than his purse

would allow ; and actually written, such was his indomitable
pertinacity, with a child on his knee or rocking the cradle !
No wonder he afterwards attained to fame—a man who could
write under such circumstances could do anything short of a
miracle. In October 1782, after Scott had been at Olney
about a year and a half, Lady Austen, the friend of Cowper,
came to lodge at the Vicarage, taking his first floor and other
accommodation he could easily spare ; and she remained here
for nearly two years.

It was in the room used by Lady Austen as a dining-room
that the incident occurred that suggested the subject of
Cowper's beautiful poem, "The Rose," the flower in question
being one given to Lady Austen by Mrs. Unwin.

> " The rose had been washed, just washed in a shower,
>   Which Mary to Anna conveyed ;
> The plentiful moisture encumbered the flower,
>   And weighed down its beautiful head.
>
> The cup was all filled, and the leaves were all wet,
>   And it seemed, to a fanciful view,
> To weep for the buds it had left, with regret,
>   On the flourishing bush where it grew.
>
> I hastily seized it, unfit as it was,
>   For a nosegay, so dripping and drowned,
> And swinging it rudely, so rudely, alas !
>   I snapped it, it fell to the ground.
>
> And such, I exclaimed, is the pitiless part
>   Some act by the delicate mind ;
> Regardless of wringing and breaking a heart
>   Already to sorrow resigned.
>
> This elegant rose, had I shaken it less,
>   Might have bloomed with its owner a while ;
> And the tear that is wiped with a little address,
>   May be followed perhaps with a smile."

The year after Scott left Olney Lady Hesketh took up her
abode in the Vicarage, where she stayed about six months (from
June 1786 to the following November).

In 1788, at the death of Moses Browne, the Rev. James
Bean became vicar, and resided at Olney. A sufficient

guarantee as to the excellence of Mr. Bean's character is the fact that he was loved and esteemed by Cowper, who observes (March 12, 1788), "He is a plain, sensible man, and pleases me much; a treasure for Olney, if Olney can understand his value." At Mr. Bean's request Cowper wrote a hymn to be sung by the children of the Sunday-school. Melville Horne became vicar in 1795, Christopher Stephenson in 1800; Henry Gauntlett was curate from 1811 to 1815, vicar from 1815 to 1834. The Rev. Henry Gauntlett was born on March 15, 1762, at Market Lavington, in Wiltshire, and at an early age was placed by his parents at the Grammar School, West Lavington. In 1786 he was ordained to the cure of the neighbouring parishes of Tilshead and Imber, and about the same time formed the acquaintance, which ripened into a friendship, of the Rev. Dr. (afterwards Sir James) Stonhouse, the gentleman introduced in Hannah More's "Shepherd of Salisbury Plain" under the fictitious name of Mr. Johnson. Mr. Gauntlett, who well knew the shepherd (David Sanders) and his family, furnished the authoress with some of the materials for this instructive and once popular narrative. In 1800 Mr. Gauntlett removed to Botley, near Southampton; thence he removed to Wellington (Salop), and thence to the neighbourhood of Reading. In January 1811 he came to Olney as curate to Mr. Stephenson, upon whose death, four years later, he succeeded to the living, being inducted on May 15, 1815, the day on which he completed his fifty-third year.

In 1813 he published "The Proverbs of Solomon, with Observations," and in 1821 his "Exposition of the Book of Revelation" (which rapidly passed through three editions), "being the substance of forty-four discourses preached in the parish church of Olney, Bucks, on evening services of the Lord's Day in the years 1819 and 1820." These and his other works were written in the study of his predecessors, the Revs. John Newton and Thomas Scott.

A pleasing incident in connection with the publishing of this "exposition" was the kindness to Mr. Gauntlett of Cowper's kinsman and friend, "Johnny of Norfolk." "The Rev. Dr. Johnson," says Mr. Gauntlett in his preface, "to whom I sent a copy of the prospectus of this work, in writing to desire me to consider him as a subscriber, informed me that, though he was at present in circumstances which kept him constantly employed, he might nevertheless have it in his power to procure me a few others. This modest and unsolicited pledge was redeemed by sending me immediately from himself, or through his respectable connections, names for more than two hundred copies." After its publication, Mr. Gauntlett received a large number of letters expressing the high degree of pleasure his work had yielded to his readers. In reference to these expressions of approbation and commendation, his daughter observes, "Such repeated testimonies to the excellence of this work from a numerous and superior class of readers were extremely gratifying to the author. Its publication was at the same time useful to himself, as by it he realised about £700."

Twenty-six of his sermons and a memoir of his life, by his daughter, were published in 1835.

In a Buckinghamshire Directory, of 1830, occurs the following passage :—

"In the literary world Olney has been long recognised as having had for its vicars and curates worthies of the highest literary attainments ; of the ten ministers who have resided here, from the year 1753 down to the present period, seven have been authors of valuable works, estimable either for their pious breathings, scriptural elucidations. or theological reasonings."

The names of two of the seven, John Newton and Thomas Scott, are familiar in every Christian household, not only in England, but in every English-speaking country ; but the renown of the other five, earnest, sincere, thoughtful, and pious as they probably were, has proved merely ephemeral, and their names call up in our minds no precious memories ; but, if they were faithful, they will have their reward, for, to adapt that beautiful saying of the Caliph Omar, uttered after a battle, when among the names of slain Moslems many were mentioned with whom he was unacquainted—"If we know them not, God does."

After the death of Mr. Gauntlett Dr. Langley was appointed vicar.

In 1856 he was presented to the Rectory of Yardley Hastings, by the Marquis of Northampton, when his son, the Rev. J. P. Langley, M.A., who had been curate here from 1852 to 1856, was inducted to the living.

Dr. Gauntlett.[1]—Dr. Henry John Gauntlett, the distinguished church musician, was the eldest son of the Rev. Henry Gauntlett, vicar of Olney. He was born at Wellington in 1805, and consequently when the family moved to Olney was about six years old.

There was at this time no organ in the parish church, the musical part of the service being performed by persons in the gallery, who played the trombone and bassoon. To Mr. Gauntlett, who was himself a good musician, this state of affairs was intolerable, and soon after he succeeded to the living he told the parishioners that if they would subscribe and buy an organ, he would undertake to provide an organist as long as he was vicar of the parish. He had intended that his two elder daughters, Arabella, then thirteen, and Lydia, ten years old, should play the hymn tunes, chants, and voluntaries arranged as duets, because he was afraid one child would not be able to produce sufficient effect in the large church. This arrangement, however, was never carried out, for his little son Henry, then nine years old, solemnly informed his father "that it was not fitting for girls to take such a prominent part in the service of the sanctuary, and that if his mother would teach him to play, he would be ready to take the service by the time the organ was built."

Six months later the organ was put up, and, remarkable to say, the promise was redeemed. Thus early did the youthful musician display his genius, and also his intense reverence for the house of God—a reverence which distinguished him all through life. He played the organ regularly in Olney church for more than ten years, and the crowds that came from the neighbouring villages to hear the vicar preach would remain after the service to hear the young organist extemporise on the organ.

---

[1] From notes kindly furnished by Mrs. Pole (*née* Matilda Gauntlett) and Miss S. M. Russell.

Soon after he had completed his twentieth year he was articled to a solicitor in London, and subsequently practised as a solicitor in that city; but his heart was not in his profession, and all his spare time was devoted to music. About 1838 he entirely severed his connection with the law, and took up music as a profession.

In spite of the most bitter opposition and unbelief, he designed the first Bach organs ever made in England. They were built by Mr. Hill, and erected in the churches of Christ Church, Newgate Street, and S. Peter's, Cornhill. There must be many who remember Dr. Gauntlett's magnificent performance of Bach's music on those noble instruments.

In 1841 he married a lady of Kent, who survives him, and by whom he had five sons and three daughters.

In 1843 he received at the hands of the Archbishop of Canterbury the degree of Doctor of Music, a distinction that had not been conferred upon any one since the time of Archbishop Sancroft and Dr. John Blow. From the year 1844 Dr. Gauntlett devoted himself entirely to church music. He created the present school of four-part hymn tunes or chorals; during the last forty years of his life he composed some thousands, and they remain unsurpassed for melody and perfection of harmony. The influence of Dr. Gauntlett upon church music has justly been compared with that of S. Ambrose, Luther, and Bach in their respective centuries. He has been styled "the father of church music;" and "The Church Hymn and Tune book, by the Rev. W. J. Blew, and Dr. H. J. Gauntlett," has been called the "father of tune-books."

Dr. Gauntlett died suddenly at his house in Kensington on the 21st of February 1876, and was buried at Kensal Green.

VI.

THE POET COWPER.

" Cowper is certainly the sweetest of our didactic poets."—Dr. DORAN.

" I have always considered the letters of Mr. Cowper as the finest specimen of the epistolary style in our language. To an air of inimitable ease and carelessness they unite a high degree of correctness, such as could result only from the clearest intellect, combined with the most finished taste."— ROBERT HALL.

" If there is a good man on earth, it is William Cowper."—LORD THURLOW.

I. FIRST THIRTY-SIX YEARS (1731–1767).

OF the places resided at or visited by the poet Cowper, it is natural that none should have been remembered by him with more affection than Great Berkhampstead; for here, in the Rectory House, on the 26th of November 1731, he was born, and here he spent the happy days of his childhood, becoming attached to every tree, gate, and stile in the neighbourhood, preferring his own house to a palace, and supposing as a matter of course that he and his father and mother were going to live in it always. His father, the Rev. John Cowper, D.D., was rector of the parish, and chaplain to King George II.; his mother, Anne, daughter of Roger Donne, Esq., of Ludham Hall, in Norfolk, was of the same family as Dr. Donne, the poet and satirist of James the First's reign. She died in 1737 at the age of thirty-four. Her affection and tenderness made such an impression on the mind of her son, that fifty years afterwards, on receiving her picture, he "dwelt as fondly on the cherished features as if he had just mourned her death." Writing to his cousin Mrs. Bodham, who had sent him the portrait, he says, "I received it the night before last, and viewed it with a trepidation of nerves and spirits somewhat akin to what I should have felt had the dear original presented herself to my embraces. I kissed it, and hung it where it is

THE OLD PARSONAGE (NOW DEMOLISHED), GREAT BERKHAMPSTEAD,
BIRTHPLACE OF COWPER.

the last object that I see at night, and, of course, the first on which I open my eyes in the morning." His lines "On the receipt of my Mother's Picture out of Norfolk" form one of the most beautiful and touching elegies in the language. How pathetic, for example. is the following :—

> " My mother ! when I learned that thou wast dead,
> Say, wast thou conscious of the tears I shed ?
> Hovered thy spirit o'er thy sorrowing son,
> Wretch even then, life's journey just begun ?
> Perhaps thou gavest me, though unfelt, a kiss :
> Perhaps a tear, if souls can weep in bliss—
> Ah, that maternal smile !—it answers—Yes.
> I heard the bell tolled on thy burial day,
> I saw the hearse that bore thee slow away,
> And, turning from my nursery window, drew
> A long, long sigh, and wept a last adieu !"

Soon after his mother's death. William, who was the elder of her two sons (John being at this time an infant), was sent, at the age of six, to a large boarding school, where he experienced much cruel treatment from older and rougher boys, and the two years spent there were remarkable only for their wretchedness.

He was removed on account of serious inflammation in his eyes, and placed under the care of an eminent oculist ; and at the age of ten, when sufficiently recovered, was entered at Westminster, where he was the schoolfellow of Warren Hastings, Elijah Impey, Robert Lloyd, Charles Churchill, Richard Cumberland, George Colman the elder, and Bonnell Thornton, all of whom rose to distinction and fame.

He left school when about eighteen, and after spending nine months at Berkhampstead, was sent to acquire the practice of law with Mr. Chapman, an attorney. But his time was spent not so much at Mr. Chapman's as in Southampton Row, with his cousins Harriet (afterwards Lady Hesketh) and Theodora, where, as he himself tells us, he and his fellow-student, Thurlow, the future Lord Chancellor, were " constantly employed from morning to night in giggling and making giggle, instead of studying the law." In 1752 he took chambers in the Temple, and here it was that he first experienced that melancholy and depression of spirits that afterwards assumed so serious a form.

Among his acquaintances at the Temple were Carr, Allston and Clotworthy Rowley, and it may have been to one of these that he wrote the earliest preserved letters of his, one of which is dated Feb. 21, 1754, and which begin "Dear Toby." He was also a member of a society of wits called the Nonsense Club, which included among its members Cowper's lifelong friend Joseph Hill. He was called to the Bar in 1754. In the meantime he had fallen in love with his cousin Theodora, the Delia of his early poems, but Mr. Ashley Cowper firmly refused his assent to the union. The decision of the father was accepted on both sides as final; Cowper took his farewell of her about 1756, and they never again met. After many years had passed by, when in the height of his fame, he received at different times several handsome presents from an anonymous donor, who, though he himself never suspected it, was doubtless his cousin Theodora. Now it was a writing-desk, the same that figures in his portrait by Abbot, now an elegant snuff-box, with a representation of the Peasant's Nest on the lid. Sometimes even sums of money came just as anonymously. Theodora Cowper died unmarried in 1825.

In 1756, shortly after the death of his father, Cowper bade his last adieu to Berkhampstead, its fields, and woods, and the old parsonage that was so familiar to him. Whilst at the Temple he was a member of the Nonsense Club, a society of literary triflers, Westminster men all of them, who dined together every Thursday; and he contributed a few papers to "The Connoisseur," and "produced several halfpenny ballads, two or three of which had the honour to become popular." He was now presented by his kinsman, Major Cowper, to the office of Clerk of the Journals to the House of Lords, a desirable and lucrative appointment, but doubly welcome to Cowper, for his patrimony was small, and fear of poverty was making his life miserable. But no sooner had he accepted it than he found he would be obliged to qualify himself at the bar of the House; and such was his sensitiveness, that the dread of the examination threw him into the deepest distress and misery. Having brooded over his accumulated troubles till worked up to a fit of madness, he attempted to commit suicide, and,

thereupon, was removed to a private asylum at St. Albans kept
by Dr. Cotton, where, although his health and reason were
regained in about four months, he stayed altogether a year and
a half. Through the kindness of his relations, his income
having been made enough to keep him, he determined not to
return to London, but to retire to some quiet place in the
country; and, so as to be near his brother John, who resided
at Cambridge, decided on Huntingdon. It was about the
time this change was made that he wrote the Hymns, "How
blest Thy creature is, O God," and "Far from the world, O
Lord, I flee," of which the latter contains the following well-
known and beautiful lines :—

> " The calm retreat. the silent shade,
>   With prayer and praise agree ;
> And seem by Thy sweet bounty made,
>   For those who follow Thee.
>
> There, if Thy Spirit touch the soul,
>   And grace her mean abode,
> Oh, with what peace. and joy, and love,
>   She communes with her God."

At Huntingdon he formed an intimacy, and took up his
abode with the Unwins, the amiable family with whose virtues
and graces his letters have made us so familiar. The father,
the Rev. Morley Unwin, was "a Parson Adams in simplicity,"
the daughter, Susanna, a young lady of eighteen, " handsome
and genteel ; " but to us the more interesting members of this
little circle are the mother, Mary Unwin, "of a very uncommon
understanding, who had read much to excellent purpose, and
was more polite than a duchess ; " and the son, William Caw-
thorne, known to posterity as the beloved friend and one of
the four most favoured correspondents of the poet.[1] In June
1767 Mr. Unwin met with his death from an accident, and
thereupon Mrs. Unwin and Cowper, towards whom " her behaviour had always been that of a mother to her son," resolved
to leave Huntingdon, desiring to remove to some town or village

[1] The other three were Rev. John Newton, Lady Hesketh, and Mr Hill.

where they would be under an evangelical minister of the Gospel. Whilst undecided whither to go, a visitor arrived, the Rev. John Newton, who had been requested to call on them by Dr. Conyers, a Cambridge friend of young Unwin, and it was soon arranged that they should come and reside either at Olney or the neighbouring village of Emberton.

II. Cowper at Olney.

1. *The Newton Period,* 1767–1780 *(about Twelve Years).*

At first Emberton was decided upon, the principal induce-ment being that the house they proposed to take was com-modious and well-built, and had a large garden. Cowper and Mrs. Unwin visited Olney on August 3, but had not made up their minds when they returned. The question was whether they should take a comfortable house at Emberton, with a mile of road, often well-nigh impassable, between them and Mr. Newton, or a less convenient house at Olney, where they would be close to him. On the 18th of August Newton writes to them : "I shall expect to hear from you soon, whether Mrs. Unwin pitches upon Olney or Emberton. I hope it will be the former ; but if the latter, you will not be far from us, and I shall try to see her, if the weather or roads should con-fine her from being constantly amongst us." This letter seems to have decided them, for at their request Mr. Newton engaged the house in the Market-place at Olney called "Orchard Side," the one now called "Cowper's House," and arranged that until it was ready for their reception they should take up their abode with him. It must be borne in mind that the sole motive which induced them to settle in this neighbour-hood was that they might be under the pastoral care of Mr. Newton.

They removed to Olney on September 14, 1767. The Vicarage, which Lord Dartmouth was renovating, was not finished until October 23, on which day Newton removed thither, Cowper and Mrs. Unwin accompanying him. It was not until December 9 that they at length settled at "Orchard

Side." These first three months were spent very happily. So far from being a recluse, Cowper, in company with Newton, visited all the country round. Now they are together at Kettering, now they are riding to Winslow; one day they walk to Lavendon Mill, on another occasion pastoral work calls them to Weston. "On September 19," writes Newton in his pocket-book, "breakfasted at Yardley, spoke from Matt. v. 6; at Denton, from Phil. iv. 4. Mr. Cowper went with me, a pleasant walk both ways;" and entries like "a pleasant walk with Mr. Cowper" are frequent in the record of Newton's pocket-book during this period. The intercourse between the friends now became close and affectionate. "For six years," says Newton, "we were seldom separate, when at home and awake." As his garden was divided from Cowper's by an orchard, they had a doorway made in the Vicarage garden wall to enable them to visit each other without going through the street, and paid a guinea a year for right of way; hence the name "Guinea Field," which has attached itself to the orchard. Much of their time was spent in visiting the poor, ministering to the sick, and praying at the bedside of the dying. In the midst of these labours Cowper lost his only brother John, to whose character and worth he alludes in "The Task," II.

In February 1771, one of their servants having fallen ill with the smallpox, Cowper and Mrs. Unwin were obliged to leave Orchard Side and take up their abode for a short time at "the Bull." Later on in the year, struck with the increasing gloom that was enveloping his friend, Newton suggested the writing of the Olney Hymns, in the hope that concentration of mind on holy themes would afford relief; but ere the former had completed his share the old and dreaded malady again seized him, and he was deranged for a third time (January 1773). A month later he had an awful Dream in which "a word was spoken," and this dream had such an effect on him that ever after he believed himself to be damned.[1]

The first of the hymns by Cowper is that entitled "Walking with God:"

---

[1] See the Author's "Life of William Cowper."

"Oh for a closer walk with God!
A calm and heavenly frame;
A light to shine upon the road
That leads me to the Lamb!"

By many this hymn is considered Cowper's masterpiece, but "Hark, my soul! it is the Lord," and "Jesus, where'er Thy people meet," are perhaps its equals; and the hymn of which the following is the opening verse is not less excellent:—

"Sometimes a light surprises
The Christian while he sings;
It is the Lord who rises
With healing in His wings:

When comforts are declining,
He grants the soul again
A season of clear shining,
To cheer it after rain."

"Jesus, where'er Thy people meet," was composed for the use of the worshippers at the "Great House;" the hymn on "Submission," was probably suggested by the loss of his brother John, as was also the beautiful hymn entitled "Welcome Cross:"

"Tis my happiness below
Not to live without the cross,
But the Saviour's power to know,
Sanctifying every loss;
Trials must and will befall,
But with humble faith to see
Love inscribed upon them all,
This is happiness to me."

The last written by Cowper, and perhaps the finest of all, is said to have been composed after the frustration of a plan to destroy himself:

"God moves in a mysterious way
His wonders to perform:
He plants His footsteps in the sea,
And rides upon the storm."

In consequence of his derangement the engagement of marriage which had been contracted between Cowper and Mrs. Unwin two or three years previously was broken off. They were to have been married in a few months. Mrs.

Unwin was now forty-eight years of age, Cowper forty-one.
After about fourteen months he slowly regained his mental
powers, and as he recovered began to amuse himself with
carpentering, drawing, gardening, and keeping pet animals, of
which at one time he had as many as twenty.

He also continued the delightful series of letters to his
friends. They are written in a beautiful and distinct hand,
and are almost without an erasure or a blot.

His correspondents during the Newton period were Joseph
Hill, Mrs. Cowper, and William Unwin.   Joseph Hill, his
schoolfellow at Westminster and his friend throughout life,
he describes as—

> "An honest man, close-buttoned to the chin,
> Broadcloth without and a warm heart within."

Mrs. Cowper was the sister of Martin Madan (attacked in
"Anti-Thelyphthora") and the wife of Major, afterwards
General, Cowper, the poet's cousin.   Mr. Unwin, Mrs. Unwin's
son, was at this time Rector of Stock, in Essex.   A great
change now took place in Cowper's mode of life; in 1780,
the year that Newton removed to London, he began to give
himself up altogether to literary work.

Before leaving Olney Newton introduced him to his friend,
the Rev. William Bull of Newport Pagnell, who for so many
years was equally beloved by them both.   Newton looked
upon a quiet pipe with "Dear Taureau" as one of the chief
pleasures of this life :—

> "A theosophic pipe with Brother B.
> Beneath the shadow of his favourite tree,
> And then how happy I ! how cheerful he !"

And Cowper, though no smoker, who had even been satirical
on smoking in one of his poems,[1] seems never to have been so
delighted as when he could get Bull and his pipe into the
Summer-house—"the smoke-inhaling Bull," "always filling,
never full."

Whether the influence of Newton on Cowper was beneficial
or injurious has long been a disputed point; consequently it

[1] See "Conversation," line 245.

will not here be out of place to lay before the reader the able
confutation by the Rev. J. H. Overton of the serious charges
that have been brought against Newton by those who have
laid the mental depression of Cowper at his door. Mr.
Overton, after pointing out that the germs of this distressing
melancholy which cast a gloom over Cowper's later years are
clearly traceable before his acquaintance with Newton began,
makes the assertion that the most that can be said is that
the depression of spirits was increased by his intimacy with
the pious and energetic curate of Olney, and then inquires
whether there is any real foundation for this supposition.   To
answer this question Mr. Overton examines the nature of the
relationship which subsisted between Cowper and Newton,
and points out that although at first sight no two men could
be more opposite in character, yet the differences were really
superficial.   Cowper's apparent effeminacy was all on the sur-
face ; "his mind, when not unstrung, was, as his letters as well
as his poems testify, of an essentially masculine and vigorous
type; whilst, on the other side, within Newton's hard and
rough exterior there beat a heart as tender and delicate as that
of a child."   "Newton," continues Mr. Overton, "had a point
of contact with every side of Cowper's character.   He had at
least as strong a sympathy with the author of 'John Gilpin'
as with the author of 'The Task.'   For one of the most
marked features of John Newton's intellectual character was
his strong sense of humour.   Many of his 'ana' rival those of
Dr. Johnson himself; and now and then, even in his sermons,
glimpses of his humorous tendency peep forth.   (See Fourth
Sermon on 'The Messiah.')   Again, he could fully appreciate
Cowper's taste for classical literature ; considering how utterly
Newton's education had been neglected, it is perfectly mar-
vellous how he managed, under the most unfavourable circumstances, to acquire no contemptible knowledge of the
great classical authors.   Add to all this that Newton's native
kindness of heart made him feel very deeply for the misfortune
of his friend, and it will be no longer a matter of wonder that
there should have been so close a friendship between the two
men.   It is readily granted that there was a certain amount of

awe mingled with the love which Cowper bore to Newton, but Newton was the very last man in the world to abuse the gentle poet's confidence."

Mr. Overton next examines seriatim the various counts of the indictment brought against Newton, pointing out—

(1.) That Cowper's mental depression was not even aggravated by Newton's Calvinistic views; for, in the first place, although Newton was a Calvinist, it was only in a very modified sense—the gloomy, repulsive side of Calvinism found no place in Newton's system; in the second place, Cowper never regarded himself as one of those predestined to be lost, do what they would, but, on the contrary, always held that he had once been a child of God. "To follow all the aberrations of a disordered intellect is of course impossible; but it is quite clear that the dreadful hallucination which possessed Cowper's mind had nothing to do with any of the five points of Calvinism."

(2.) There is no evidence to show that either hymn-writing or visiting the poor tended in any way to induce a return of Cowper's malady. "Newton may well have thought that the consciousness of being usefully employed was the very best means of diverting Cowper's mind from the gloomy thoughts in which a want of occupation would have given him leisure to indulge."

(3.) Newton ought not to be charged with narrow-mindedness because he disapproved of Cowper's translating Homer. "He thought that one who, like Cowper, was gifted with an original genius was capable of better things than merely reproducing another man's thoughts." And who among the poet's admirers at the present day can help regretting that five years were wasted over Homer?

(4.) It is not fair to accuse Newton of unwarrantable interference because he wrote from London "to inquire into the truth of a report which he had heard" that Cowper and Mrs. Unwin had entered "into worldly society." That meddlesome busybody of Olney (whoever he was) rather should be blamed that wrote and misled Newton, and consequently gave origin to a misunderstanding between the two friends. I cannot help thinking, too, it was the same informant that afterwards made unpleasantness between Cowper and Scott. Was it not said of old, "A whisperer separateth chief friends"?

2. *The Literary Period*, 1780-1786 (*about Seven Years*).

We now come to the most interesting portion of Cowper's life —the period at Olney during which were produced his principal works. Hitherto he had written nothing of merit besides two hymns composed at Huntingdon, and sixty-six others at Olney; for his "Early Poems" are devoid of intrinsic value. His history as a poet really commences in 1780. In the course of that year he wrote several short pieces for his own amusement; and then, at the instance of Mrs. Unwin, began and finished the "Progress of Error." This was rapidly followed by "Truth," "Table-Talk," "Expostulation," "Hope," "Charity," "Conversation," and "Retirement." A few minor pieces were added; and the volume, which was published in March 1782, met with moderate success, its merit being acknowledged, though grudgingly, by the most captious critics of the day. "The Task" has been read, and read again, by almost everybody, but these earlier poems, although containing many passages of exquisite beauty and a whole mine of Addisonian and Hogarthian humour, have been somewhat neglected. What can be droller than "the smirking, smart Abbé," in the "Progress of Error," "the Splenetic" in "Conversation," or "the Persian" in the same poem ?—

> "A Persian, humble servant of the sun,
> Who, though devout, yet bigotry had none,
> Hearing a lawyer, grave in his address,
> With adjurations every word impress,
> Supposed the man a bishop, or at least,
> God's name so much upon his lips, a priest ;
> Bowed at the close with all his graceful airs,
> And begged an interest in his frequent prayers."

What more exquisitely beautiful than the account of the two disciples journeying to Emmaus in "Conversation," the contrast between Voltaire and the Cottager in "Truth," or the lines on Whitefield (Leuconomus) in "Hope"? To quote from the last—

" He loved the world that hated him : the tear
  That dropped upon his Bible was sincere :
  Assailed by scandal and the tongue of strife,
  His only answer was a blameless life ;
  And he that forged and he that threw the dart
  Had each a brother's interest in his heart."

But perhaps the greatest charm of all is the abundance of delightful couplets, often proverbial verses, that, as Hayley says, "express a simple truth with perfect grace and precision." You meet with them on almost every page.   To take a few of the best :—

" None sends his arrow to the mark in view
  Whose hand is feeble or his aim untrue."
                              —*Progress of Error.*

" Called to the temple of impure delight,
  He that abstains, and he alone, does right."
                              —*Progress of Error.*

" 'Tis hard if all is false that I advance,
  A fool must now and then be right by chance."
                              —*Conversation.*

" Vociferated logic kills me quite,
  A noisy man is always in the right."
                              —*Conversation.*

" Where men of judgment creep and feel their way
  The positive pronounce without dismay."
                              —*Conversation.*

" A moral, sensible, and well-bred man
  Will not affront me, and no other can."
                              —*Conversation.*

" An idler is a watch that wants both hands,
  As useless when it goes as when it stands."
                              —*Retirement.*

In the summer of 1781 Cowper became acquainted with Lady Austen—the history of whose sojourn in Olney forms a subsequent sketch, "The Threefold Cord." "John Gilpin" was published anonymously in November 1782 ; and in July 1783, at the suggestion of Lady Austen, was commenced his great work, "The Task."

This poem, which was published in July 1785, has beauties on almost every page, but certain portions far outshine the rest; and we agree with Hazlitt that among the very finest must be reckoned the description of the preparations for tea (Book IV.), of the unexpected fall of snow (Book IV.), of the frosty morning, with the fine satirical transition to the Empress of Russia's palace of ice (Book V.), and the winter's walk at noon under the oaks and elms of Weston Park (Book VI., lines 57–117); but of equal beauty are the description of the walk by the Peasant's Nest and the Alcove in Book I., and the story of Crazy Kate; the last forcibly reminding us of that beautiful ballad of Gay's, "'Twas when the seas were roaring," for which Cowper in one of his letters expresses so much admiration.[1]

> " A serving-maid was she, and fell in love
> With one who left her, went to sea, and died.
> Her fancy followed him through foaming waves
> To distant shores, and she would sit and weep
> At what a sailor suffers; fancy too,
> Delusive most where warmest wishes are,
> Would oft anticipate his glad return,
> And dream of transports she was not to know.
> She heard the doleful tidings of his death,
> And never smiled again. "

The following passage from Book V. (lines 177–188) is also in his best style :—

> " Great princes have great playthings. Some have played
> At hewing mountains into men, and some
> At building human wonders mountain high.
> Some have amused the dull, sad years of life,
> Life spent in indolence, and therefore sad,
> With schemes of monumental fame; and sought
> By pyramids and mausolean pomp,
> Short-lived themselves, to immortalise their bones.
> Some seek diversion in the tented field,
> And make the sorrows of mankind their sport.
> But war's a game, which, were their subjects wise,
> Kings would not play at. "

---

[1] To Rev. W. Unwin, August 4, 1783.

But undoubtedly the noblest lines in the whole poem are those at the end of the Fifth Book, the "Address to the Creator." We can here give only the last eleven, but the reader would do well to turn to his "Cowper" and read carefully all of them.

> " Thou art the source and centre of all minds,
> Their only point of rest, Eternal Word!
> From Thee departing, they are lost, and rove
> At random, without honour, hope, or peace.
> From Thee is all that soothes the life of man,
> His high endeavour and his glad success,
> His strength to suffer and his will to serve.
> But oh, Thou bounteous Giver of all good!
> Thou art of all Thy gifts Thyself the crown!
> Give what Thou canst, without Thee we are poor ;
> And with Thee rich, take what Thou wilt away."

The acquaintance of Cowper with Mr. John Courtenay Throckmorton (afterwards Sir John) commenced in May 1784.

"You say well, my dear," he wrote to Lady Hesketh a few years later, " that in Mr. Throckmorton we have a peerless neighbour; we have so. In point of information upon all important subjects, in respect, too, of expression and address, and, in short, everything that enters into the idea of a gentle-man, I have not found his equal (not often) anywhere. Were I asked who in my judgment approaches nearest to him in all his amiable qualities and qualifications, I should certainly answer, his brother George."

The publication of " The Task " made its author famous, and his relations were now only too pleased to communicate with him. Their letters were warmly welcomed ; but the person with whom it gave him most pleasure to correspond was Lady Hesketh, and his series of letters to her is perhaps the most delightful in the language. As the reader is probably aware, the two most important editions of Cowper's letters are those of Grimshawe [1] and Southey. The former, however, has a very serious blemish, and one that should here be pointed out. Of course, as regards literary style and method of dealing with the subject, Grimshawe is a long, long way behind Southey.

---

[1] Grimshawe was Rector of Biddenham, near Bedford.

But that is not the point. His chief fault is that in many of the letters he leaves out the very cream. He also omits most of those droll or spicy little paragraphs with which so many of the letters are wound up. For example :

March 14, 1782, to Newton :—

"We return you many thanks, in the first place for a pot of scallops excellently pickled, and in the second for the snuff-box. We admired it, even when we supposed the price of it two guineas; guess then with what raptures we contemplated it when we found that it cost but one. It was genteel before, but then it became a perfect model of elegance, and worthy to be the desire of all noses."

Again, March 21, 1784, to Unwin : —

"Your mother wishes you to buy for her ten yards and a half of yard-wide Irish, from two shillings to two shillings and sixpence per yard; and my head will be equally obliged to you for a hat, of which I enclose a string that gives you the circumference. The depth of the crown must be four inches and one-eighth. Let it not be a round slouch, which I abhor, but a smart, well-cocked, fashionable affair. A fashionable hat likewise for your mother ; a black one if they are worn, otherwise chip."

Again, December 13, 1789, to Lady Hesketh :—

"Received from my master, on account current with Lady Hesketh, the sum of——one kiss on my forehead. Witness my paw,   BEAU [1] ×, his mark."

But even Southey's edition is extremely defective. In the first place, the so-called " Private Correspondence " having been refused him, he was unable to keep to chronological order ; in the second, through his misfortune in being obliged to copy Hayley, many of his letters are mutilated (though not so badly as those in Grimshawe) ; and in the third, many letters have been brought to light since. The author hopes, before many months have passed, to be able to put into the hands of the public the whole of Cowper's correspondence in consecutive order, with annotations.

In June 1786 Lady Hesketh visited Olney, and stayed at

---

[1] Cowper's little dog.

the Vicarage till the following November; tnen, thinking that a change of residence would be beneficial to Cowper, she hired for him the house called Weston Lodge, to which he removed on the 15th. His correspondents during the second period of his residence in Olney were the Rev. John Newton and Mrs. Newton, the Rev. W. Unwin, Joseph Hill, the Rev. W. Bull, Lady Hesketh and the Rev. W. Bagot, brother of Mr. Chester of Chicheley Hall.

III. WESTON UNDERWOOD, 1786-1795 (ABOUT TEN YEARS).

In November 1784, a few days after the completion of the "Tirocinium," Cowper had commenced a translation of Homer, and he now devoted almost the whole of his time to it. Within a fortnight after his arrival at Weston a heavy calamity fell upon him and Mrs. Unwin. This was the death of her only son, the Rev. William Unwin of Stock. Cowper was now fifty-five. The shock of his friend's death proved too severe for him, and in January 1787 he was deranged for the fourth time. In about six months, however, he suddenly recovered, and resumed at once his Homeric labours.

On February 25, 1790, he received from his niece, Mrs. Bodham, "the only picture of his mother to be found in all the world," a picture which he prized "more highly than the richest jewel in the British crown," and which inspired the beautiful elegy already alluded to and quoted.

In May 1791 the Rev. John Buchanan, curate of Ravenstone, who lived at the house in Weston now an inn under the title of "Cowper's Oak," made the observation to Cowper, that no poet, ancient or modern, had expressly treated on the four divisions of human life, infancy, youth, manhood, and old age, suggesting at the same time that it was a suitable subject for a poem. Pleased with the idea, the poet requested him to draw out his thoughts at length, and on Mr. Buchanan's compliance, wrote to him as follows :—"My DEAR Sir,—You have sent me a beautiful poem, wanting nothing but metre. I would to Heaven you would give it that requisite yourself; for he who could make the sketch cannot but be well qualified to finish.

But if you will not, I will, provided always, nevertheless, that God gives me ability, for it will require no common share to do justice to your conceptions."[1] Accordingly he made a start, hoping to produce a work of about the same length as "The Task." But of this intended poem only thirty-eight lines were written; it was laid aside for the lines on Yardley Oak, and this second remarkable fragment was in its turn laid aside for his notes on Milton. The last proved a complete failure, and Cowper often wished "this Miltonic trap" had never caught him; but out of it grew his acquaintance with the amiable Hayley, who afterwards became his biographer. In December 1791 Mrs. Unwin was seized with paralysis, and although she soon recovered, was never actually herself again. May 1792 saw Hayley at Weston; and in August of the same year Cowper and Mrs. Unwin paid the return visit to Eartham, near Chichester, where they remained for six weeks.

Whilst at Hayley's house at Eartham his portrait was drawn by Romney. A few weeks previously it had been painted by Abbot. A year later it was drawn by Lawrence.

There exist altogether five different likenesses of the poet Cowper, all of which are reproduced in our frontispiece.

1. The shadow or profile already spoken of, taken at Olney.

2. The oil painting by Abbot. Painted in July 1792 at Weston.

3. The portrait in crayons by Romney. Drawn in August and September 1792 at Eartham.

4. The sketch by (Sir) Thomas Lawrence. Drawn at Weston in October 1793.

5. A painting now in the possession of Earl Cowper, at Penshangar, Herts. It was painted after the poet's death, probably from the portraits by Abbot and Lawrence, and is ascribed to Jackson, R.A.

It will be interesting to speak more particularly of 2, 3, and 4.

Abbot's oil painting represents the poet in a periwig, green

---

[1] Mr. Buchanan was as much respected by the Throckmortons as by Cowper. There was always a place laid for him at dinner at the Hall.

coat, yellow waistcoat, and breeches; the first being probably the identical article concerning which he wrote to "Mrs. Frog" (Throckmorton) in March 1790—"My periwig is arrived, and is the very perfection of all periwigs, having only one fault; which is, that my head will only go into the first half of it, the other half, or the upper part of it, continuing still unoccupied. My artist in this way at Olney has, however, undertaken to make the whole of it tenantable, and then I shall be twenty years younger than you have ever seen me." The desk represented is the one already spoken of as the gift of his cousin Theodora. "My desk, the most elegant, the compactest, the most commodious desk in the world, and of all the desks that ever were or ever shall be, the desk that I love the most."[1] In a letter to Hayley (July 15, 1792) he writes—

> " Abbot is painting me so true,
>   That (trust me) you would stare,
> And hardly know, at the first view,
>   If I were here or there."

And a few days later he said to the same correspondent, "Well! this picture is at last finished, and well finished, I can assure you. Every creature that has seen it has been astonished at the resemblance. Sam's boy bowed to it, and Beau walked up to it, wagging his tail as he went, and evidently showing that he acknowledged its likeness to his master. It is half length, as it is technically but absurdly called: that is to say, it gives all but foot and ankle." Cowper thought Abbot's likeness of him the "closest imaginable;" and according to the Rev. Dr. Johnson, Lady Throckmorton ("Catharina"), and John Higgins, Esq., all friends of Cowper, it was a better resemblance than either Romney's or Lawrence's.

Romney was the contemporary and rival of Sir Joshua Reynolds. His portrait was regarded by Hayley as one of the most masterly and faithful resemblances he ever beheld. Romney himself considered it as the nearest approach he had ever made to a perfect representation of life and character. It had, however, an "air of wildness in it expressive of a dis-

---

[1] To Lady Hesketh, December 7, 1785.

ordered mind, which the shock produced by the paralytic attack of Mrs. Unwin was rapidly impressing on his countenance."[1] Cowper, as the following lines from a sonnet show, thought the picture an excellent one, and did not notice, though all his friends did, the "symptoms of woe" in it.

"To GEORGE ROMNEY, ESQ.,

"On his picture of me in crayons, drawn at Eartham, in the sixty-first year of my age, and in the months of August and September 1792.

"Romney, expert infallibly to trace
      On chart or canvas, not the form alone
      And semblance, but, however faintly shown,
The mind's impression too on every face,
With strokes that time ought never to erase ;
      Thou hast so pencilled mine, that though I own
      The subject worthless, I have never known
The artist shining with superior grace."

In Lawrence's portrait, as in Romney's, the poet is represented in the cap which he was accustomed to wear in a morning, presented to him by Lady Hesketh, the same immortalised in his lines entitled "Gratitude :"—

"This cap, that so stately appears,
      With ribbon-bound tassel on high,
Which seems by the crest that it rears
      Ambitious of brushing the sky ;
This cap to my cousin I owe,
      She gave it, and gave me beside,
Wreathed into an elegant bow,
      The ribbon with which it is tied."

After their return to Weston in September Mrs. Unwin's health rapidly declined, and she at length sank into a state of second childishness. The worse she became, however, the brighter burned Cowper's affection for her ; and it was in the autumn of 1793, whilst she was in this pitiable state, that he wrote those affecting stanzas "To Mary" of which the following are three of the most beautiful :—

[1] Grimshawe.

" Thy spirits have a fainter flow,
I see thee daily weaker grow ;
'Twas my distress that brought thee low,
    My Mary !

Thy needles, once a shining store,
For my sake restless heretofore,
Now rust disused, and shine no more,
    My Mary !

Thy silver locks, once auburn bright,
Are still more lovely in my sight
Than golden beams of orient light,
    My Mary ! "

The beautiful sonnet commencing, " Mary ! I want a lyre with other strings," was written in the preceding May.

The anxiety occasioned to Cowper by Mrs. Unwin's illness now began to tell upon him ; his gloom and melancholy came on again, and once more he sank into a state bordering on imbecility, from which he never fully recovered. A change of scene was thought to be desirable, and accordingly in July 1795 his affectionate kinsman Johnson conveyed the invalids into Norfolk.

Cowper's life at Olney appears, with the exception of the periods of derangement, to have been on the whole a happy one. When, however, the proposal was made that he should remove to Weston, the thought of the great happiness he was to enjoy in the more comfortable house, Weston Lodge, and in being so near the Throckmortons and their beautiful grounds, caused him to depreciate " Orchard Side," and to forget the happy days he had spent there.

The halcyon time he had so counted on, however, was of but short duration ; his malady increased as he advanced in years ; and instead of long periods of happiness interspersed with short ones of melancholy and madness, as at Olney, he gradually sank into an almost unintermittent state of gloom.

His manner towards children, and the light in which they regarded him, may be considered, perhaps, as matters of but little consequence, but they show that the Cowper of Weston was a very different person from the Cowper of Olney.

Calling to mind his allusion to "infants clamorous, whether pleased or pained," and other expressions in his works as little complimentary to the juvenile world, we might naturally suppose that he had little sympathy with their troubles or pleasures. But in reality it was the reverse of this at Olney; for, as many old persons have testified, he ever had a kind word for the children he came in contact with, and not infrequently, especially at Fair time, made them trifling presents. "Nanny Stowe," one of the last persons in Olney who remembered the poet, and who died, we believe, some thirty years ago, was proud of telling how, one Cherry Fair (June 29), when she was a child, he gave her money to go into a sway-boat which had been planted just opposite his house, and how they waved hands to each other, he at his parlour window, and she going up and down in the sway-boat.

At Weston he was spoken of very differently. When Dr. Eccles went there as priest in 1826, he was often told by the people that in their childhood, whenever they saw the poet, who, poor sufferer, though he took no notice of them, would not have hurt a hair of their heads, they ran frightened to the protection of their mothers, and were doubly alarmed if he happened to be in his dressing-gown and cap; for by this time his eccentricities and frequent attempts at suicide were bruited in every cottage in the parish.

IV. NORFOLK, 1795–1800 (ABOUT FIVE YEARS).

Dr. Johnson and his invalids first proceeded to the village of North Tuddenham, near East Dereham, where they were accommodated with an untenanted parsonage house, in which they were received by Mr. Johnson's sister and her friend Miss Perowne.

In August the invalids were taken to the village of Mundesley, on the Norfolk coast, so as to have the benefit of the sea air, and here they resided until October. From Mundesley Cowper wrote once more to his friend, Mr. Buchanan of Weston, his chief motive being "the desire I feel to learn something of what is doing and has been done at Weston (my beloved

Weston !) since I left it." "Gratify me with news from Weston ! If Mr. Gregson [1] and your neighbours the Courtenays are there, mention me to them in such terms as you see good." Cowper seems on his departure from Weston to have handed over his pets to Mr. Buchanan's mercy, for he writes—"Tell me if my poor birds are living? I never see the herbs I used to give them without a recollection of them, and sometimes am ready to gather them, forgetting that I am not at home." When Dr. Johnson and his invalids had explored all the walks in the neighbourhood of Mundesley, they made a journey by way of Cromer, Holt, and Fakenham to look at Dunham Lodge, a house to which they removed in October.

The few years spent in Norfolk were sad in the extreme.

It was told Dr. Currie by the Rev. Dr. Johnson that "Cowper firmly believed that good and evil spirits haunted his couch every night, and that the influence of the latter generally prevailed. For the last five years of his life a perpetual gloom hung over him—he was never observed to smile. I asked Johnny (Dr. Johnson) whether he suspected the people about him of bad intentions, and he said that he very often did. 'For instance,' observed he, 'he said there were two Johnnies; one the real man, the other an evil spirit in his shape; and when he came out of his room in the morning, he used to look me full in the face inquiringly, and turn off with a look of benevolence or anguish, as he thought me a man or a devil !'"

In the summer of 1796 the invalids were at Mundesley again, and finally in October of that year they removed to East Dereham.

Mrs. Unwin died on December 17, 1796, at the age of seventy-two. Cowper never afterwards mentioned her name.

On December 20, 1799, he wrote his last original piece, those pathetic and despondent lines entitled "The Castaway," and he died on the 25th of April 1800, in the sixty-ninth year of his age. He was buried on the 2nd of May in St. Edmund's Chapel, in the church of East Dereham, where a monument was erected to his memory with an inscription from

---

[1] Dr. Gregson, the priest at Weston.

EAST DEREHAM CHURCH, NORFOLK, BURIAL-PLACE OF COWPER.

the pen of Hayley. The poet, as we may see from the following lines from the end of "The Task," had once hoped that he
might be buried in Olney or his beloved Weston :—

> " So glide my life away ! and so at last,
> My share of duties decently performed,
> May some disease, not tardy to perform
> Its destined office, yet with gentle stroke,
> Dismiss me weary to a safe retreat,
> Beneath the turf that I have often trod."

"Cowper," says Hayley, "was of a middle stature, rather
strong than delicate in the form of his limbs ; the colour of

COWPER'S STOCK-BUCKLE.

his hair was of a light brown, that of his eyes a bluish gray, and
his complexion was ruddy." According to persons in Olney
who remembered him, he always walked with his head slightly
bowed, as if in thought, but was by no means sorrowful-look-
ing. He was unobtrusive and retiring, and to avoid persons
chancing to come towards him in his walks would go out of
his way, turn down a lane, for instance, or cross a field.

Among the relics of Cowper still preserved are :—His fly-
table and silver stock-buckle, in the possession of Mrs. Welton
of Olney ; his profile (see p. 10) and a chair (Mr. Hollingstead,
Olney) ; his Bible and one of his muslin caps (Rev. J. Barham
Johnson, Norwich) ; his shoe-buckles and coffee-pot (Mrs.
Higgins, Turvey Abbey) ; his watch, and the desk given to
him by Theodora (Canon W. Cowper Johnson, Northwold,
Norfolk) ; the MS. of "Yardley Oak" (Mr. W. H. Collingridge,

of the City Press, London) ; and his snuff-box, with picture of
Peasant's Nest and hares on the lid (C. A. Godfrey, Esq., 41
Devonshire Place, Portland Place, W.).

PRINCIPAL WORKS OF COWPER.

POEMS.

1. Early poems (published posthumously).
2. The Olney Hymns (the sixty-eight by Cowper were distinguished by a C), 1779.
3. His first volume of poems, 1782.
4. His second volume of poems, which contained "The Task,"
&c., 1785.
5. About sixteen short poems added in subsequent editions.
6. Posthumous poems of middle and later life.
7. Translations from Madame de la Mothe Guyon (published
in 1801); Milton (published in 1808); Vincent Bourne ;
the Latin Classics ; and the Latin of Owen. Translations
of Greek and English verses.
8. Translation of Homer.

PROSE WRITINGS.

1. His Letters. Some were published by Hayley in 1803 ; others
by Cowper's kinsman, John Johnson, in 1814. Grimshawe's Cowper was published in February 1835, Southey's
in October 1835. As soon as the copyright in the Private
Correspondence ceased, which Southey was debarred from
printing, it was placed at the end of his edition as a
supplement.
2. Memoir of the Early Life of William Cowper. A painful
narrative, written at Huntingdon when he was in a state
of despondency, meant only for the private reading of his
friends. It was not published till 1816.
3. Adelphi. A sketch of the life and character of his brother
John. Not published until 1816.
4. He also contributed a few papers to the second volume of *The
Connoisseur*, a weekly periodical, published in 1756.

VII.

THE REV. JOHN NEWTON.[1]

"So valuable are some of Newton's hymns, from their deep knowledge of the human heart, their experience of our wants, and their application to our need, that probably no hymns have ever been written which have given greater help to depressed and anxious minds."—J. C. COLQUHOUN, *W. Wilberforce: His Friends and Times.*

"In speaking of his characteristics as a letter-writer,[2] we have to notice mainly his intense earnestness. . . . They are often affectionate addresses, rather than vivid, various, and life-reflecting letters. But he could be witty and graphic. Many of his letters to Mr. Bull ('My dear Taureau') abound in playfulness, while his letters to Dr. Haweis are as graphic as anything in Scott."—C. MITCHELL CHARLES.

I. THE FIRST THIRTY-NINE YEARS (1725–1764).

JOHN NEWTON was born in London on the 24th of July 1725. His father, a stern and severe, but at the same time a sensible and moral man, was captain of a ship in the Mediterranean trade. Like Cowper, Newton at a very early age lost his mother (he was only seven when she died), a kind and affectionate woman, who made it the chief business of her life to instruct him, stored his memory with Bible truths, and "often commended him with prayers and tears to God." Abandoned as he became in early manhood, he never entirely forgot the lessons she had striven to inculcate, and, indeed, "afterwards considered his own case as affording much encouragement to parents to be diligent and persevering in the religious instruction of their children."

From his eighth to his tenth year he was at a boarding school at Stratford, in Essex, where he was severely and improperly treated, but whilst there made considerable progress in Latin.

---

[1] Founded on Newton's Narrative, his Life by the Rev. R. Cecil, and the Writings of Rev. Josiah Bull, M.A.

[2] Extracts from several of Newton's letters are given in "The Second Earl of Dartmouth."

When in his twelfth year he was taken to sea, and continued
to make voyages with his father until 1742. In the December
of this year his father, not intending to go to sea again, was
desirous of settling his son, and at length it was arranged that
he should go out to Jamaica with a Liverpool merchant. In
the meantime, being sent on business into Kent, Newton paid
a visit to some relations of his mother, by whom he was very
kindly treated, and upon making the acquaintance of their
daughter, Mary Catlett, fell in love with her, almost at first
sight. Speaking afterwards of this occurrence. Newton says,
" I was impressed with an affection for her which never abated
or lost its influence over me. None of the scenes of misery
and wretchedness I afterwards experienced ever banished her
for an hour together from my waking thoughts for the seven
following years." Feeling that it would be intolerable to live
at such a distance from her as Jamaica, and that for four or
five years, he determined not to go thither, and stayed in Kent
three weeks, instead of three days, in the hope (which was
realised) that the ship would sail without him. His father was
greatly displeased; but as there was no help for it, the Jamaica
scheme was given up, and Newton made a voyage to Venice.
Soon after his return (1743), owing partly to his own imprudence, he had the ill-luck to be impressed, and sent on board
the Harwich man-of-war. But his father, though unable to
obtain his release, was fortunate enough to procure a recommendation to the captain, who took him on the quarter-deck
as a midshipman. Thus a second time Newton had a capital
chance of doing well; but by breaches of discipline and other
imprudences he gradually lost all favour, and at length foolishly
determined to desert the ship while she lay at Plymouth. He
was discovered and brought back by a party of soldiers, put in
irons, publicly whipped, and degraded to a level with the lowest
sailor on board.

The ship was bound for India, but at Madeira, at his own
request, he was transferred to a ship bound for the Guinea
coast. Here again he might have fared well, for he found that
his new captain was a friend of his father; but we cannot
wonder at his troubles, for he tells us that one reason why he

rejoiced in the exchange of vessels was that he could then be as abandoned as he pleased without any control. When the ship was about to leave the coast he determined to remain in Africa; and, obtaining his discharge, was landed on one of the Plantanes, a group of islands near Sierra Leone, where he entered into the service of a slave-dealer. Being attacked by a severe fit of illness, he experienced the greatest cruelty from his master's wife, a black woman, who from the first had been strangely prejudiced against him. His bed was a mat, spread on a board; his pillow a log of wood. She lived in plenty herself, but hardly allowed the poor sufferer sufficient food to sustain life, and could scarcely be prevailed on to let him have a drop of water, though he was burning with fever.

Even after his recovery Newton's sufferings were intense; often he had to go about half-starved and ill-clad, and was sometimes exposed for as many as thirty hours together to incessant rains.

On this island he beguiled his wretchedness by studying a copy of Barrow's "Euclid," the only book that happened to have been brought on shore, making himself master of its contents by drawing his diagrams on the sand.

"I remember," he says, "that on one of these memorable days to which I have referred I was busied in planting some lime-trees. My master and mistress stopped to look at me. 'Who knows,' he said, 'but by the time these trees grow and bear, you may go home to England, obtain the command of a ship, and return to reap the fruit of your labours? We see strange things sometimes happen.'" Curiously enough, what was intended as a sarcasm turned out to be a prediction. Newton did return, commander of a ship, to that very spot, and plucked some of the first limes from those very trees! While in this deplorable situation he wrote to his father, who at once instructed a captain of a vessel then about to sail from Liverpool to seek for and bring his son home. In the meantime, having found another and a better master, Newton had become reconciled to his situation; so when the captain, after great difficulty, found him, he was at first disinclined to go; then he thought of Mary Catlett, and "the hope of seeing her, and still greater hopes," caused him to consent to embark.

Whilst returning home he spent his whole time in the greatest wickedness. Even the captain, who was not at all circumspect in behaviour, often reproved his profanity. But this voyage was the turning-point of his life. Several occurrences combined brought him to a sense of his folly and sin; but two were of particular effect—and before he had again reached England he had fully made up his mind to give up his evil habits. In the first place, he happened to pick up a copy of that remarkable book, "The Imitation of Christ," by Thomas à Kempis, and the thought darted through him, "What if these things should be true?" For a time he put aside his serious reflections and joined in the idle talk of his companions ; but another effective occurrence was at hand. The next day he was awakened from sleep by the force of a violent sea which broke on board. The water filled his cabin, and a cry was heard that the ship was sinking. In the awfulness of this storm he began to reflect on all his past life, and for the first time in many years made earnest supplications to God. "About this time," says Newton, "I began to know that there is a God who hears and answers prayer." He had no Christian friend with whom to take counsel, and consequently it was only very gradually that the truth in its fulness dawned upon his mind. Upon his arrival in Liverpool a kind friend named Mr. Manesty offered him the command of a ship, but this he declined for the present, and accepted the station of mate. The voyage, which was to the Guinea coast, commenced in August 1748. His duty was to sail in the long-boat from place to place, in order to purchase slaves. It may seem strange to us that a man who had just given up what he called his evil ways, and whose religiousness was certainly sincere, should, without scruple, engage in such business. In after years he himself unsparingly denounced the slave-trade, and confessed with shame that he had formerly been an accessory to so much misery and mischief. At the same time he observed, "Perhaps what I have said of myself may be applicable to the nation at large. The slave-trade was always unjustifiable, but inattention and self-interest prevented for a time the evil from being perceived."

His leisure hours were employed in picking up Latin, which by this time he had almost forgotten.

On his return to Liverpool he repaired to Kent, and was married to Miss Catlett in February 1750. He sailed for his first voyage to Guinea, as commander of a ship, in the following June, and returned to England in November 1751. During the interval between the preceding voyage and the next he was led, he tells us, into further views of Christian doctrine and experience by Scougal's "Life of God in the Soul of Man," " Hervey's Meditations," and the "Life of Colonel Gardiner" (killed at the battle of Prestonpans in 1745, fighting against the rebels). Some passages in the last affected him even unto tears, which he hoped proceeded from sincere repentance and shame.

His second voyage to Guinea as commander lasted from July 1752 to August 1753, his third from September 1753 to the following August.

Although Newton had no scruples as to the rightfulness of the slave-trade, he could not help thinking himself a sort of jailer, and was sometimes "shocked with an employment so conversant with chains, bolts, and shackles." On this account he had often prayed that he might be fixed in a more humane profession. His prayers were answered, but in an unexpected way. When about to set out once more, he was taken with a violent fit, which, although he recovered from it in about an hour, incapacitated him from taking the command of his vessel.

In August 1755 he obtained an appointment of tide surveyor of the port of Liverpool, and "his circumstances became as smooth and uniform as they had before been stormy and various."

The leisure now at his command he spent in study, and before he had been long at Liverpool began to turn his attention towards the work of the ministry. Whether to go into the Established Church or to join with the Dissenters he was undecided. At first he inclined towards the latter, and preached for six weeks on probation to the Independents of Warwick, but it is said that the disputes which he knew to be common in so many Dissenting congregations at that time caused him to decide for the Establishment. During his resi-

dence at Liverpool he enjoyed the privilege of an intimate
acquaintance with Whitefield and Wesley, both which remarkable men continued to correspond with him after his arrival in
Olney; and Whitefield in one letter entertains the hope of
coming, when bodily strength should allow, to join his testimony in Olney pulpit with that of Newton that " God is love."

II. Curate of Olney, 1764-1780 (Sixteen Years).

In 1764 Newton, at the request of his friend Mr. Haweis,
was presented by Lord Dartmouth with the curacy of Olney.
On April 29 he was admitted to deacon's orders by the
Bishop of Lincoln, and the next day came to Olney to take a
glance at the place and the people.   His first sermon in Olney
Church was preached on May 27 from Ps. lxxx. 1 ; he was
ordained priest at Buckden on June 17 of the same year, and
on the next day returned to Olney.   The well-known work of
Bishop Ryle, "The Christian Leaders of the Last Century,"
and other books of the same class that have been issued during
the last few years, have made almost every reading person
aware of the religious, or rather the irreligious state of England
a hundred or a hundred and twenty years ago.   "The Church
of England," says the Bishop, "existed in those days, with her
admirable articles, her time-honoured liturgy, her parochial
system, her Sunday services, and her ten thousand clergy.   The
Nonconformist body existed, with its hardly won liberty and
its free pulpit.   But one account unhappily may be given of
both parties.   They existed, but they could hardly be said to
have lived.   They did nothing ; they were sound asleep.   The
curse of the Uniformity Act seemed to rest on the Church of
England.   The blight of ease and freedom from persecution
seemed to rest upon Dissenters.   Natural theology, without a
single distinctive doctrine of Christianity, cold morality, or a
barren orthodoxy formed the staple teaching in church and
chapel.   Sermons everywhere were little better than miserable
moral essays, utterly devoid of anything likely to awaken,
convert, or save souls.   Both parties seemed at last agreed on
one point, and that was to let the devil alone, and to do nothing

for hearts and souls. And as for the weighty truths for which Hooper and Latimer had gone to the stake, and Baxter and scores of Puritans had gone to jail, they seemed clean forgotten and laid on the shelf."

Many of the so-called teachers of religion were disinclined either to do good themselves or to let others do it for them; and in 1768 the vice-chancellor of Oxford actually expelled six students from the university because they "held Methodistic tenets, and took on them to pray, read, and expound Scripture in private houses." Two of the six, Mr. Jones and Mr. Middleton, afterwards came into this neighbourhood. The Rev. Erasmus Middleton, in his old age. was presented with the living of Turvey; and the Rev. Thomas Jones, who married Lady Austen's sister, and of whom we shall have more to say by and by, became curate of Clifton Reynes. A few years previous another clergyman connected with this neighbourhood, the Rev. Matthew Powley, got into trouble at Oxford because he entertained Methodistical tenets. Mr. Powley, who had been excluded from the foundation of his college and threatened with expulsion, subsequently married Miss Unwin, became the friend and correspondent both of Cowper and Newton, often visited at Olney and Weston, and frequently preached at Olney for Newton.

Enough has now been said or quoted to show the low state to which religion had got in England in the middle of the last century. Then came a revival, and the country was stirred to the core by the labours of noble men whose names are now loved and honoured. Whitefield and Wesley led the way, preaching at all times and in all places. The labours of others of this noble brotherhood were more confined, but their earnestness was the same. Grimshaw and Venn raised the standard of Evangelicalism in Yorkshire, Rowlands in Wales, Walker in Cornwall, Toplady in Devon, Fletcher in Shropshire, Romaine and Haweis in London; whilst nearer to us James Hervey of Weston Favell, John Berridge of Everton, in Beds., and at a somewhat later date Simeon of Cambridge, preached in the same earnest manner. They were called Methodists, but it should be borne in mind that the term was then applied only to evangelical clergymen of the Church of England.

Thus in 1764, at a time when all England was aroused and all classes were led to inquiry, John Newton came to Olney, full of desire to promote the same work that had been commenced by these eminent men, with most of whom he had become personally acquainted, and in a few years he rose to be one of the most distinguished ornaments of the Evangelical party. It will be interesting at this point to look round and make some inquiry concerning his most celebrated clerical contemporaries. Newton's own age was thirty-nine. John Wesley was sixty-one, in full vigour, and twenty-seven more years of industry lay before him. Grimshaw was fifty-six, and had only two years more to live; Whitefield, Romaine, Rowlands, and Berridge were each about fifty. Whitefield had only six more years to live, but Romaine had thirty-one, Rowlands twenty-six, and Berridge twenty-nine. Henry Venn was forty, and for thirty-three more years continued a life of usefulness. To Toplady yet remained fourteen years, and to Fletcher twenty-one. Walker had been dead three years, James Hervey six.

No sooner was Newton in Olney than he threw himself with his whole heart into the work, filling up his time with his schools, cottage lectures, public services, and prayer meetings. One of his most frequent resorts was the cottage of Molly Mole, or, as he called it, "the Mole Hill," and when the favoured Molly removed to another cottage, called by Newton "the new Mole Hill," the prayer meetings followed her.

To Mrs. Newton, who did not come to Olney until several weeks after her husband's arrival here, Newton on the 28th of July wrote the following letter, which reveals the way in which his life was spent during part, at any rate, of his stay in Olney. It will be seen that his forenoons were occupied chiefly in reading and writing, his afternoons in visiting :—

"My housekeeper suits me well. In many respects she supplies your place : she calls me out of the garden when it is cold, puts me on my great-coat, watches my countenance, and asks me if I am well several times a day, tells me if she is

afraid this or the other will not agree with me. On the other
hand, I read some of my letters to her before I send them
away, read books to her; in short, in all common matters she
does as well as the finest and politest lady in England would
do. I want no other company till I can have yours. About
ten o'clock I bolt her out, and let her in at six. I come down
to breakfast at eight, find all ready, up again to study" (at the
top of the house, as the reader will remember) "till one. When
the clock strikes I go down, to find dinner upon the table. In
the afternoon we entertain one another, as I have said—only
when I take my rounds among the people or my walks in an
evening. And thus we go on regularly as the chimes, or much
more so, for they have been out of order several times."

In August he published his narrative, the preface of which
was written by Dr. Haweis, a series of fourteen letters in which
he gives the history of his life until the time when he first had
thoughts of entering the ministry. It awakened a good deal
of attention, and Newton hoped that its publication would give
additional weight to his ministry in Olney. "The people stare
at me since reading them, and well they may. I am indeed a
wonder to many, a wonder to myself, especially I wonder that
I wonder no more."

Amongst those to whom Newton presented his Narrative
was Mr. Thornton, a wealthy and liberal Russia merchant, with
whom he had previously been acquainted.

After reading the Narrative, and becoming further acquainted
with Newton, Mr. Thornton formed a very high estimation of
his character, and for many years gave him great assistance in
pecuniary matters. "Be hospitable," he wrote, "and keep
open your house for such as are worthy of entertainment: help
the poor and needy. I will statedly allow you £200, and
readily send whenever you have occasion for more." Whilst
at Olney Newton received upwards of £3000 in this way.

Early in 1765 he first commenced the services in what was
called the "Great House," a mansion, the property of Lord
Dartmouth, that stood between the church and the mill.
The gateway through which it was approached stood near the
east window of the chancel. The piers of this gateway and

the two stone balls that surmounted them are now at the entrance of the churchyard; the building itself and everything else appertaining to it were done away with about 1830.

This house being unoccupied, Newton got permission to make use of it, in the first instance for the meetings of the children, "where he could talk, preach, and reason with them in their own little way," and afterwards for prayer meetings.

It was his particular pleasure to get his friends, when they visited Olney, to take part in the services at the Great House. Berridge and Venn, Rowland Hill, Symonds of Bedford, Bull of Newport, and many other eminent or earnest divines were inveigled hither and called upon to speak. Newton's own addresses were practical to a degree, and he always spoke bearing in mind some circumstance of recent occurrence: on one occasion he chooses a text because " Sir Cowper[1] is down in the depths;" on another he speaks from 2 Peter i. 10, "chiefly on account of my maid Molly, who is perplexed and tempted on the point of election." Cowper after his arrival in Olney frequently took part in the services, and Mr. Bull speaks of a paper in his possession containing a list of those who engaged in prayer at the meetings. It gives weekly dates for nearly twelve months, with a single name attached to each; Cowper's appears about eight times.

Newton's exertions soon began to have visible results; the accommodation at the church was insufficient for the large numbers who now regularly flocked to hear him, and even when a large gallery was erected and opened (July 1765) "there seemed no more room in the body of the church than before." Short days, uncertain weather, dirty roads—none of these made any sensible diminution in the assemblies; and the seriousness of his hearers gave Newton hope that his congregations did not come in vain. His powers of endurance seem to have been exercised almost as much in his self-imposed tasks at Olney as they were on the shores of Guinea. "I have been engaged," says he, "about six hours in speaking at church and at home, yet find myself in good case, little or

---

[1] In Olney the poet was sometimes called Sir Cowper, and sometimes "the Squire."

nothing fatigued; but if there was occasion, I could readily go and preach again."

In January 1767 he published a volume of "Sermons, preached in the Parish Church of Olney." " My design," he says, "in printing them was twofold. First, to exhibit a specimen of the doctrines I taught, to satisfy those who desired information, and, if possible, to stop the mouth of slander; and secondly, to promote the edification of my people."

On the 14th of September 1767, as we have seen, the poet Cowper came to Olney, and two years later (in November 1769) Newton published his "Review of Ecclesiastical History," the "Apology," as he calls it, "of Evangelical Christianity, to obviate the sophistry and calumnies which have been published against it." When asked at a later date why he did not continue this work (it reaches only to the end of the first century), he said he had not read enough Church History; but added, " I was the remote cause of Milner writing his. He got the first hint from me."

The "Review," which was highly appreciated in many quarters, was considerably overrated by Cowper, who, blinded by his friendship for Newton, went so far as to declare that its style is incomparably better than that of Robertson or Gibbon.

Most of the events of the next eight years of Newton's life were such as need not here arrest our attention; but we ought to notice that on the 11th of November 1770 he preached in Olney Church a funeral sermon for his friend, the celebrated George Whitefield (who had died the last day of the preceding September), taking as his text the appropriate words, " He was a burning and shining light" (John v. 35); that in 1773 commenced Cowper's dreadful derangement of fourteen months; and that in 1774 were published the letters of Omicron, to which were afterwards added those of Vigil. Newton's attachment to Olney was now to receive a rude shock. After a dreadful fire had broken out and destroyed a deal of property he took an active part in comforting and relieving the sufferers, collecting a large sum of money for them. This was in October 1777; and on the 5th of November, on which day his weekly lecture happened to fall, he exerted himself to preserve some degree of quiet in the evening, hoping that he had sufficient influence with the people to restrain the rioting in which they were accustomed to indulge. "But instead of hearkening to his entreaties, the looser sort exceeded their former extravagance, drunkenness, and rioting, and even obliged him to send out money, to preserve his house from violence." Newton, over whom pecuniary advantages had no influence, afterwards told Mr. Cecil that he should never have made a change "had not so incorrigible a spirit prevailed in a parish which he had long laboured to reform." The town of Olney, it may be remarked, has obtained an unenviable notoriety for fires. In 1786 as many as forty-three houses were burnt down; but the most serious fire of all occurred in 1854,[1] when almost the whole of the northern half of the town was destroyed.

The Olney Hymns, 348 in all. Cowper having written 68, Newton 280, were published in 1779. The two chief motives for writing them were, as Newton says in his preface, "a desire to promote the faith and comfort of sincere Christians, and secondly, to raise a monument to perpetuate the remembrance of an intimate and endeared friendship." Before, however, the plan was half completed Cowper was seized with one of those fearful indispositions that throw so much sadness over the story of his life, and Newton, after suspending his work for a time through grief and disappointment, at length went on with the task alone.

Of the hymns by Cowper we have already spoken.

Among the best of Newton's must certainly be reckoned the three of which the following are the opening verses :—

> "Safely through another week
>   God has brought us on our way ;
> Let us now a blessing seek
>   On the approaching Sabbath-day,
> Day of all the week the best,
> Emblem of eternal rest."

> "Come, my soul, thy suit prepare,
> Jesus loves to answer prayer :
> He Himself has bid thee pray,
> Therefore will not say thee nay."

---

[1] A short account of this fire, with an illustration, appeared in the *Illustrated London News* for July 8, 1854.

"Begone, unbelief;
　　My Saviour is near,
　　And for my relief
　　Will surely appear.
　　By prayer let me wrestle,
　　And He will perform;
　　With Christ in the vessel,
　　I smile at the storm."

But finest of all is that beautiful hymn, justly considered as second to none in our language :—

"How sweet the name of Jesus sounds
　　In a believer's ear,
　　It soothes his sorrows, heals his wounds,
　　And drives away his fear."

The circumstances that gave origin to these beautiful productions were various.[1] Newton was in the habit of making one hymn for every Sunday evening service at the "Great House," and that commencing—

"O Lord, our languid souls inspire,"

was written for the first service of prayer held in the mansion; hence the second verse runs :—

"Dear Shepherd of Thy people, hear,
　　Thy presence now display;
　　As Thou hast given a place for prayer,
　　So give us hearts to pray."

It chanced one day that a lion was brought into the town. "He was wonderfully tame," says Newton, "as familiar with his keeper and as docile and obedient as a spaniel; yet the man told me he had his surly fits, when they dare not touch him." "I got a hymn out of this lion," he writes to Mr. Bull, "which you shall see when you come to Olney if you please me" ("The lion though by nature wild," ii. 93).

---

[1] The best of Newton's hymns are very fine; a large number, however, of the 280 are entirely devoid of merit.

F

The subjects of many of them were suggested by Mr. Barham of Bedford, an intimate friend of Newton, of Cowper, and of the "good Lord Dartmouth." Like other men who produce anything worth reading, Newton, although he could sometimes throw off beautiful lines with but little effort, often laboured painfully over his productions. On the 26th of June, for example, he tells us that he spoke in the evening from a hymn which took him the most of two days to finish.

Newton's ministry in Olney now drew to a close. At this period the right of presentation to the living of St. Mary Woolnoth, in the city of London, was vested in his friend and patron, Mr. John Thornton, who, feeling the importance of fixing a sound and able preacher of Christ's Gospel in such a post, pressed the living on Newton; and the latter, on September 21, 1779, wrote to Bull, "My race at Olney is nearly finished; I am about to form a connection for life with one Mary Woolnoth, a reputed London saint in Lombard Street." His last sermon in Olney previous to his departure for London was preached on Tuesday evening, January 11, 1780.

It had long been his custom to conduct services not only in the church, but also in the villages and isolated houses in the neighbourhood; for, like the other great evangelical preachers, he did not confine his labours to his own parish. One of his favourite resorts was Lavendon Mill, where he would take tea with his friend Mr. Perry the miller, and preach afterwards to the people who had assembled to hear him in a large barn. It was the custom of both Mr. Bull and Mr. Newton to spend the whole of the Friday of Whitsun-week at Mr. Perry's, which custom, kept up by the Bulls, father and son, after Newton's removal, lasted sixty-seven years.

Newton's departure was deeply regretted by his friends in the neighbourhood. Cowper especially greatly missed him. The Vicarage seemed a melancholy object; and as he walked in the garden in the evening it seemed lonely to think that when the smoke issued from the study chimney it was no longer a sign that Newton was there. And Newton himself, notwithstanding the unpleasant circumstances that occurred towards the end of his ministry here, did not leave without considerable regret the town for which he had so long retained an affection, and to which he so frequently alludes as "dear Olney."

III. Rector of St. Mary Woolnoth, Jan. 1780–Dec. 1807 (Twenty-eight Years).

Newton's life in London was of a very different kind from that which he had led at Olney; not only was he beset with crowds and noise on every side, instead of being able to wander among woods and fields, but instead of having five or six hours a day to himself, for many days he could scarcely save one half-hour from morning to night. Amid all this hurry and bustle, how to satisfy his numerous correspondents he at first could scarcely tell. But to the able navigator—and Newton was one—every wind is favourable; hence in the present case the happy idea struck him of *publishing* his letters, so that, in this way, he could send his friends and correspondents a whole bundle at once. This was the origin of Cardiphonia, or "the utterance of the heart."

So many strangers came to hear him in London that the parishioners complained that Sunday after Sunday either their seats were taken or they could not get to them for the crowd in the aisle. Relating this in a letter to his wife, who was at Olney, after saying that he told the churchwarden who made the complaint how sorry he was, but knew not how to prevent it, he adds, with his usual quiet humour—"He proposed with many apologies my letting another clergyman preach now and then for me, hinted that it should be no expense to me, and thought that if it was uncertain whether I preached or not the people would not throng the church so much. I could not but admire the scheme. I thought it would exactly answer the design. But I said I could not possibly comply with it." A similar occurrence had happened some twenty-five years previous to Newton's friend Romaine when he was morning preacher at St. George's, Hanover Square, with this difference, that Romaine, because he attracted too many hearers, and thereby inconvenienced the parishioners, was actually dismissed.

In May 1783 died Mrs. Cunningham, Newton's sister; and her daughter Eliza, who was dearly beloved by both Mr. and Mrs. Newton, was adopted by them, and received into their home; but, to their great grief, she died about two years after, at the age of but little more than fourteen. In the spring of 1786 Newton published his "Messiah," and at Lady Day of this year he removed from Charles Square, Hoxton (his first residence in London), to No. 6 Coleman Street Buildings,[1] where he continued to reside till his death.

The year 1790 proved for him a sad and eventful one. On November 7 died his "best friend," Mr. Thornton; and on the 15th of December his beloved wife, with whom he had lived upwards of forty years, was removed by death. His grief was excessive; but his "term of preaching had very much led him to endeavour to comfort the afflicted by representing the Gospel as a catholicon, affording an effectual remedy for every evil, a full compensation for every want or loss, to those who truly believe it," and reflecting on this, he endeavoured by his own practice to confirm the doctrine he had preached to others. Thereupon he nerved himself up, and besought God to help him; and through the whole of this painful trial he attended all his stated and occasional services as usual, and a stranger would scarcely have discovered, either by his words or looks, that he was in trouble. For several years after her death he used to vent his grief and affection in verses on its anniversary, which he published in a small tract, "Ebenezer;" and some of them are very beautiful :—

> " Forget her ! No; can four short years
>   The deep impression wear away?
> She still before my mind appears,
>   Abroad, at home, by night, by day !
> Oft as with those she loved I meet,
>   Her looks, her voice, her words recur ;
> Or if alone I walk the street,
>   Still something leads my thoughts to her !"

---

[1] "Coleman Street Buildings," he writes to Mr. Bull, "is about half-way between London Wall and King's Arms Yard," in which was Mr. Thornton's counting-house.

After the death of Mrs. Newton his chief companion was his niece, Miss Elizabeth Catlett, a young lady who had been brought up by him with Miss Cunningham. Twenty-one letters written to her when she was at school at Northampton, the first of which is dated Olney, September 8, 1779, have been published. Writing in October 1783 he says, "I remember when you were a little girl at Northampton school. . . . I found such an affection for you that I would not part with you for your weight in gold. And though you are much heavier now than you were then, I can say the same still."

She became quite necessary to him in his later years; she watched him, walked with him, visited wherever he went, and when his sight failed him read to him.

In the spring of 1797 Mr. Wilberforce published his well-known book, "A Practical View of the Prevailing Religious Systems, &c." Newton's impression of its value was so great, and so deeply was he interested both in the author and his work, that he says, "I can scarcely talk or write without introducing Mr. Wilberforce's book." The copy presented by the author to Newton is now in the possession of a lady of Olney. Above the inscription on the title-page are the words, in Newton's handwriting, "Second reading began 20 April 1797;" and at the end of the book, "Finished the second reading 10 May 1797. Finished the third reading the 11 June '97. Fourth reading begun 19 Oct."

On the second page, also in Newton's handwriting, is the following :—

"My regards for the author, who gave me this book, will not permit me to part with my property in it, and therefore I can only *lend* it to my dear Elizabeth[1] during my life. If she survives me, it will then be her own. I commend it to her as one of the best books (in my judgment) extant, and I hope she will find much pleasure and much profit from a frequent perusal of it. The Lord accompany her reading with His especial blessing. Amen. 10 May 1797."

Some years previous he had been in correspondence with

---

[1] Miss Catlett.

Dr. Carey, who had sent him an account of the progress of the Mission in India. Writing in 1802 to Dr. Claudius Buchanan, the eminent preacher and promoter of Christian Missions in the East, whom he had been the means of bringing to a knowledge of the Saviour, and who had for a time been his curate, Newton, after expressing his high opinion of Carey, and his regret that Dr. Buchanan should have spoken slightingly of the enormous labours of the Baptist triumvirate of missionaries, concludes with, "I do not look for miracles, but if God were to work one in our day, I should not wonder if it were in favour of Dr. Carey."

As Newton approached his eightieth year his memory and physical powers began to fail, but he would not give up preaching. "I cannot stop," he replied, when a friend about this time suggested that he might now consider his work as done. "What! shall the old African blasphemer stop while he can speak?"

He died on the evening of Monday, December 21, 1807, in his eighty-third year, and was buried at St. Mary Woolnoth's, of which he had been Rector twenty-eight years.

THE PRINCIPAL WORKS OF JOHN NEWTON.

Liverpool—   *Published*
Discourses intended for the Pulpit   . Jan. 1760.

Olney—
The Authentic Narrative . . . . Aug. 1764.
Sermons preached in the Parish Church of
    Olney . . . . Jan. 1767.
Review of Ecclesiastical History . . . Nov. 1769.
Omicron's Letters, twenty-six in number . July 1774.

> They were written at various times for the *Gospel Magazine.* The fifteen letters signed Vigil were added afterwards.

Olney Hymns .   . Feb. 1779.

JOHN NEWTON'S TOMB IN OLNEY CHURCHYARD.

The small Monument to the left, with a stone ball on the top, is to Mrs. Newton's father, George Catlett.

London— *Published*

Cardiphonia . . . . . . 1781.

Tracts—
{
A Plan of Academical Preparation for the Ministry . . . May 1782.

Apologia, or Four Letters to a Minister of an Independent Church . . . . March 1784.

A Monument to the Memory of Miss Eliza Cunningham . Oct. 1785.
}

Messiah, or Fifty Expository Discourses on the series of Scriptural Passages which form the subject of Handel's celebrated Oratorio . . . . . . April 1786.

Letters to a Wife . . . . . April 1793.

Seven Occasional Sermons preached between { Dec. 19, 1779, and Dec. 19, 1797.

Life of Grimshaw . . Feb. 1799.

VIII.

THE REV. THOMAS SCOTT AND HIS COMMENTARY.[1]

"The longer I live the more I am certain that the great difference between men, between the feeble and the powerful, the great and the insignificant, is energy—invincible determination—a purpose once fixed, and then death or victory. That quality will do anything that can be done in this world."
—Sir FOWELL BUXTON.

I. BRAYTOFT, 1747–1772 (TWENTY-FIVE YEARS).

"I WAS born," says the Rev. Thomas Scott, "on the 4th of February 1746–7, answering since the change of the style, and the beginning of another century, to February 16, 1747. A small farm-house at Braytoft (near Burgh), in Lincolnshire, was the place of my birth. My father, John Scott, was a grazier, a man of a small and feeble body, but of uncommon energy of mind and vigour of intellect; by which he sur-mounted, in no common degree, the almost total want of education. His circumstances were very narrow, and for many years he struggled with urgent difficulties. But he rose above them; and though never affluent, his credit was supported, and he lived in more comfortable circumstances to the age of seventy-six years. I was the tenth of thirteen children, ten of whom lived to maturity; and my eldest brother was twenty-three years older than my youngest sister." Scott's father greatly desired to have a son educated for one of the learned professions, and for this reason sent his eldest son, who showed a talent for learning, to Scorton school, in Yorkshire; but, to the great grief of the father, this son of promise, who, after finishing an apprenticeship at Burgh, had risen rapidly in his profession, fell a victim to a malignant

[1] Compiled chiefly from "The Life of the Rev. Thomas Scott," by John Scott, A.M.

disease, being cut off in his twenty-fourth year. The father, nevertheless, was still bent on having a son in the medical profession; and seeing that Thomas seemed capable of readily learning Latin, it was settled that he should be the one; so at the age of ten he was sent to Scorton, where his brother had been before him. At the age of sixteen he left school, and was bound apprentice to a medical practitioner at Alford, but his ill behaviour so displeased his master that at the end of two months he was dismissed, and returned home in disgrace. The whole of the lad's premium, it appears, had not been paid, and the father, who was greatly angered at both his son and the apothecary, resolutely refused to pay the remainder. The master as decidedly refused to give up the indentures till it was paid, and, in consequence, as no compromise was attempted between these two high-spirited men, the lad was finally excluded from the profession for which he had been designed.

Being obliged to remain at home, Scott now began to experience much harsh treatment from his father, and was set to do the most degrading, laborious, and dirty work belonging to a grazier. Yet a kind of indignant, proud self-revenge kept him from complaining; and as, after a few unsuccessful attempts, his father gave up all thoughts of placing him out in any other way, for above nine years he worked on the farm, and "was nearly as entire a drudge as any servant or labourer in his father's employ." During this period he several times tried to amend his ways, and, although his relapses were frequent, gave up many of his bad habits, and seems to have become more and more desirous of leading a Christian life. Curious to say, notwithstanding all his troubles he continued to entertain thoughts of the university and of the clerical profession; for this reason he occupied all his leisure in reading whatever books he could procure, keeping up his school learning as well as he could with a few torn Latin books and a Greek grammar; and, discouraging as were his circumstances, began to exhibit that indefatigable application and undaunted resolution which were part and parcel of him throughout the rest of his career. Soured as had become his temper, through his father's sternness—and the punishment seems to us to have been out of all proportion to the offence—discontented and rebellious as he was, one consideration still made him cling to home. "I had only one surviving brother," he tells us, "and he was well situated in a farm. My father was far advanced in life, and not of a strong constitution; and I supposed, as most of my family did, that I should succeed to his farm." As soon, therefore, as Scott discovered that such was not to be the case, but the lease of the farm was to be left to his brother, he determined to make some effort, however desperate, to extricate himself. He threw aside his shepherd's frock, declared that he would not again resume it, set off for Boston, where a clergyman lived with whom he had contracted some acquaintance, and to him, though with hesitation and trepidation, opened his mind, and declared his purpose of attempting to take orders. The surprise which the clergyman first exhibited disappeared somewhat when the shepherd, in which light Scott had long been regarded, proved his acquaintance with Greek and Latin, and he promised to speak a word for him to the Archdeacon at the ensuing visitation. This being settled, Scott returned to his father for the intervening days and worked as usual about the farm. At the appointed time he readily found access to the Archdeacon, who concluded the interview by assuring him that he would state the case to the Bishop.

Although now in the twenty-sixth year of his age, wholly without the prospect of a decent subsistence, yet his father most decidedly set himself against the design. But Scott's mind was now made up. He procured a title to a small curacy near Horncastle, sent his testimonials and other papers to the Bishop, and waited on him in London at the appointed time. But the Bishop refused to admit him as a candidate at that ordination. He told him too that he could not be admitted at the next ordination unless he could procure his father's consent; and Scott, who regarded this difficulty as insuperable, quitted London almost in despair. "At length I reached Braytoft," says he, "after walking twenty miles in the forenoon; and, having dined, I put off my clerical clothes, resumed my shepherd's dress, and sheared eleven large sheep in the afternoon." The difficulty, however, which at first had seemed so great, was in a most unexpected manner surmounted. His father, at the urgent solicitation of all the family, gave his consent in writing; and at the ensuing Michaelmas ordination (Sept. 20, 1772) Scott was admitted a candidate without objection, and passed both his examinations with credit. On the Saturday before the ordination a letter had been received by the Bishop from Mr. (afterwards Dr.) Dowbiggin, Rector of Stoke Goldington and Gayhurst, in Bucks. He wanted a curate for Stoke, jointly with Weston Underwood, a perpetual curacy held by another person, the whole salary £50 a year, with some trifling additions. " This," says Scott, " the Secretary proposed to me, the Bishop being disposed to favour my accepting it, if I had no particular attachment to the parish from which I had my title." It appears that he had no pecuniary inducement to accede to the proposal, but the idea of appearing a clergyman in a neighbourhood where he had not been known in any other character induced him to listen to it. In " The Force of Truth," a kind of autobiography afterwards published by him, he severely judges his own conduct in the whole transaction, calling it, in fact, the most atrocious wickedness of his life. " As far as I understand such controversies, I was nearly a Socinian and Pelagian, and wholly an Arminian. . . . While I was preparing for the solemn office I lived, as before, in known sin and in utter neglect of prayer, my whole preparation consisting of nothing else than attention to those studies which were more immediately requisite for reputably passing through the previous examination. . . . Thus with a heart full of pride and wickedness ; my life polluted with many unrepented, unforsaken sins ; without one cry for mercy, one prayer for direction or assistance, or for a blessing upon what I was about to do ; after having concealed my real sentiments under the mask of general expressions ; after having subscribed articles directly contrary to what I believed ; and after having blasphemously declared in the presence of God and of the congregation, in the most solemn manner, sealing it with the Lord's Supper, that I engaged myself to be ' inwardly moved by the Holy Ghost to take that office upon me '—not knowing

or believing that there was any Holy Ghost ;—on September
20, 1772, I was ordained a deacon." He concludes this
severe judgment upon himself by praying, "May I fervently
love, and very humbly, devotedly, serve that God who hath
multiplied His mercies in abundantly pardoning my com-
plicated provocations!"

II. THE BUCKS CURACIES, 1772–1785 (THIRTEEN YEARS).

Thus in October 1772 Scott came to Stoke Goldington, and
entered on his new curacies; "boarding with a parishioner (of
the name of Brice) for twenty guineas a year." "My regular
services," he tells us, "were at Stoke and Weston Underwood;
but my rector was sub-dean of Lincoln; and when he went
thither into residence, he procured other supplies for Weston,
and I officiated at Gayhurst, where George Wrighte, Esq."
(grandson of the George Wrighte mentioned in the article on
Gayhurst), "had a seat." "This commenced an acquaintance
with him which produced important effects on my future life."
At Stoke Scott applied himself with astonishing diligence to his
studies : he spent three hours a day at Hebrew, read Herodotus
in the original, in Latin, and in English, paid considerable
attention to other studies, and at the same time was engaged
on a course of sermons upon our Saviour's Sermon on the
Mount. "I find my taste for study," he says, "grow on me
every day. I only fear I shall be, like the miser, too covetous.
In fact, I really grudge every hour that I employ otherwise.
Others go out by choice, and stay at home by constraint; but
I ever stay at home by choice, and go out because I am persuaded it is necessary. In every other expense I am grown a
miser : I take every method to save : but here I am prodigal.
No cost do I in the least grudge to procure advantageous
methods of pursuing my studies. So far is a multiplicity of
studies, a diversity of pursuits, from overburdening my memory,
that by exercising it I find it in a high degree more retentive,
as well as the comprehending faculty more quick." In after
days he judged far too severely his course of life at Stoke, and
in "The Force of Truth" only gives himself credit for having

there "attended just enough to the public duties of his station
to support a decent character," which he deemed "subservient
to his main design." Nevertheless, the letters written by him
at the time show that he was already realising the seriousness
of his work, and that he was not so enamoured of his literary
pursuits as altogether to forget the more important business
which claimed his attention as a parochial minister.

From the first he took great pains in preparation for the
pulpit, but lamented that his sermons were but little appreciated. After preaching two of the most forcible discourses
in his power he had been able to collect only twenty-six or
twenty-seven communicants. "Whether," he says, "I shall be
able to make any reformation among my parishioners I much
doubt; but I tell them their duty pretty freely." It did not
seem to strike Scott just then that he himself wanted reforming
nearly as much as the people of Stoke Goldington. But there
is this extenuating circumstance as regards the minister: the
Stoke people did have some one to exhort them to mend *their*
ways, whereas he had nobody to exhort him to reform, and
nobody to tell him *his* duty pretty freely. What effect Scott's
sermons had on his parishioners we cannot very well tell; but
when afterwards he found himself preached at, in a sermon
far more eloquent, though not in words, than those just
referred to, he was filled with remorse for his previous indiffer-
ence, and resolved, God helping him, to become a new man.
The eloquent sermon I refer to was Newton's visit, by and by
to be spoken of, to the dying couple at Weston.

In November 1773 Scott quitted his residence at Stoke, and
from that time to his marriage, somewhat more than a year
afterwards, lodged at Weston.

At Stoke, he tells us with his usual candour, he had been
diligent in his clerical profession for outward show; and at
Weston, where there was a considerable number of Roman
Catholics, he was equally diligent, but for the reason that he
"would not have it said that *they* have all the religion."

During his residence at Stoke an event occurred that,
although at first he regarded it lightly, had an important influence on his subsequent career. At the instance of an apothe-

cary at Olney he was induced to walk over and hear one of Mr. Newton's famous Thursday evening sermons.

"I sat fronting the pulpit," he says, "and verily thought Mr. Newton looked full on me when he came into the desk;" and, to Scott's great astonishment, the text named was Paul's speech to Elymas. "As I knew he preached *extempore*, I took it for granted that he had chosen the text purposely on my account. . . . But I thought his doctrine abstruse, imaginative, and irrational, and his manner uncouth; and the impression that, though Elymas was named, I was intended, abode with me for a long time: nor was it wholly effaced till I discovered, some years afterwards, that he was regularly expounding the Acts of the Apostles, and that this passage came in course that evening; and that, in fact, he neither saw nor thought of me." The idea that he was aimed at served Scott at the time as a subject of merriment, but it had nevertheless a lasting and beneficial influence on his mind; and he afterwards confessed that the passage was but too appropriate to his character and conduct. "Thou enemy of all righteousness, wilt thou not cease to pervert the right ways of the Lord"—the words long after rang in his ears, and pursued him wherever he went. Such was the effect of the first sermon preached by Newton, unwittingly, at Scott. The effect of the next was far greater; Scott himself tells us all about it:—

"In January 1774 two of my parishioners, a man and his wife" (Andrew and Sarah Blower), "lay at the point of death. I had heard of the circumstance; but, according to my general custom, not being sent for, I took no notice of it; till one evening, the woman being now dead and the man dying, I heard that my neighbour, Mr. Newton, had been several times to visit them. Immediately, my conscience reproached me with being shamefully negligent in sitting at home, within a few doors of dying persons, my general hearers, and never going to visit them. Directly it occurred to me that, whatever contempt I might have for Mr. Newton's doctrines, I must acknowledge his practice to be more consistent with the ministerial character than my own. He must have more zeal and love for souls than I had, or he would not have

walked so far to visit and supply my lack of care to those
who, as far as I was concerned, might have been left to perish
in their sins. This reflection affected me so much, that, without delay, and very earnestly, yea with tears, I besought the
Lord to forgive my past neglect; and I resolved thenceforward to be more attentive to my duty: which resolution,
though at first formed in ignorant dependence on my own
strength, I have, by Divine grace, been enabled hitherto to
keep. I went immediately to visit the survivor; and the
affecting sight of one person already dead, and another ex-
piring in the same chamber, served more deeply to impress
my serious convictions: so that from that time I have constantly visited the sick of my parishes, as far as I have had
opportunity, and have endeavoured, to the best of my knowledge, to perform that essential part of a parish minister's
duty."

The tombstone to these two parishioners of Scott's, with
the sculpture of two coffins on a trestle, is in Weston churchyard, in the angle between the chancel and the south aisle of
the church.

At Weston Scott became acquainted with the Higgins
family,[1] from whom he received so many favours during the
time he lived in this neighbourhood.

On December 5, 1774, he was married at Gayhurst church
to Miss Jane Kell, the housekeeper of Mrs. Wrighte of Gayhurst, with whom he had become acquainted through his
intimacy with the Wrightes. Miss Kell, who had long been
with Mrs. Wrighte, was well educated, being the daughter of a
gentleman formerly of good circumstances, but who had been
impoverished by a sudden heavy loss. At Gayhurst she had
been greatly respected, and treated almost as a relative.

A few days after her marriage Mrs. Scott wrote—" Mr. and
Mrs. Wrighte accompanied me to church—though it was the
first time of her being out to walk after a long and dangerous
illness—and Mr. Wrighte gave me away." After his marriage
Scott returned for a few months to Stoke, and in the following

---

[1] Bartholomew Higgins, Esq., sen., was the friend mentioned in " The Force
of Truth."

spring (1775) exchanged his curacy of Stoke for that of Raven-stone.

In May 1775 began his correspondence with Newton, but it was dropped in the December of the same year, and their acquaintance for a season was almost wholly broken off.

During part of the time that Scott resided at Ravenstone he daily attended as tutor the son of Mr. Wrighte of Gayhurst, but differences having arisen about the management of the child, he was dismissed from the employment; he also gave great offence to the Wrightes (who were staunch and orthodox Churchmen) by openly proclaiming his Socinian principles (which he afterwards abandoned), "whereby he excluded himself from all hope of preferment through their influence, and as nearly as possible severed all connection with them."

In the spring of 1777 Scott again removed to Weston Underwood, and took up his abode at Weston Lodge, afterwards the residence of the poet Cowper.

His intercourse with Newton was now renewed. At Ravenstone he had already begun a deep practical study of God's Word, with constant prayer for Divine teaching; and now that change of sentiments and of character resulting from it described in "The Force of Truth" was making itself apparent. Day after day he might have been seen in the park at Weston, since immortalised by the poems of Cowper, with his Greek Testament in his hand, reading and meditating as he walked. "Slowly and laboriously, and without help from any living man, except perhaps Newton, Scott worked his way from point to point, until he was finally established in the Evangelical faith." [1]

"After some time," he tells us, "a house at Weston belonging to Mr. Charles Higgins became vacant, and was offered me at less than half the rent (of £12) which I had previously paid; and I accordingly removed to it. In fact, Mr. Higgins took no rent of me but a hamper of pears annually from a fine tree in the garden, for which he regularly sent me a receipt." In this house, which is the one near the church, and which commands a view of the whole village street, he wrote "The Force of Truth," the most important work of his life, with the

1 J. H. Overton.

exception of the "Commentary." It was revised by the poet
Cowper (who then lived at Olney), "and as to style and exter-
nals, but not otherwise, considerably improved by his advice."
"The Force of Truth," says J. H. Overton, "is one of the most
striking treatises ever published by the Evangelical school."

"Breakfasted with Mr. Scott," wrote Newton in his diary
(December 11, 1778). "Heard him read a narrative of his
conversion" ("The Force of Truth") "which he has drawn up
for publication. It is striking and judicious, and will, I hope,
by the Divine blessing, be very useful. I think I can see that
he has got before me already. Lord, if I have been useful to
him, do Thou, I beseech Thee, make him now useful to me."

It had been Newton's wish on removing to London that
Scott should at once succeed him; but the people of Olney,
as soon as that wish became known, raised so general and
violent an opposition that Newton wrote, "I believe Satan has
so strong an objection to your coming to Olney, that it would
probably be advisable to defer it for the present." Scott, therefore, did not take possession of the Olney pulpit till about a
year after. The people of Olney, however, had reason to
repent of their obstinacy, for in Mr. Page, who came instead
of Scott, they caught a veritable Tartar. He fell out with his
patron, with his vicar, and with his people. "He quarrelled
with most of his acquaintance, and the rest grew sick of him."
"He even quarrelled," says Cowper, "with his auctioneer in
the midst of the sale of his goods, and would not permit him
to proceed, finishing that matter himself;" and culminated his
vagaries by taking leave of his parishioners in these words,
"And now let us pray for your wicked vicar," meaning, of
course, the excellent Mr. Browne. All opposition to Scott's
coming to Olney had now vanished; but the people did not
receive him heartily, neither did he ever experience here a tithe
of the popularity enjoyed by Newton. From Weston, February
15, 1781, he writes—"I have undertaken the curacy of Olney
along with Weston, leaving Ravenstone; which will be attended
with my removal to Olney at Lady Day. . . . I have this day
finished my thirty-fourth year. I lived without God in the
world for nearly twenty-eight: then He did not starve me:

G

nay, He provided well for me, though I knew Him not. I have now in some measure trusted and poorly served Him the other six years, or nearly, and He has not failed me."

Among Scott's occasional hearers at Olney was William Carey, afterwards the celebrated missionary, who had recently joined the church under Mr. Sutcliff. The agreeable information that his preaching had been instrumental in directing the genius of Carey was communicated to Scott in February 1821, a few weeks before his death, by Dr. Ryland, who wrote as follows :—"What led me to write now was a letter I received from Dr. Carey yesterday, in which he says, ' Pray give my thanks to dear Mr. Scott for his history of the Synod of Dort. I would write to him if I could command time. If there be anything of the work of God in my soul, I owe much of it to his preaching, when I first set out in the ways of the Lord.' "

In some of his letters to Newton the poet Cowper, although all along he had been on friendly terms with Scott, brings the charge against him that he was in the habit of scolding his people. Scott, in defence, however, stated that neither Cowper nor Mrs. Unwin ever heard him preach. "Mr. Cowper's information concerning my preaching was derived from the very persons whose doctrinal and practical antinomianism I steadily confronted." In explanation of the statement that Cowper never heard Scott preach, "it should be remembered that at the time Scott was in Olney one feature of the unhappy illusion under which Cowper laboured was a persuasion that it was his duty to abstain from religious worship."

At Christmas 1785, having been appointed to the chaplainship of the Lock Chapel, Grosvenor Place, Scott quitted Olney for London, having resided in the neighbourhood about thirteen years—one year at Stoke Goldington, two years at Ravenstone, five and a half at Weston, and four and a half at Olney.

III. The "Commentary."

The great work of Scott's life, the famous "Commentary," was commenced on January 2, 1788. In his own words we have the account of its origin. "As I had read over the whole of the Scriptures repeatedly, I trust with constant prayer, considering how almost every verse might be applied, as if I had been called to preach upon it, I had often thought that I should like to preach through the Bible, for instruction from every part crowded upon my mind, as I read and meditated, from day to day. While I was in this frame of mind a proposal was made to me to write notes on the Bible, to be published with the sacred text in weekly numbers. . . . I had hardly an idea of the arduousness of the work and of the various kind of talent and knowledge which it required, of most of which I was at that time destitute. My inclination biassed my judgment. I must also own that a guinea a week, with some collateral advantages which I was to receive, promised to be no unacceptable addition to my scanty income."

To give an account of the troubles, vexations, anxieties, and difficulties that accompanied the writing and publication of this work would only weary the reader ; suffice it to say that they were enough to make almost any other man throw up the whole thing in despair ; but Scott had put his hand to the plough, and go back he would not. "The indomitable perseverance exercised in carrying out this work," says Sir James Stephen, "is beyond all praise. Animated by one changeless purpose—devoted to one inexhaustible task, . . . blest with a resoluteness of understanding which turned aside from no difficulty, and with a mental energy which trampled down the whole brood of doubts, sophisms, and delusions,—and sustained by a vigour of body which baffled all fatigue and triumphed over all disease,—on he went interpreting the Word of his God, and onward he could not but go though '*fractus illabatur orbis*,'—though publishers should cheat and chancellors restrain him,—though asthma should choke and fever unnerve him,—though want should hang on him heavily, and critics censure, and congregations desert him,—and though the wife of his bosom should be taken from him (Mrs. Scott died September 1790). It mattered not. These things could not move him, nor prevent his writing and enlarging, and yet again enlarging, his ' Commentary.'"

"When the first edition was completed I calculated," says

Scott, " in the most favourable manner, my own pecuniary
concern in the work ; and the result was, that, as nearly as I
could ascertain, I had neither gained nor lost, but had performed the whole for nothing. As far as I had hoped for
some addition to my income I was completely disappointed ;
but as Providence otherwise supported my family and upheld
my credit, I felt well satisfied, and even rejoiced in having
laboured often far beyond what my health and spirits could
well endure, in a work which had been pleasant and profitable
to me, and which I hoped would prove useful to others. The
sale of the second edition scarcely cleared more than the prime
cost. By the third edition he fared somewhat better; but except
the sum given for the copyright since that edition was concluded,
he tells us that he certainly did not clear as much as £1000
for the labours of above twenty-one years, and yet the copies
disposed of in his lifetime sold for nearly £200,000. The spirit
in which the " Commentary " was written is admirably shown
by Sir James Stephen in the " Evangelical Succession." After
referring to Scott's lack not only of imagination, but also of the
various kinds of knowledge without which at first sight the
writing of a Commentary would appear to be an impossibility,
Sir James Stephen goes on to say, " But in this poverty he
found his wealth, and illustriously vindicated, in his own person,
the paradox, ' When I am weak then am I strong.' He proposed to himself a canon of Biblical criticism more perfect
than any which had been followed by Origen, Jerome, Erasmus,
or Beza. Believing God to be the common Father of us all,
and the Word of God to be the common patrimony of all His
children, he was assured that the real meaning of it must have
been placed within the reach, not only of the learned few, but
also of the unlearned many. But how (he inquired) should
that book, which was so often found by the wise to be sealed
and inscrutable, be thus intelligible to the simple ? He returned
the answer to his own inquiry—God is truth, and His Word is
truth, and all truth must be consistent with itself. He, therefore, who shall diligently, humbly, and devoutly collate every
passage of the Divine oracles with the rest will possess himself
of the key to that inexhaustible treasury. . . . Mr. Scott's efforts

to elucidate the sacred text by the juxtaposition and comparison of the various parts of it with each other were such
that a review of them must affect any ordinary student with
shame and admiration. It is scarcely possible to count, and
it is vain to conjecture, the number of the illustrations of the
sense of scriptural words and phrases with which this method
furnished him. The labour expended in collecting, verifying,
and arranging them all must have oppressed any mind of less
than herculean vigour. Yet this was but one, and not the
most arduous, of the many employments to which he devoted
the scanty leisure allowed to him by the daily and severe
pressure of his pastoral and domestic duties." Perhaps we
may best get an idea of the feeling with which for many years
ministers have regarded the "Commentary" by the following
acknowledgment :—" I never like to preach a sermon," says the
Rev. J. H. Evans (1852), "without having seen what Scott
says about it. If he takes the same view, I consider then that
I am tolerably safe." The latter days of Scott were passed in
the quiet and seclusion of the tiny village of Aston Sandford,
in the middle of Buckinghamshire, to which he had removed
in the spring of 1803, and here in April 1821 he breathed his
last. In the north wall of the chancel is a tablet of white
marble bearing this inscription—"Near this spot are deposited
the remains of the Reverend Thomas Scott. twenty-one years
rector of this parish. He died April 16, 1821, aged seventy-
four years. But in his writings he will long remain and widely
proclaim to mankind the unsearchable riches of Christ." An
inscribed slab in the pavement covers his remains.

THE WORKS OF THE REV. THOMAS SCOTT.

1. "The Force of Truth," written at Weston Underwood.
   Published in 1779.
2. "Occasional Sermons." Seven on national occasions, the
   first being that preached at Olney in 1784 on the close
   of the American War.

3. "Theological Treatises," the first being the "Discourse on Repentance," written at Olney, and published in 1785.
4. "The Commentary," first published between the years 1788 and 1792.
5. "Works directed against the Infidelity and Disaffection of the Times." These are, "The Rights of God" and "The Tract on Government."
6. Other Controversial Works, as "The Answer to Bishop Tomline's Refutation of Calvinism," and "The History of the Synod of Dort."

IX.

THE SECOND EARL OF DARTMOUTH.

" We boast some rich ones whom the Gospel sways,
  And one who wears a coronet and prays ;
  Like gleanings of an olive-tree they show
  Here and there one upon the topmost bough."
                          —COWPER : *Truth.*

THE nobleman alluded to in the above lines of Cowper as
" one who wears a coronet and prays " was, it is scarcely necessary to say, William Legge, second Earl of Dartmouth ; and at
a time when the practice of religion was very much more
unusual among the nobility than it now is, it argued a man of
no common mould to declare for Christ, to brave the sneers
and ridicule of the great and wealthy, and to openly befriend
the most faithful ministers of the day. " The good Lord Dartmouth," as he has been affectionately called, was born in the
year 1731. Early in life deprived of his father, his education
devolved on his surviving parent, and he continued to reside
with her after her marriage with Francis, first Earl of Guild-
ford. After the death of his mother he left England to make a
tour on the Continent. In 1750 he succeeded his grandfather
as Earl of Dartmouth, and three years after espoused the only
daughter and heiress of Sir Charles Gunter Nicholl, by whom
he acquired the Manor of Olney and other considerable additions to his fortune. Shortly after his marriage he was introduced to the Countess of Huntingdon, of whom he soon became
the intimate friend ; and at her house made the acquaintance
of Whitefield, Romaine, the Wesleys, and other distinguished
men of the same class. Indeed, Lord and Lady Dartmouth
very soon attracted general attention for the profession of religion they made and the countenance they afforded to faithful
ministers suspected of what was called Methodism.

"I have not the honour of Lord Dartmouth's acquaintance," wrote Hervey of Weston Favell in 1757, "but I hear he is full of grace and valiant for the truth—a lover of Christ and an ornament to His Gospel." Lady Fanny Shirley, a reigning beauty of the court of George I., and aunt to Lady Huntingdon, was extremely intimate with Lord and Lady Dartmouth, and frequently corresponded with them. Receiving a letter from his Lordship with which she was particularly delighted, she enclosed it to Mr. Hervey, who in reply said—"It is indeed a delightful sight to see a person of Lord Dartmouth's dignity and politeness closing a letter with the name of Jesus Christ. May we all know more and more of that just One! Then it will appear meet and right, not a pious extravagance, but a most rational determination, *to count all things but loss for the excellency of Jesus Christ our Lord.*"

At Lord Dartmouth's residence at Sandwell that faithful and laborious minister of the Gospel, Henry Venn, frequently took duty, and always received a warm welcome, and in 1759, at his Lordship's solicitation, he was appointed vicar of Huddersfield, in Yorkshire. Of Mr. Venn's immense labours during the twelve years of his residence in this place, and the good work subsequently performed by him at Yelling, where he became the pastor of pastors, Simeon of Cambridge and scores of less distinguished men have borne grateful testimony.

Lord Dartmouth now began to experience a portion of that contempt and ridicule which all who live a godly life must expect some time or other to encounter, one of his greatest trials being the conduct towards him of his uncle, the Honourable Henry Bilson Legge, then Chancellor of the Exchequer, who treated him with unmerited severity, and for a time refused to hold intercourse with him. "But through the kind interference of Lady Huntingdon, who obtained several private interviews with his Lordship's aunt, the Baroness Stawell, he was restored to the friendship of his relations, who ever after entertained a more favourable opinion of him and of the sentiments which he espoused.[1] . . . Indeed, for some years after, the Chancellor of the Exchequer and Lady Stawell were not

[1] See the "Life and Times of Lady Huntingdon."

infrequently to be found amongst the circle who attended Mr. Whitefield's preaching at Lady Huntingdon's residence; and so much did his Lordship conciliate the esteem of his noble relatives, by a prudent and consistent line of conduct, that several of them became of the congregation at the Countess's. His Lordship was considered a tolerable speaker in the House of Lords. He connected himself early in life with the Rockingham party, and when they came into power in 1765 he was made First Lord of Trade and sworn of the Privy Council." Few persons, we are told, were more highly esteemed by his Majesty George III., who appointed him principal Secretary of State for the American Department, which office his Lordship afterwards exchanged for the place of Lord Keeper of the Privy Seal; and some years after was constituted Lord Steward of his Majesty's household. "They call my Lord Dartmouth an enthusiast," observed the King, "but surely he says nothing on the subject of religion but what any Christian may and ought to say."

His Lordship patronised the college for American Indians, and contributed largely towards Whitefield's orphan-house in Georgia. He was also one of the chief patrons of the evangelical preaching at the Lock Chapel. How deeply he felt himself indebted to Lady Huntingdon will be seen by the following letter of sympathy addressed to her, under date Blackheath, May 18, 1763, shortly after the death of her daughter, Lady Selina Hastings :—

"MY DEAR MADAM,—Permit Lady Dartmouth and myself to sympathise with you on the recent departure of the amiable and excellent Lady Selina Hastings. Mr. Romaine was so good as to let me see your Ladyship's letter to him, announcing the solemn event, and detailing the supports and Divine consolations which she enjoyed in her last moments. Little did we imagine when we had the pleasure of seeing her so lately in London that she was so near the confines of the eternal world. Lady Dartmouth feels most sensibly for your Ladyship on this occasion, and has been deeply affected by the touching close of your daughter's earthly course. We are deeply indebted to your Ladyship—more deeply than we can express. Our obligations are of a nature never to be repaid by us; but you will be rewarded

openly before an assembled world, when we shall swell that
innumerable train of children which the Lord hath given you.
There, Madam, we shall hope to meet you and join your beatified
child. God grant you grace to feel resigned and submissive
under this event. To His never-failing kindness and mercy we
commend you—living and dying may you be the Lord's!

"With a grateful sense of your kindness, I remain, my dear
Madam, your very affectionate humble servant,

"DARTMOUTH."

The connection of the Rev. John Newton with Lord
Dartmouth commences in 1759, when the former acquainted
his Lordship of his design of episcopal ordination. Five years
later Mr. Browne, the vicar of Olney, removed to Morden
College, Blackheath, in the vicinity of Lord Dartmouth's seat,
and the curacy of Olney was offered to Dr. Haweis, who at the
time he declined it drew his Lordship's attention to Newton.
"How much," exclaims the author of the "Life and Times of
Lady Huntingdon," "the Church of Christ owes to this introduction and his Lordship's kindness!" Newton, as we have
seen, had preached a good deal in Warwickshire and Yorkshire, and, from his previous connection with the Dissenters
and Methodists, had been refused ordination by the Archbishop
of York. Lord Dartmouth, however, not only prevailed on
Dr. Green, Bishop of London, to ordain him, but in a dozen
other different ways exhibited great kindness towards him.
Of the letters written by Newton to Lord Dartmouth, twenty-
six, extending from March 1765 to July 1777, are published
in the "Cardiphonia."

In June 1766 his Lordship paid a long-expected visit to
Olney. "It was a good time!" writes Newton. "What do I
owe the Lord for such countenance on every side! My house
is now to be enlarged to my mind. I preached twice on
Sunday, and Mr. Madan" (Rev. Martin Madan, who had accompanied Lord Dartmouth) "in the evening—a great audi-
tory and an excellent sermon. My noble guest left us on
Tuesday. Much affected with his kindness and generosity and
the Lord's goodness to us."

Lord Dartmouth was an ardent admirer of Whitefield. On

one occasion the church door having been closed against him,
that great preacher addressed the multitudes that had assembled
to hear him from a tombstone in Cheltenham churchyard.
The scene, one never to be forgotten, has been described by
Mr. Venn, one of the four Evangelical ministers present :—The
preacher pouring forth a wonderful torrent of eloquence—Lord
and Lady Dartmouth and the ministers at his side—the
immense throng of people, some sobbing deeply, some weeping
silently, a solemn concern appearing on the countenance of
almost every one—the awful pause of a few seconds made by
the preacher. "Oh with what eloquence," says Mr. Venn,
"what energy, what melting tenderness, did Mr. Whitefield
beseech sinners to be reconciled to God." In the evening the
Sacrament was administered by Mr. Whitefield at his Lordship's
residence, which the next day was thrown open for preaching.
In the morning he addressed a prodigious congregation from
the passage, and in the evening of the same day, exhausted as
he was, preached again, standing upon a table near the front
of the house.

Lord Dartmouth, as we have said, on account of his Christian principles, had to encounter the misrepresentations and
ridicule of many of his friends ; and to the noble lord's isola-
tion on this account Newton refers in a letter dated December
8, 1774.

"The believer's call," he says, "is beautifully and forcibly
set forth in Milton's character of Abdiel, at the end of the Fifth
Book :—

> ' Faithful found
> Among the faithless, faithful only he,
> Among the innumerable false, unmoved,
> Unshaken, unseduced, unterrified,
> His loyalty he kept, his love, his zeal :
> Nor number, nor example, with him wrought
> To swerve from truth or change his constant mind,
> Though single.'

Methinks your Lordship's situation particularly resembles that
in which the poet has placed Abdiel. You are not indeed
called to serve God quite alone ; but amongst those of your
own rank, and with whom the station in which He has placed

you necessitates you to converse, how few there are who can understand, second, or approve the principles upon which you act, or easily bear a conduct which must impress conviction or reflect dishonour upon themselves! But you are not alone. The Lord's people (many of whom you will not know till you meet them in glory) are helping you here with their prayers. His angels are commissioned to guard and guide your steps. Yea, the Lord Himself fixes His eye of mercy upon your private and public path, and is near you at your right hand, that you may not be moved! That He may comfort you with the light of His countenance and uphold you with the arm of His power is my frequent prayer."

As we may see from the following letter, dated June 1773, Newton reckoned his various interviews with Lord Dartmouth among the greatest pleasures of his life. After stating his knowledge that it would be impracticable for his Lordship to visit Olney for some time to come, he goes on to say—" I must content myself with the idea of the pleasure it would give me to sit with you half a day under my favourite great tree, and converse with you, not concerning the comparatively petty affairs of human government, but of things pertaining to the kingdom of God. How many delightful subjects would suggest themselves in a free and retired conversation! The excellency of our King, the permanency and glory of His kingdom, the beauty of His administration, the privileges of His subjects, the review of what He has done for us, and the prospect of what He has prepared for us in the future; and if while we were conversing He should be pleased to join us (as He did the disciples when walking to Emmaus), how would our hearts burn within us! But we cannot meet. All that is left for me is to use the liberty you allow me of offering a few hints upon these subjects by letter, not because you know them not, but because you love them."

Many distinguished leaders of the Evangelical party besides those already named received great kindness from Lord Dartmouth. Romaine in 1764 (shortly before he was inducted to the living of St. Anne's, Blackfriars) was offered a living in the country; Powley (who married Miss Unwin) was in 1777,

through the interest of his Lordship, presented by the King to
the living of Dewsbury, in Yorkshire; Scott in 1780 obtained
the curacy of Olney, and four years later, partly through his
Lordship's influence, was made chaplain of the Lock Hospital.
From what has been said, it will be seen that the motive
power that brought Newton, Cowper, and Scott to Olney was
the Earl of Dartmouth. He first appointed Newton to the
curacy; and Cowper and Mrs. Unwin, solely because they
had been used to evangelical preaching, and had heard of
Newton's excellence, left Huntingdon and settled at Olney.
His Lordship and Cowper were schoolfellows at Westminster,
and sat side by side in the sixth form, and the former, when
he visited Olney, made a point of calling on the poet. They
had previously corresponded, and Cowper makes mention of
Cook's Voyages and other books which his Lordship at various
times had been kind enough to lend him. Newton's income
at Olney was small, only £60 a year, but as soon as his
worth became known, his patron was ever ready to help him.
We have noticed that his Lordship rebuilt the Vicarage, and
that he allowed Newton the use of the Great House at Olney
for prayer-meetings and lectures; it should also be mentioned
that we frequently read of his sending considerable sums of
money for distribution among the poor and needy of the
town; nor do we doubt that, had not Mr. Thornton's muni-
ficence made pecuniary aid quite unnecessary, the noble Earl
would have as readily assisted Newton himself in the same
way that he did so many other excellent, though impecunious,
ministers of the Gospel.

Lord Dartmouth died in the year 1801. Of his public career
we have spoken at some length; in private life it will only be
necessary to say that he gained the affection of all about him;
that "he bore the character of a good husband, a good father,
and a kind master," and that it was his daily endeavour to
put into practice the precepts of the Lord Jesus Christ.

X

THE THREEFOLD CORD, OR LADY AUSTEN AT OLNEY.

> " Now, Sister Anne, the guitar you must take,
> Set it, and sing it, and make it a song."

THE humorous poem of the " Distressed Travellers," addressed
to Lady Austen, who was to " set it, and sing it, and make it
a song," consists mainly of an imaginary dialogue between the
poet himself and Mrs. Unwin, whom he represents as sticking
in the mud, sinking in a hole, slipping and sliding on the
grass, and wading through a flood, as they toil through the wet
and difficult fields between Olney and the neighbouring village
of Clifton Reynes. But the poet made many other journeys
to Clifton amid more agreeable circumstances ; and one at least,
though unsung, was an event of no little importance in his life,
a journey (though a walk of but little over a mile can scarcely
be so called) accomplished when the fields, and even the streams,
were aglow with summer flowers, and when if he did not pay
his customary tributes to the beauties of nature, it must have
been because his attention was entirely absorbed by the fasci-
nating conversation of his new companion. Looking out at
one of his parlour windows a few days previously—it was in
July 1781—he had seen two ladies enter the draper's shop on
the opposite side of the way, one of whom he recognised as
Mrs. Jones, wife of the curate of Clifton, the

> " Martha, ev'n against her will,
> Perched on the top of yonder hill "—

a lady with whom both he and Mrs. Unwin were already intimate. Having been much struck with the appearance of the
stranger, and discovering upon inquiry that she was the sister
of Mrs. Jones, he got Mrs. Unwin to invite the ladies to tea ;

but upon their arrival, in acceptance of the invitation, the poet, who had since repented of his boldness, could not at first muster sufficient courage to join the little party.

But, having at length forced himself into their company, he found Lady Austen such a vivacious and sympathetic companion that he speedily lost all shyness, with which in her presence he seems never afterwards to have been troubled. In his own words, she was "a lively, agreeable woman, who had seen much of the world, and accounted it a great simpleton, as it is—one who laughed and made laugh, and could keep up a conversation without seeming to labour at it." In the evening he escorted the ladies home, and a few days after, with Mrs. Unwin, returned the visit. Although the walk from Olney to Clifton is not described in connective verse, like that at Weston by the Peasant's Nest and the Alcove, its beauties and principal features are frequently alluded to both in his poems and letters. The path leads first through level meadows intersected by narrow arms of the river, and about half-way to Clifton, a few yards beyond the main stream, takes us past the pleasant spot where stood the picturesque old water-mill to which Cowper alludes in "The Winter Morning Walk" ("Task," V.). The current is spoken of as stealing silently and unperceived beneath its sheet of ice and snow, but at the mill it bursts asunder its icy shackles, and

> " Scornful of a check, it leaps
> The mill-dam, dashes on the restless wheel,
> And wantons in the pebbly gulf below :
> No frost can bind it there ; its utmost force
> Can but arrest the light and smoky mist
> That in its fall the liquid sheet throws wide."

The music of its familiar clack and splashing waters has long ceased ; even the mill itself, with all its appurtenances, has disappeared ; but the site is still very beautiful, especially in summer time, when the shallow streams that surround it are yellow with irises, and bristle with reeds, and rushes, and waxlike umbels of butomus.

A few years ago a tall poplar hereabouts having been blown down, the upturned earth revealed a number of flat stones that doubtless belonged to the pavement of some portions of the mill.

The view from the ridge of Clifton Hill is one not soon to be forgotten. The visitor carries away remembrance of the smooth line of the horizon broken by the conspicuous spire of Hanslope church (eight miles distant); the nearer prospect of the Weston uplands (in front of whose woods and spinnies could formerly be seen the old mansion of the Throckmortons); the steep white road leading to Weston; the river winding through the level meadows, and, here and there lost to sight, appearing in the evening sun like a succession of silver lakes; the lines of willows marking the smaller watercourses; the roof-tops of the long town of Olney; the church with its many-lighted steeple and great east window; the mill at Olney; and the straight run of river at the foot of the declivity, lined on the near side by a row of willows, doddered with age, and grown with polypodies and wild raspberry.

The outcome of this meeting of Cowper and Lady Austen was a friendship which, as the former said, gave them and Mrs. Unwin an opportunity to verify Solomon's word that "a threefold cord is not soon broken."

Many pleasant walks and conversations were enjoyed by the friends that summer, and as the following extract from Cowper's rhyming letter to Newton testifies (July 12, 1781), their dissipation extended even to picnicing :—" Mrs. Jones proposes, ere July closes, that she and her sister, and her Jones Mister, and we that are here, our course shall steer, to dine in the Spinnie; but for a guinea, if the weather should hold, so hot and so cold, we had better by far stay where we are. For the grass there grows, while nobody mows (which is very wrong), so rank and so long, that, so to speak, 'tis at least a week, if it happen to rain, ere it dries again."

Everything, however, turned out favourably; so Cowper and Mrs. Unwin, Mr. and Mrs. Jones and Lady Austen, "all dined together in the Spinnie—a most delightful retirement, belonging to Mrs. Throckmorton of Weston. Lady Austen's lackey and a lad that waits on me in the garden drove a wheelbarrow full of eatables and drinkables to the scene of our *fête champêtre.* A board laid over the top of the wheelbarrow served us for a table ; our dining-room was a root-house, lined with moss and ivy. At six o'clock the servants, who had dined under the great elm upon the ground, at a little distance, boiled the kettle, and the said wheelbarrow served us for a tea-table. We then took a walk into the Wilderness, about half a mile off, and were at home again a little after eight, having spent the day together from noon till evening without one cross occurrence, or the least weariness of each other, a happiness few parties of pleasure can boast of."

By the time Lady Austen set out for London in October she and the poet (or rather Sister Anne and Brother William, as they now preferred to call each other) were closest friends. Lady Austen, indeed, made up her mind to disturb Dick Coleman, his wife, and the thousand rats that inhabited one portion of the house occupied by Cowper, and live there herself. "Next spring twelvemonth she begins to repair and beautify, and in the following winter she intends to take possession." In December, to all appearance, the affection between the brother and sister was undiminished, for on the 17th was despatched the " Poetical Epistle to Lady Austen ; " but before February had flown a disagreement occurred, which culminated when the poet wrote a letter that " gave mortal offence." And that was the end of the friendship that promised so much—at least so thought Cowper. Far otherwise it proved, for Lady Austen, soon after, sent a present of three pairs of ruffles, with advice that he should soon receive a fourth. " I knew they were begun before we quarrelled. I begged Mr. Jones to tell her, when he wrote next, how much I thought myself obliged, and gave him to understand that I should make her a very inadequate though the only return in my power by laying my volume at her feet. This likewise she had previous reason given to expect." The volume of poems referred to was published in February 1782. The passing cloud that had obscured his friendship having now blown over, Lady Austen revisited Clifton in August, and once again there were pleasant journeyings to and from Clifton ; she even proposed that Cowper and Mrs. Unwin should leave Olney and hire Clifton Hall.

"We are as happy," he writes to Mr. Unwin (July 16, 1782), "in Lady Austen, and she in us, as ever. Having a lively imagination, and being passionately desirous of consolidating all into one family (for she has taken her leave of London), she has just sprung a project which at least serves to amuse us and to make us laugh ; it is to hire Mr. Small's house, on the top of Clifton Hill, which is large, commodious, and handsome, will hold us conveniently, and any friends who may occasionally favour us with a visit. The house is furnished ; but if it can be hired without the furniture, will let for a trifle."

By and by the walks to Clifton were suddenly interrupted by the autumn rains, which swelled the river and covered the meadows with one great sheet of water. But although parted from his affectionate "sister," the poet, instead of suffering himself to be depressed by the weather, amuses himself by striking off, from a small printing-press she had given him, a short poem on the flood, which poem, by the bye, is said to have been the earliest matter printed in Olney ; and with characteristic drollery, instead of expressing a wish that the waters may abate, cries rather, "Oh that I were a Dutchman, that I need not repine at the mud !"

> "Or meadows deluged with a flood,
> But in a bog live well content,
> And find it just my element."

This Dutch weather seems to have penetrated even the parlour walls, for the printed lines "turn up their tails like Dutch mastiffs." Thus Cowper acted something like the irrepressible Cardinal de Retz, who avenged his captivity by writing an account of his jailer.

An unexpected occurrence now brought the brother and sister together again. Mr. Jones soon after the commencement of the floods had occasion to go to London, and no sooner was he gone than Clifton Rectory, or the "château," as Cowper calls it, "being without a garrison, was besieged" during the night and broken into by thieves ; and the frightened ladies, not daring to stay there alone, came to Olney, and took refuge with Mrs. Unwin. "Men furnished with firearms were put into the house, and the rascals, having intelligence of this circumstance, beat a retreat." Mrs. Jones and Miss Green, her daughter, returned to Clifton ; but Lady Austen, who had not quite recovered from a recent indisposition, had been so scared and terrified that she resolved to remain with Mrs. Unwin until apartments could be prepared for her at Olney Vicarage. This occurrence was subsequently turned to account, for we doubt not that it suggested the Rural Thief in "Task," IV., whose poverty results from idleness, and who prowls abroad for plunder, that

> "He may compensate for a day of sloth
> By works of darkness and nocturnal wrong."

The Vicarage was soon ready for the reception of Lady Austen, and henceforward she and the poet and Mrs. Unwin allowed never a day to pass without meeting ; and so intimate did they become that "a practice obtained at length of dining with each other alternately every day, Sundays excepted."

Then Lady Austen would play on the harpsichord and sing the songs Cowper wrote for her—" No longer I follow a sound," "When all within is peace," or the noble dirge commencing, "Toll for the brave." So the halcyon days went by ; but in the autumn of '82 a dark time seemed at hand ; the poet's brow clouded, a dull heavy feeling pervaded his mind, and he moved about with a vacant woebegone look. Nothing seemed to afford him pleasure ; his books, his favourite hares, his birds, were unnoticed, and he cared not to pace his thirty yards of gravel walk, or to meditate among his apple-trees and holly-hocks in the garden of which he had formerly been so fond.

Mrs. Unwin saw with apprehension the dejected brow and the altered demeanour, and did all that an affectionate woman could do to dispel the darkness, but apparently in vain, and both she and Lady Austen feared that a winter of distress and sorrow was about to succeed a summer of so much happiness. Ten years had elapsed since his last attack, ten had interposed between that and the second attack, and ten between that and the first ; and to all appearance another of these decennial periods of madness awaited the poet. The tenderness of Mrs. Unwin and the vivacity of Lady Austen were equally unavailing, and a foreboding gloom was thrown over the little circle. But one evening, in the famous parlour, the three friends being seated, a droll tale, that she had heard when a girl, came into Lady Austen's mind, and she proposed to tell it. Mrs. Unwin readily assented, but Cowper was silent, for by this time he had got into that pitiable state in which nothing seemed to interest him. This was not very encouraging to Lady Austen, but she began her story, and told how on a time a citizen of the Chepe, Beyer by name, rode out to celebrate the twentieth anniversary of his wedding—how he went farther than he intended, and all his misadventures. The poet, indifferent at first, and apparently paying no attention to what was going on, gradually grew interested as the story proceeded, and Lady Austen, seeing his face brighten, and delighted with her success, wound up the story with all the skill at her command. Cowper could now no longer control himself, but burst out into a loud and hearty peal of laughter. The ladies joined in the mirth, and the merriment had scarcely subsided by supper-time. The story made such an impression on his mind that at night he could not sleep ; and his thoughts having taken the form of rhyme, he sprang from bed, and committed them to paper, and in the morning brought down to Mrs. Unwin the crude outline of " John Gilpin." Only the outline, however. But all that day and for several days he secluded himself in the green-house, and went on with the task of polishing and improving what he had written. As he filled his slips of paper he sent them across the Market-place to Mr. Wilson, to the great delight and merriment of that jocular barber, who on several other occasions had been favoured with the first sight of some of Cowper's smaller poems. This version of the origin of " John Gilpin" differs, we are aware, from the one generally received, which represents the famous ballad as having been commenced and finished in a night ; but that the facts here stated are accurate we have the authority of Mrs. Wilson ; moreover, it has always been said in Olney that " John Gilpin " was written in the " green-house," and that the first person who saw the complete poem, and consequently the forerunner of that noble army who have giggled at its drolleries, was William Wilson the barber. "The story of 'John Gilpin,'" observes Hazlitt, "has perhaps given as much pleasure to as many people as anything of the same length that ever was written."

The ballad was first printed in November 1782, in the *Public Advertiser*, and it not only did the hearts good of its numerous readers, it acted in a similar manner upon the poet himself, for in this same month of November we read of his growing plump, and the ladies told him that he was looking as young as ever.

In July 1783. at the instance of Lady Austen, who playfully suggested the Sofa as a suitable subject to write upon, and to please whom it was written in blank verse, Cowper commenced his *magnum opus*, "The Task;" but long before its publication another rupture had taken place between them. The reason is not clearly known, but it is probable that, finding Lady Austen's attachment to him growing more serious than he had ever intended—for since his dreadful derangement at the Vicarage he had given up all thoughts of marriage (it should be remembered too that he was in his fifty-fourth year)—and seeing himself called on to renounce either one lady or the other, he felt it to be his bounden duty to cling to Mrs. Unwin, to whose kindness he had been indebted for so many years.

The short poem (twelve lines) written by Cowper which Lady Austen interpreted too literally, and which she afterwards showed to Hayley, was printed for the first time in 1870 in the Globe edition of Cowper. It is entitled, "To a lady who wore a lock of his hair set with diamonds," and contains the lines—

> " The heart that beats beneath that breast
> Is William's, well I know :
> A nobler prize and richer far
> Than India could bestow."

Hayley, who was not permitted to print the verses, makes the remark—"Those who were acquainted with the unsuspecting innocence and sportive gaiety of Cowper would readily allow, if they had seen the verses to which I allude, that

they are such as he might have addressed to a real sister ;
but a lady only called by that endearing name may be
easily pardoned if she was induced by them to hope that they
might possibly be a prelude to a still dearer alliance. To
me they appeared expressive of that peculiarity in his character, a gay and tender gallantry perfectly distinct from amorous
attachment."

When matters could go on no longer as they were, "Cowper,"
says Hayley, "wrote a very tender yet resolute letter, in which
he explained and lamented the circumstances that forced him
to renounce her society." She in anger burnt the letter,
and ere long left Olney. The threefold cord was broken !
But "all's well that ends well :" Lady Austen married, soon
after, M. de Tardiff, an accomplished Frenchman, who was
passionately attached to her, and appears to have spent the
remainder of her life very happily (she died in Paris in 1802) ;
whilst the poet and Mrs. Unwin became greater friends than
ever, and the former, setting more earnestly about his literary
work, occupied himself in finishing the great poem that owed
its origin to Lady Austen's suggestion.

XI.

"KILWICK'S ECHOING WOOD."

" There is a field, through which I often pass,
Thick overspread with moss and silky grass,
Adjoining close to Kilwick's echoing wood."
—COWPER : *The Needless Alarm.*

How welcome and exhilarating is the first bright day that
follows the cold, mist, wind, and rain of the dull months of
February and March! Spring came in with a bound last year,
and a single flood of sunshine put the whole country-side into
good-humour; it coaxed the budded sprigs of alehoof till
they purpled every bank, it poured new vigour into the veins
of Jack-by-the-hedge till he and his companions rose as if by
magic in serried and stately ranks, it shed its genial and irresistible influence over field and lane till sloe blossom whitened
the hedges, and every bush and tree, lately so bare, were
burgeoning in tender green. In so goodly a garment, indeed,
was the earth arrayed that this first bright April day seemed
to more than compensate for all the dull months that preceded
it; and we at once made up our minds to take advantage of
the fine weather, and attempt a walk to "Kilwick's echoing
wood," and the venerable hollow tree that is now called
"Cowper's Oak." The way we took, the pleasantest and most
direct one, is the path that gradually rises from the close called
the Pightle, through several enclosures on the west side of
Olney, and is parallel to the road leading from Olney to
Weston, the highest portion being that called by Cowper in his
letters "the Cliff." "One morning last week," he tells Lady
Hesketh (November 26, 1786), "they (the Throckmortons)
both went with me to the cliff—a scene, my dear, in which you
would delight beyond measure, but which you cannot visit
except in the spring or autumn. The heat of summer and

the clinging dirt of winter would destroy you. What is called
the cliff is no cliff, nor at all like one, but a beautiful terrace,
sloping gently down to the Ouse, and from the brow of which,
though not lofty, you have a view of such a valley as makes
that which you see from the hills near Olney, and which I
have had the honour to celebrate, an affair of no consideration."
He thus alludes to it in " The Task : "—

> " How oft upon yon eminence our pace
> Has slackened to a pause, and we have borne
> The ruffling wind, scarce conscious that it blew,
> While admiration, feeding at the eye
> And still unsated, dwelt upon the scene."

By a few vivid touches he then lays the charming panorama
before his readers, the "slow winding Ouse," the square tower
of Clifton church, the tall spire of Olney, "groves, heaths, and
smoking villages remote." From this elevation may be descried,
in clear weather, the village of Steventon, in Beds, and also the
faint profile of Bow Brickhill. In Cowper's day Clifton Hall
could be seen peeping through the trees on Clifton Hill, whilst
on the right stood out conspicuously Weston Hall, the mansion
of the Throckmortons. After leaving this eminence and passing through several other fields we crossed the railway (the
Midland branch from Bedford to Northampton), the scream
of whose engine when first heard probably gave as much alarm
to the sheep of these fields, as the sound of the huntsman's
horn did to their progenitors who obtained celebrity by " The
Needless Alarm." Next we passed the farm-house of Hungry
Hall, and its spinnie-trees dotted with magpies' nests ; and
thence by hedge and ditch, still starred by the celandine, or, to
call it by its local name, the crow-pightle, made for the field
called "Danes' Close." Surely every acre of English ground
is historical, and if one would take the trouble to investigate,
would be found to be interestingly connected either in name
or associations with some stirring epoch in our nation's story :
you can enter scarcely a hamlet or farm-house without hearing
some tradition of Dane or Briton, robber or wizard, bishop or
king. Our interest in the close was heightened by information
concerning two other enclosures hard by, Broadroad and

Watts' Field, both of which, in addition to crops of turnips, occasionally yield broken sword-blades and rusty fragments of armour. But who the combatants were, when they fought, or why they fought, nobody has ascertained : they may have been Britons and Romans, hacking one another, and being hacked, at the time the eagles of Rome were advancing through the island ; they may have been Cavaliers and Roundheads riddling one another with bullets in one of the frequent skirmishes between Rupert and Skippon—all that we know is, that a few of their rusty weapons, from which it would be idle to attempt to extract the secret, are now and again picked up. Then our conversation turned to the hawks that frequent the neighbouring woods and occasionally help themselves to the farmers' chickens, woodpeckers speckled and green, and the last badger that was dug out of Yardley Chase. Luckless little mammal! But why was he not let alone? This English propensity for digging out, knocking down, and knocking over everything that crosses our path is rapidly clearing the fields of all things animate and wild. But it is not the death of a badger, "the last of England's wild beasts," as Phil Robinson aptly calls it, or of any other comparatively harmless little animal, that is most lamented by those who love the country ; and it is not even the slaughter of the larger of our English birds though I am sure the reader would have been grieved had he seen the jackdaw that lay dead, but still warm, at a stile—a poor unfortunate that was stigmatised by the labourer who killed it as a "mischievous young beggar," and would heartily have wished that jackdaws were less sinful or ploughmen's hearts more tender. All this havoc is undesirable enough, but what is most to be deplored is the wholesale destruction, every spring, and for no earthly reason except the mere love of mischief, of the eggs of the smaller birds, even the sweetest songsters. Our woods and hedgerows are rapidly depeopling, and North Bucks is unhappily as badly off in this respect as other districts, many species of small birds that were once common having in recent years quite disappeared. Surely those who love birds and delight in their song should not rest satisfied, as many do, with talking regretfully of the gradual disappearance

of our songsters. Ought they not rather to point out to
thoughtless schoolboys over whom they may have any influence or control (for schoolboys are the chief delinquents)
the cruelty and folly of such procedure, and do their best to
prevent it. Surely it should at the present day be instilled
into the minds of the young that

> " He prayeth best who loveth best
>   All things both great and small."

It is pleasing, whilst speaking on this subject, to be able to
state that several gentlemen in Olney and its neighbourhood
have long exhibited their humanity and good taste by strictly
forbidding the disturbance of nests in their gardens and
plantations.

We now gained the confines of Dinglederry and Kilwick;
and as if to bring to our minds even more vividly the scenes
in Cowper's poem, "The Needless Alarm," the cry of the
hounds was heard as we passed through Kilwick Wood, and
we stood aside to see the hunt ride picturesquely among the
trees; whilst

> " With the high-raised horn's melodious clang
>   All Kilwick and all Dinglederry rang."

The primrose had only just begun to show its yellow, but
numbers of anemones were nodding their fragile cups about
the tree stumps, and mercury stained the ground in dark
green patches. Emerging from the wood our eye naturally
roves towards the ancient tree, the object of our pilgrimage,
and a few more steps bring us under its branches, the whole
walk from Olney being about two and a half miles. How
can we better speak of the veteran than in Cowper's own
words, for though it has lost a few stout limbs and upholds a
little more dead wood, it has not greatly altered since he
wrote the poem entitled "Yardley Oak." Behold then a
"hollow trunk" with "excoriate forks deform."

> " A giant bulk,
> Of girth enormous, with moss-cushioned root
> Upheaved above the soil, and sides emboss'd
> With prominent wens globose."

" Time made thee what thou wast—king of the woods ;
And time hath made thee what thou art—a cave
For owls to roost in."

Writing from Weston to Mr. S. Rose, September 11, 1788, Cowper says :—"Since your departure I have twice visited the oak, and with an intention to push my inquiries a mile beyond it, where it seems I should have found another oak much larger

COWPER'S OAK.

and much more respectable than the former ; but once I was hindered by the rain, and once by the sultriness of the day. This taller oak has been known by the name of Judith many ages, and is said to have been an oak at the time of the Conquest. If I have not an opportunity to reach it before your arrival here, we will attempt that exploit together ; and even if I should have been able to visit it ere you come, I shall be glad to do so; for the pleasure of extraordinary sights, like other pleasures, is doubled by the participation of a friend." The oak first referred to is that now called ' Cowper's Oak," and the one to which Cowper's noble poem is addressed.

The second oak, the one called Judith, situated near Yardley Lodge, and a mile farther from Weston than the first, is now called Gog (the larger of the two trees Gog and Magog). As is easily seen by any one who visits these trees, Cowper's description of their situation is as clear as daylight. But he is not only clear—he makes a similar statement in another letter written September 13, 1788 (two days after), to Lady Hesketh. We quote from this also:—"I walked with him " (Mr. Gifford) "yesterday on a visit to an oak on the border of Yardley Chase, an oak which I often visit, and which is one of the wonders that I show to all who come this way and have never seen it. I tell them all that it is a thousand years old, believing it to be so, though I do not know it. A mile beyond this oak stands another, which has from time immemorial been known by the name of Judith, and is said to have been an oak when my namesake the Conqueror first came hither. And beside all this, there is a good coachway to them both, and I design that you shall see them too."

Notwithstanding the perfect clearness of Cowper's description, almost every person who has hitherto spoken of the trees has curiously confused them, and it has been repeatedly, though erroneously, said that what is now called " Cowper's Oak " is the one that was formerly called Judith, whilst all mention as to the situation of the other tree has been forborne. How the mistake arose is easy to see. Hayley, instead of reading carefully Cowper's description, wrote to Dr. Johnson of Norfolk to ask for particulars. Dr. Johnson wrote in reply a letter which completely muddles up the affair. It may be seen in Hayley's " Life of Cowper." This letter misled Hayley, and has misled almost every person who has dealt with the subject ever since. The facts, then, are these. Firstly, the Yardley Oak, the tree to which the poem is addressed, the hollow tree, the tree said by Cowper to be 22 feet

6½ inches in girth, is the one now called "Cowper's Oak," situated three miles from Weston, just beyond Kilwick Wood, near Cowper's Oak farm-house. Secondly, the oak at Yardley Lodge, the perfectly sound tree, the tree that was formerly called Judith, the tree said by Cowper to be 28 feet 5 inches in girth, is the one now usually called Gog, and is situated a mile farther from Weston than the last mentioned, near the old-fashioned farm-house of Chase Farm, which was formerly called the Ranger's Lodge. These facts, which are gathered from Cowper's letters, tally exactly with local tradition. Indeed, had it not been for Dr. Johnson's letter there would never have been any confusion. The name Judith, by which Gog was originally known, was possibly obtained from its having been planted by the Lady Judith, niece to the Conqueror, and wife of Earl Waltheof.

The following memorandum was found among the poet's papers after his death :—"Yardley Oak, in girth, feet 22, inches 6½. The oak at Yardley Lodge, feet 28, inches 5." The poem on Yardley Oak was written in 1791, but owing to Cowper's engrossment in other matters it was thrown aside unfinished, and never published during his lifetime. We owe its preservation to the diligence of Hayley, who alighted upon it after a long search among the piles of books and papers that had been consigned to his keeping. "I could hardly have been more surprised," observed the delighted biographer, "if a noble oak in its material majesty had started up from the turf of my garden, with full foliage, before me." Gog and Magog are both larger than "Cowper's Oak." Gog is now 32 feet in girth, measured at about 5 feet from the ground. Close to the ground, by reason of the huge protuberances and mighty roots, it is, of course, far greater. Magog, which stands at a distance of fifty yards from its tremendous brother, is 29 feet in girth, and its trunk is not nearly so irregular.

XII

TWO OLD MEETING-HOUSES.

I. THE BAPTIST MEETING.

THE Upper or Baptist Meeting, or, as it has latterly been
styled, in memory of its distinguished minister, the Sutcliff
Chapel, is a quaint and exceedingly plain seventeenth-century
Meeting-house, and presents, we should imagine, as regards
internal arrangement, much the same appearance to-day as it
did in the reign of King William III. It is oblong in plan ;
the pulpit, which is narrow, is placed against the middle of
the back long wall, whilst to the other three walls are affixed
cumbrous galleries supported by wooden pillars. The lofty
panelling at the back of the pulpit attracts our attention, and
our imagination furnishes it again with the large peg, " on
which," in the words of Dr. Halley, " on occasion of funeral
sermons hung solemnly the preacher's hat, with its silken
tokens of mourning." We are interested too in that indispen-
sable and often costly article with the early Dissenters, the
great red cushion, with its tassels, or, as one old church-book
has it, the " Pulpitt Quishion," whilst just below stands the
stiff-looking deacon's chair. The pews are deep and perpen-
dicular-backed, with doors fastened by wooden buttons. The
larger pews, which are square, with green baize and rows of
brass-headed nails, appear to be a modern innovation ; for in
the indentures of the Meeting-house of the 19th of January
1694 it is stipulated that " every such pew or seat shall not
contain or extend above four foot and a half in length and
four foot in breadth," a regulation of more importance than
we in the present day might suppose, seeing that " the families who rented these great pews regarded them almost as
private property, and would have been nearly as much offended

by the intrusion of a stranger as if he had gone uninvited into their dining-room." [1]

Just in front of the pulpit is the "Communion or table pew," so called on account of the table placed therein for the celebration of the Lord's Supper.

In the tops of the pews still remain the holes into which the old-fashioned wooden candlesticks were inserted, reminding us of the days, before gas was dreamt of, when some grave old brother used periodically and solemnly to march round the meeting with the snuffers, and of the boys of the last generation nudging one another naughtily as now and again a candle was inadvertently snuffed out.

The exterior of the building, as would be expected, is altogether destitute of ornament. In the front wall are two stones bearing dates, one 1694, when the Meeting was erected, the other 1763, when it was enlarged.

The oldest monument in the burying-ground is that to the memory of Samewell Finding, who died 2nd of March 1695. There is a large altar-tomb to the Rev. John Sutcliff,[2] and a stone to William Wilson, several times spoken of in this book as Cowper's barber. In the graveyard too is a flourishing tree which sprang from an acorn from "Cowper's Oak" planted by Mr. Wilson on January 1, 1800.

The earliest date in the church-book is 1752, but the articles of the covenant are copied from a much older volume, which is now lost. All are more or less quaint, but the palm undoubtedly belongs to the twelfth and thirteenth.

"XII. Though in some respects a woman is allowed to speak in the church, yet not in such as carries in it direction, instruction, government, and authority; for she must be in subjection under obedience, not to teach nor to resist authority over the man, 1 Cor. xiv. 34, 35—1 Tim. ii. 11 and 12, but to be and learn in silence. We therefore have agreed that no sister shall be permitted to speak in the church except it be in a way of submission and in subjection, or in answer to any question proposed to her by the church ; and that order might be observed, and confusion be

---

1 Rev. R. Halley's "Lancashire : Its Puritanism and Nonconformity," 1869.
2 There is a mural monument to his memory in the chapel.

prevented at our church meetings, the Brethren are not to speak above one at a time in any matter of debate there.

"XIII. And whereas we are not all of one mind respecting the ordinance of singing, we have in this our covenant agreed to allow each member their liberty to act according to their consciences therein without offence."

Curiously, this thirteenth article has been crossed out since; so, as the covenant now stands, liberty of conscience is not allowed in respect to singing. Willy-nilly, sing you must.

A few of the entries must here be quoted :—

"Had our church meeting, our messengers who admonished E. Burditt brought word that she remained stupid and unimpressed. Agreed to let her case rest as it is for the present."

Of one person it is said—and matters are not minced in an early Baptist church-book—" Excluded, her sin was lying;" of another, "Excluded, for a failure in the world, attended with such circumstances as were very reproachful to religion." One of the members, William Ashburner, "was suddenly translated," and another "sweetly fell asleep in Jesus."

The following, too, is well worthy of our notice :—

"John Tupp attempted to exhibit a charge against Thomas Osborn for an offence of a private nature, but being asked whether or not he had taken the divine rule in Matt. xviii. 15, and answering in the negative, the church refused to admit it."

This is as it should be. How very many misunderstandings might be set right if only, when offended with one another, we would carry out the precept of the Saviour and go and tell our brother privately. The following extract shows the importance of some acquaintance with the phraseology of early Dissent if we would rightly understand its records, for it was doubtless written by some grave-faced deacon into whose head the thought never entered that it was not without a trace of humour :—

"An inquiry was made relative to Hugh Webb, viz., what situation he was in. It appeared that at a church meeting some years ago he had leave given him to *sit down*, that he had refused to accept of it, and *never had sat down*. He never having accepted what was offered, and some freely expressing their dissatisfaction with him, it was agreed by the church that he should be looked upon by the church as *standing at a distance.*"

The next page tells us that " Hugh Webb desired that his name might be erased," and adds, " He had long been an *irregular walker*, and as such was excluded."

II. The Early Days of Nonconformity in Olney.

It is not to be wondered at that at an early period Nonconformists were numerous in this neighbourhood, for hereabouts laboured and suffered three of their most indomitable leaders. At Northampton during the latter part of his life dwelt Robert Brown, the founder of the Brownists, from whom sprang the Independents, and in Northampton jail in 1630 he died at the age of eighty-one; at Bedford John Bunyan preached and wrote, and in Bedford jail underwent an imprisonment of twelve years; and at Newport Pagnell and Olney the distinguished and influential John Gibbs spent the greater part of his life. The Rev. John Gibbs, who for about fourteen years had been vicar of Newport Pagnell, was ejected from his living about 1660, on account, we are told, of his refusal to admit to the Lord's Table a parishioner who possessed considerable influence but was notoriously immoral. Whether such was the case or not, it is asserted by both Baxter and Calamy that for conscience' sake, and for conscience' sake alone, Mr. Gibbs was ejected from the living; moreover, the ejectment took place too long before the Act of Uniformity to have had any connection with that enactment, which did not become law until the 24th of August 1662. Mr. Gibbs, too, must have been ejected in or before 1660, as his successor, the Rev. Robert Marshall, was inducted on the 24th of March of that year, that is, during the brief period of anarchy that immediately preceded the accession of Charles II., who landed at Dover on May 25.

The occasion on which Mr. Gibbs's name first appears prominent is in connection with a public controversy (a common occurrence in those days) which took place whilst he was yet

I

vicar, between him and another native of Newport Pagnell, the quaint, versatile, pedantic, and conceited Richard Carpenter. After the controversy the latter published a book on the subject with the following title, "The Anabaptist, washt, and washt, and shrunk in the washing : or a scholasticall discussion of the much agitated controversie concerning Infant Baptism ; occasioned by a publicke disputation, before a great assembly of ministers and other persons of worth, in the church of Newport Pagnell, between Mr. Gibbs, minister there, and the author, Richard Carpenter, Independent."

Mr. Gibbs, who, by the bye, was called by Carpenter "a heady enthusiast" and "a lean, lone, Pagnell saint," became after his ejectment the local leader of Nonconformity, and preached in a large barn, near the site of which now stands the Newport Pagnell Independent Meeting. He was frequently imprisoned, and, to quote a quaint elegy written shortly after his death, was engaged " in dangers great and perils night and day," and " wicked ones . . . his hair pulled off, his person much abused." We first hear of his name in connection with Olney in 1669. In the deeds which were drawn up at the time of the erection of the Baptist Meeting he is styled "pastor of a congregated church in Newport Pagnell and Olney." Hence we infer that although Mr. Gibbs resided at Newport Pagnell he was looked upon by the Nonconformists of Olney as their head or pastor, in other words, that the two churches were regarded as one. As will presently be seen, he was assisted in his labours here by several other persons ; but it is not improbable that many of the Olney Nonconformists would spend their Sundays in Newport, people in those days thinking nothing of going five, ten, or even twenty miles to hear preaching ; but it is also probable that during part of the time the Five Mile Act was in operation Mr. Gibbs preached constantly at Olney in Joseph Kent's barn, on the site of which stands the Baptist Meeting, and if so would undoubtedly be followed every Sunday by his Newport congregation, who would get here about nine in the morning, in time for the first service, and leave about nine in the evening, soon after the last.

In the Lambeth MSS. (Tenison), "An Account of the Conventicles in Lincoln Diocese, 1669," we find the following notice of Olney and neighbourhood :—" Parishes and Conventicles in them : Olney 2, at the house of Widow Tears ; Newton Blossomville in private houses." As regards sect, &c., those at Olney are called Anabaptists ; their number was "about 200, but decrease." Their quality is not described, but their " Heads or Teachers " are stated to be, " Mr. Gibbs, Mr. Breeden, and James Rogers, Lace-buyers, and one Fenne, a Hatter."

The number at Newton Blossomville is put at fifty or sixty, who are described as "meane people, but such as say they value not His Majesty's clemency one pin."

This account was drawn up at a time when Nonconformists were being treated with great severity, but three years later their prison doors were thrown open and persecutions suspended by the "Indulgence of 1672," in which it was stated "that the experience of twelve years had proved the inefficiency of coercive measures in matters of religion ; that the King found himself obliged to make use of that supreme power in ecclesiastical matters which was not only inherent in him, but had been declared and recognised to be so by several statutes and acts of Parliament ; . . . that it was, moreover, his will and pleasure that all manner of penal laws in matters ecclesiastical against whatsoever sort of Nonconformists or recusants, should be from that day suspended ; and that to take away all pretence for illegal or seditious conventicles he would license a sufficient number of places and teachers for the exercise of religion among the Dissenters, which places and teachers so licensed should be under the protection of the civil magistrate."

This indulgence was gratefully accepted by the Dissenters, who presented by their ministers an address of thanks to the King ; and in the course of the year licenses to preach were granted to the number of upwards of three thousand. The famous John Bunyan applied not only for a license on his own account, "for Josias Roughead's house in his orchard in Bedford," but also for licenses for twenty-five other places in Beds and the adjacent counties, two of which are of peculiar interest to us: that on account of John Gibbs "for William Smyth's barn and his own house in Newport Pagnell," and of

William Hensman, "for Joseph Kent, his barn in Olney."
The application is dated May 9, 1672, and is in Bunyan's
handwriting in the Record Office, with the rest of the applica-
tions in a bundle. The indulgence, however, was cancelled in
1678, and matters went on almost as badly as before. Bunyan's
labours were by no means confined to Bedford—it was his
custom to make missionary excursions into the neighbouring
country, and consequently the community at Olney was frequently indebted to him. About this time it would seem that
to avoid notice and to obviate the capture of their ministers the
Nonconformists of Olney used to meet at Northey or Northway,
a farm-house about three miles distant, situated at only a few
yards from "Three Counties' Point;" so the ministers if inter-
fered with could evade the myrmidons of the law by escaping
into either of the neighbouring counties of Beds and Northants.

The room in which the worshippers used to meet, and in
which, according to tradition, Bunyan sometimes addressed
them, is still shown at Northway.

Thus in solitary farm-houses, mean barns, and even in the
midst of woods, did the early Dissenters worship, and in these
barns and solitudes did their pastors preach, according to
Anthony Wood and other of their enemies, "for profit's sake, to
silly women and other obstinate people," or as the obstinate
people themselves said, "to the edification of the saints and
the glory of God."

In the year 1676 was made a religious census of the Province
of Canterbury. A copy of the returns is preserved in the
William Salt Library at Stafford. This interesting record,
which was bought for fifteen guineas by Mr. Salt in 1844 at the
sale of the library of the Duke of Sussex, not only contains the
census of 1676, but also gives the number of Conformists, Nonconformists, and Papists in the various parishes of the Province.
"Careful attention lately given to the volume has shown, however, that all the parishes were not dealt with; that returns
were never all perfect, or that some portions were lost; that
the inquiry was not made in a manner methodical enough to
produce conclusive results."[1]

[1] T. J. Mazzinghi.

Nevertheless the results are extremely interesting, and although the relative numbers may not be accurate, the totals for each parish are probably not far from the mark.

The following are the results given in the Salt MSS. for Olney, Newport Pagnell, Bedford, and Northampton :—

Oulney cum Warrington—
Conformists . . 832
Papists . . . 0
Nonconformists . . 137

Newport Pagnell—
Conformists . 905
Papists . . 1
Nonconformists . 126

Bedford—
Conformists . . 1117
Papists . . 1
Nonconformists . 121

Northampton (three parishes, no return being given for St. Peter's)—
Conformists . . 2535
Papists . . . 0
Nonconformists . 43

The inquiry applied only to inhabitants above the age of sixteen, so in order to get an idea of the population of the above towns we must double the figures. Hence that of Olney would be about 1938, Newport 2064, and Bedford 2478. That of Northampton was probably a trifle over 6000.

It will be interesting to note that in 1881 the population of Olney was 2347, Newport Pagnell 3686, Bedford 19,532, Northampton 51,881.

The church at Olney, which admitted a mixed communion, grew under Mr. Gibbs's wise guidance into a large and united body, and at length, in 1694, five years after the passing of the Toleration Act, they pulled down Joseph Kent's barn and put up the Meeting-house that is now standing. In the Deeds which were drawn up at this time it is laid down that "no person or persons shall at any time hereafter be admitted or permitted to preach, pray, or perform any other religious worship or service in the aforesaid assemblies or upon the said premises or any part thereof but such as shall from time to time concur, agree, and be of the same persuasion and judgment in respect of doctrine, discipline, and worship with John Gibbs of Newport Pagnell, in the said county of Bucks, clerk, Pastor of a congregated church in Newport Pagnell and Olney aforesaid."

Mr. Gibbs died in 1699, and was buried near the south

door of the chancel of Newport Pagnell church. Of the altar-tomb erected to his memory only a few fragments now remain, but a handsome monument to him was some years ago erected in the Newport Independent chapel.

About a year after his death a division took place at Olney, and part of the congregation, with Mr. Maurice, the pastor, a Pædo-Baptist, laid the foundation of the present Independent interest. The Independent Meeting was erected in 1700.

It has been pointed out by Lord Macaulay and Bishop Ryle that with the cessation of persecution the energy, and consequently the power, of the Noncomformists sensibly declined; and Nonconformist writers themselves, whilst loud in their praises of the ministers and people under the Stuarts, record sadly the incapacity of the former and the carelessness and numerical weakness of the latter during William, Anne, and the elder Georges. In a manuscript history of Bicester Meeting to which I have recently had access, the writer thus mournfully finishes his account of the shortcomings of one of its ministers :—"Alas! in the pulpit during his ministry the gold was become dim and the most fine gold changed. Oh, how it is to be lamented that in many places after the ejected ministers and their immediate successors were dead their pulpits should be so improperly filled!" In some towns, Thame and Risboro for instance, the buildings were shut up and the congregations quite lost. If the ministers at Bicester were a fair type of those at other places, there is little reason to be surprised that everything went wrong. Of one of them the writer before quoted remarks—"Gay and light in his practice, fond of convivial company, it is no wonder to find the congregation dwindled under his pastoral care;" of another, "A slave to his ale and pipe;" another "was not only a tippler, but was subject to extreme passion and used his wife ill." Amid this general corruption, however, a considerable number of pastors and people kept themselves pure and unspotted, and now and again we read of a man, the pride of his hearers, who "had the whole Scriptures at his finger ends, and would quote text, chapter, and verse from Genesis to Revelation." What went on at the Baptist church, Olney, during the early part of the eighteenth century we cannot tell, for the old church-book is lost, and no other records are known to exist; but from the fact that the number of members was very small at the middle of the century, we should imagine that the history of this period would not be particularly edifying. Even the great revival of religion, the result of the labours of Wesley and others, seems to have had but little effect in waking up the Baptists of Olney, for both pastors and people appear to have been tainted with hyper-Calvinism; and until, in the time of Sutcliff, this was thrown off, the cause made but little headway. Mr. Walker, the immediate predecessor of Mr. Sutcliff, was called to the pastoral work on November 21, 1753, and appears to have been a very worthy man. It was during his ministry that the Rev. John Newton came to Olney. "Last night," wrote the latter (July 14, 1764), "I was at Mr. Walker's meeting, to hear Mr. Grant from Wellingborough;" and added, "I am engaged to dine with Mr. Grant at Mr. Ashburner's. I shall take this opportunity to set the door of acquaintance wide open. If they choose to keep it so, it is well; if not, I have but done my duty." The Dissenters of Olney did choose to keep open this door of friendly feeling, and in consequence the greatest harmony prevailed between Newton and their ministers.

The Rev. John Sutcliff, A.M., was pastor from November 1775 until his death in June 1814; Rev. James Simmons from February 1818 to 1834, and again from April 1842 to March 1858 (thirty-two years in all). During his absence were two short pastorates, those of Rev. John James (January 1835 to August 1839, when he died) and Rev. John Davis (August 1840 to June 1841). To Mr. Simmons succeeded Rev. Richard Hall, B.A. (October 1858 to February 1860), Rev. Frederick Timmis (November 1860 to September 1865) and Rev. Thomas Henry Holyoak (July 1866 to July 1870). The late Rev. Joseph Allen, B.A., who died 20th April 1892, had been pastor here since January 1, 1872.

III. THE INDEPENDENT MEETING.

The Lower or Independent Meeting, as already stated, was erected in the year 1700, its first pastor, Mr. Maurice, having a short time previous, together with part of his congregation, seceded from the Baptists. As it was taken down so recently, a detailed description would be unnecessary, even if it possessed (which it did not) features at all peculiar or uncommon. It was merely a plain, unpretending, square structure, very similar as regards internal arrangements to the Baptist Meeting; stood back from the street, from which it was almost entirely hidden by a house; and was approached through a gateway (which had a room over it) just wide enough for an ordinary vehicle. The front consisted of one great gable containing a circular opening, above which was a stone bearing the date 1762 (at which time, probably, the building was enlarged and a new front built); a row of plain semicircular-headed windows, similar to that in the front of the second storey of the schoolrooms (still standing); and two square-headed windows below, one each side the door, above which was a semicircular light. The galleries were originally approached from the outside, but of late years the doorway on the right had been walled up.

Mr. Maurice, who removed to Rowell, in Northamptonshire, was succeeded by Mr. Gibbons, father of the gifted Dr. Thomas Gibbons (born May 31, 1720) of Haberdashers' Hall, London, author of " Hymns Adapted to Divine Worship," published in 1784, and biographer of Dr. Watts. Many of Dr. Gibbons's hymns are well known, and several are of rare merit. Perhaps the finest is that commencing as follows :—

> " Now let our souls, on wings sublime,
> Rise from the vanities of time ;
> Draw back the parting veil, and see
> The glories of eternity."

But scarcely less beautiful is the one commencing thus—

> " Thy goodness, Lord, our souls confess,
> Thy goodness we adore ;
> A spring whose blessings never fail,
> A sea without a shore !"

One of the best of missionary hymns, too, is his—

> "Great God ! the nations of the earth
> Are by creation Thine ;
> And in Thy works, from nature's birth
> Thy power and glory shine."

The circumstances attending Dr. Gibbons's death were somewhat remarkable. In reply to a question, " How are you, Doctor ? " he answered, " Perfectly well, madam, I bless God." He then walked into that person's parlour, and a few minutes afterwards was found lying on the floor in a fit. This was on the 17th of February 1785. For three days he remained speechless, though he appeared to breathe freely, and died on the 22d of that month, in his sixty-fifth year. His remains are interred in Bunhill Fields.

" In Mr. Gibbons's time the interest was considerable, but upon his removal to Royston it sank almost to nothing, and there was no pastor for many years. About the year 1737 several serious Independents joined themselves to a little church at Yardley. Mr. Drake was pastor there. In the year 1738 he began to preach once a day at Olney and once at Yardley. He continued this for nineteen or twenty years, at which time the interest at Olney being much the larger, and the infirmities of old age rendering him incapable of riding backwards and forwards, he came wholly to Olney in 1759."[1] After a ministry of upwards of forty years he died on the 10th of August 1775.

There are several references to this excellent man in the Diary of the Rev. John Newton. On Tuesday, September 26, 1765, he writes, " Omitted our prayer-meeting to-night and attended Mr. Bradbury, who preached a very good sermon at Mr. Drake's. I am glad of such opportunities at times to discountenance bigotry and party spirit, and to set our Dissenting brethren an example, which I think ought to be our practice towards all who love the Lord Jesus Christ and preach His Gospel without respect to forms or denominations."

On December 30, 1767, Mr. Newton went to the Baptist Meeting to hear the sermon to the young people, and on the

---

[1] Extract from a MS. " History of Dissenting Churches," in the library of the Baptist College, Bristol ; kindly sent by Dr. Culross. The church-books of the Independent Meeting, Olney, are lost.

31st he put off his usual Thursday evening lecture, not to interfere with Mr. Drake's service, which he also attended. The day after, which was New Year's Day, Newton himself preached at the church. This custom of preaching New Year sermons to the young at each of the three places of worship—a custom which, as appears from the above, is of more than a hundred years' standing—has continued without intermission to the present time.

Curious to say, the minister who succeeded Mr. Drake was Mr. Whitford, who was an old friend of the Rev. John Newton, and had, in fact, at one time studied under him. Mr. Whitford, who was pastor at Olney from 1776 to 1783, had been on intimate terms with Newton during his residence at Liverpool, and "the sight of him," says the latter, "revived the remembrance of many incidents long since past." Eight of Newton's letters to him are published in the "Cardiphonia." Of the ministers of the "Independent Meeting," however, the best remembered is Mr. Hillyard, who occupied the pulpit from 1783 to 1828, and who was, we are told, "a man of superior talents, of primitive simplicity of manners, charitable in spirit, eminent in prayer, a constant observer of Providence, and a laborious and successful minister of the Gospel." "The Lower Meeting," writes Cowper to Newton, April 5, 1783, "has found a minister at last, and the people, it seems, are fond of him. His name, I think, is Hillyard. While he is new he will be sure to please." In another letter to Newton, written in the following June, he says—

"Mr. Hillyard, Mr. Whitford's successor, who came hither from Kimbolton, is very acceptable, and much followed. Though a man of no education, he has taken great pains to inform his mind. He often pronounces a word wrong, but always uses it with propriety. He is never out of temper in the pulpit, but his sermons are experimental, searching, and evangelical. He bids fair, consequently, for considerable success. A people will always love a minister if a minister seems to love his people."

About the middle of his pastorate Cowper died, and in the absence of Mr. Hillyard the Rev. Samuel Greatheed of Newport Pagnell, the friend of Cowper, preached on May 18, 1800, the well-known funeral sermon on the poet, from the appropriate text, Isa. lv. 8, 9, "For as the heavens are higher than the earth, so are my ways higher than your ways, and my thoughts than your thoughts." It was afterwards printed, and dedicated, with her permission, to Lady Hesketh.

In 1815, on account of Mr. Hillyard's declining strength, it was deemed necessary that assistance should be obtained, and at length it was arranged that the Rev. John Morris should supply the pulpit every third Sunday, with a view to becoming co-pastor. After a probation of twelve months Mr. Morris was ordained (October 1816), and the two pastors laboured harmoniously until Mr. Hillyard's death, which occurred on July 12, 1828, after a pastorate of forty-four years. After Mr. Morris's removal in December 1840 (his term of office having extended over twenty-four years) there was a succession of short pastorates, those of the following being the longest:—Rev. Isaac Vaughan (1841–1849), Rev. Wilkes Simmons (1856–1860), Rev. T. W. Mays, M.A. (1861–1865), Rev. J. T. Grey (January 1866–October 1867), Rev. T. Coop (1869–1875).

Early in 1875 the oversight of the church was accepted by the Rev. G. G. Horton, who is the present pastor. In 1879, after standing one hundred and seventy-nine years, the Independent Meeting-house, or, as it was latterly called, the Congregational Chapel, was taken down and the "Cowper Memorial Congregational Church" erected on its site.

The latter building, the front of which is about 20 feet nearer the street than that of the old one, is rectangular in plan, measuring 65 feet by 38 feet internally, seating 328 adults in the ground floors, and 122 in the gallery, making a total of 450. The walls are of local stone with Bath stone dressings. The principal features of the exterior are the large double-entrance doorway, and the two traceried windows above, with a shaft between supporting a figure of Cowper in the gable. In the same year, 1879, the opportunity was taken of securing a frontage to the street, by purchasing and removing the tenement that had hidden the old building.

XIII.

THE REV. JOHN SUTCLIFF, A.M.

I. Wainsgate and Bristol, 1752–1775 (Twenty-three Years).

The associations of this neighbourhood with those eminent men, Cowper, Newton, and Scott, have been diligently recorded by numerous writers, and most persons are to some extent conversant with them; but, singularly enough, the intimate connection between Olney and the great Missionary movement that stirred the whole nation at the close of the last and at the commencement of the present century has hitherto been completely ignored. How many are aware that Sutcliff, one of the committee of five who founded the Baptist Missionary Society, the first of English Protestant Missions, and whose home labours for the cause were second only to those of Andrew Fuller, was for nearly forty years minister of the Baptist church at Olney?—that William Carey, the founder of the Baptist Missions, studied under Sutcliff, was for two years a member of the church at Olney, and from Olney was sent into the ministry?—that William Ward, the celebrated coadjutor of Carey, and his equally enthusiastic, though less famous, companion Brunsdon were dedicated to their glorious work at Olney, on which occasion the crowded worshippers were melted to tears by the touching letter of Samuel Pearce, whose life was fast ebbing out, written almost with the death-sweat upon his forehead? How many are aware that twelve of the earliest missionaries were prepared for their labours by Mr. Sutcliff, and that the trumpet voices that subsequently roused the sleep of superstition by the sacred rivers of Bengal, in the devil-temples of Ceylon, and on the sultry plains of Java were first exercised in the quaint old Baptist Meeting-house at Olney?

We look back with pride that such scenes should have been here enacted, and that the labours of so many men who afterwards showed themselves so valiant in the cause of Christ should have here commenced; and in this and the following sketch shall give some account of Sutcliff and Carey, two of the most distinguished leaders of the great Missionary movement.

The name of John Sutcliff has long been honoured in the religious world. It is true that he was not a distinguished missionary like the indefatigable Carey, not a ubiquitous worker for the Mission and a prolific writer like Andrew Fuller; nor was he remarkable as an orator and a preacher like his gifted contemporary Robert Hall. Carey, with an enthusiasm fiercer than that which in mediæval times impelled Saint Francis of Assisi, sailed to India, and, after encountering manifold dangers and difficulties, succeeded in establishing the Baptist Mission; Fuller, the life and soul of the Society, the wonder of his own age and of ours, travelled the country through, preaching incessantly, and struggling now with Socinianism, now with East Indian directors, now with Antinomianism and Sandemanianism, and now with influential members of Parliament and Cabinet Ministers—and rarely struggling in vain; whilst the polished productions of Robert Hall's genius are reckoned among the classics of our language: each had his particular work in the world, and each, we verily believe, performed it to the best of his ability; but Sutcliff's work, though less brilliant, was equally important, and was done equally well.

Sutcliff was the clear-sighted adviser, the Nestor of the Mission, and his singular wisdom was a bulwark in which, under God, Fuller and Ryland placed entire confidence; and on him devolved the duty, so nobly performed, of training the students.

John Sutcliff was born in a sequestered spot called Strait-hey, near Hebden Bridge, in Yorkshire, on the 9th of August 1752 (O.S.). Like many other men who have laboured diligently for God, he owed much to home training; for Daniel and Hannah Sutcliff, his parents, both exemplary characters, paid strict attention to the instruction and government of their children. For a few years after he left school he appears to have assisted his father, who was a farmer. At the age of sixteen we find him teaching in a day school under the Rev. Dan Taylor, at Birch-cliffe, in the neighbourhood of Hebden Bridge; and on May 28, 1769, when in his seventeenth year, we hear of his becoming a member of the church meeting at Wainsgate, of which Dr. John Fawcett was pastor.

A year or two after joining the church he announced his desire to become a minister of the Gospel, and his friends, who saw that he was of a serious and studious turn of mind, and appeared to possess gifts suited to the ministry, having received his proposal with gladness, he for a short time underwent a course of study with Dr. Fawcett.

In January 1772, by the recommendation of Dr. Fawcett and the Wainsgate church, he was sent to Bristol College, then under the care of the Revs. Hugh and Caleb Evans. Although of a weakly constitution, it had long been his custom to perform all his journeys on foot, solely with a view to save a little money for the purchase of books; and consequently, although it was the depth of winter, he walked the whole of the way from his native place to Bristol (about two hundred miles), performing the journey in seven days, at an expense of something under twenty shillings. He left Bristol in 1774, and after staying six months at Shrewsbury, and six at Birmingham, came to Olney in July 1775.

II. First Seventeen Years at Olney (1775–1792).

Mr. Sutcliff, who was now about twenty-three years of age, appears to have supplied the Baptist pulpit from his first arrival in Olney; he was entered as a member of the church on November 26, 1775, but was not ordained pastor until August 7, 1776.

In the spring of 1776 an important Baptist Association was held in the town, and on the second day Robert Hall, senr., who was chosen Moderator, read the General Letter to the Churches, which was afterwards published as "The Doctrine of the Trinity stated: in a circular letter from the Baptist

Ministers and Messengers assembled at Olney, Bucks, May 28, 29, 1776."

The public meeting was held, not in the meeting-house, "which would not contain near half the people," but in the orchard, since called Guinea Field. The Rev. John Newton, whose garden, as we noticed, opened into the orchard, was present at all the services, and speaks in his Diary of his great interest in them ; and the poet Cowper must have been aware of what was going on, for he could not easily walk in his garden without hearing the preaching and singing. During these two days the Vicarage was full of company, and Newton was carrying out to the letter Mr. Thornton's injunction concerning hospitality "to such as are worthy of entertainment." Newton himself preached on the following evening at the church ; the ministers who remained in town went to hear him, and the next morning breakfasted with him at the Vicarage. To Sutcliff, especially, this was a memorable occasion, for then it was that he formed the acquaintance of Andrew Fuller, who little dreamt that May morning of the great work that he and Sutcliff, shoulder to shoulder, were destined to perform. Fuller had just been appointed to the pastorate of a church at Soham, where his income was the modest sum of £15 a year. About this time, too, Sutcliff made the acquaintance of John Ryland, jun., afterwards Dr. Ryland of Northampton. These three gifted men were about of an age, Sutcliff being only a few months older than Ryland, and Ryland a few months older than Fuller.

Among the ministers present at Mr. Sutcliff's ordination (August 7, 1776) were Dr. Fawcett and Rev. C. Evans, his former tutors, and Mr. Symonds of Bedford. Newton was also present, and gives a full account of the services in his Diary. The notice of them in the church-book concludes with the words, "O that it may be a day always to be remembered with joy," a wish that was signally realised.

During the early part of his ministry Mr. Sutcliff occupied rooms in the large house (since greatly altered) next to the Meeting-house, which then belonged to, and was the residence of, Mrs. Andrews ; and by the kindness of this lady he was able to expend the greater part of his income in the purchase of books. "No man had a higher value than he for literary treasures, or a more correct and extensive acquaintance with that description of books to which his attention was particularly directed. He was not a mere *helluo librorum*, but the strain of his conversation on all occasions showed that his mind was richly stored with what he read, and that he had a comprehensive view of the arguments and manner of different writers, which he readily communicated to others."[1]

No sooner had he settled in Olney than he set himself earnestly to work for the welfare of his people. His great thirst for reading we have noticed; but he was not content with storing his own mind with wholesome matter and accumulating a valuable library for himself, he tried to get his people to do the same; and could he have had his own way every cottage would have contained its little library of well-selected and well-thumbed books. Although he did not write much himself, he did what, in the way of doing good, amounted to almost the same thing; it was his custom to recommend to his people and even to write recommendatory prefaces to books that particularly pleased him and seemed likely to be beneficial to the church.

There was but little remarkable in the manner of Sutcliff's preaching besides his intense earnestness. He made use of no gestures, and never practised oratorical effect. "His aversion to ostentation," says Robert Hall, "might alone be said to be carried to excess, since it prevented him from availing himself of those ample stores of knowledge by which he could often have delighted and instructed his hearers. He had far more learning than the mere hearer of his discourses would have conjectured; for he seemed almost as anxious to conceal as some are to display." Thus when his tall form (he was six feet) rose from the pulpit his people knew that nothing would proceed from his lips but well-weighed thoughts, dressed in the simplest language, and uttered with customary earnestness.

On his first entering the ministry, like Ryland and Fuller, he had been inclined to the system of hyper-Calvinism, but

[1] Life of Dr. Fawcett.

like them too, partly by reflection, and partly by reading the writings of Edwards, Bellamy, and Brainerd, first began to doubt of that system, and afterwards to be decided against it. To the works of Jonathan Edwards he was peculiarly partial. On account of this change in his opinions his preaching was disapproved by part of his hearers, and in the early years of his ministry at Olney he had to encounter a considerable portion of individual opposition; but "by patience, calmness, and prudent perseverance," says one of his friends, "he lived to subdue prejudice; and though his beginning was very unpretentious, from a small and not united interest he raised it to a large body of people and a congregation most affectionately attached to him." When he first came to Olney (in 1775) there were only 38 members, even as late as 1784 there were only 48; but the number steadily increased, and during the last seven years of his ministry there were upwards of 100.

In October 1782 Andrew Fuller removed from Soham to Kettering, where, instead of being sixty or seventy miles from his friends, Ryland, Sutcliff, and the elder Hall, he was within twenty miles of each of them. The younger Hall, afterwards the celebrated Robert Hall, aged about nineteen, was at this time at Aberdeen, reading "much of Xenophon and Herodotus, and more of Plato," with his companion James (afterwards Sir James) Mackintosh.

Sutcliff's name first became widely known beyond the neighbourhood of Olney in 1784, in the spring of which year it was agreed on his motion to set apart an hour on the evening of the first Monday in every month for social prayer for the success of the Gospel, and to invite Christians of other denominations to unite with them in it. The measure thus recommended was eagerly adopted by great numbers of the churches, and so marked a revival of religion ensued that it was afterwards regarded by the associated ministers and the missionaries as the actual commencement of the Missionary movement.

This same year Sutcliff became acquainted with William Carey, afterwards the famous missionary. Carey was a member of Mr. Sutcliff's church from July 14, 1785, to April 29, 1787; but as we shall deal with the career of this distinguished

K

man in the next sketch, it will suffice for the present to say that he was assisted in his studies by Mr. Sutcliff, who lent him books, aided him with advice, and right along manifested the greatest kindness towards him.[1]

Nothing is more erroneous than to suppose that Sutcliff and Fuller were dragged into the missionary project by the importunities of Carey. All the meetings from 1784, when the motion for extraordinary prayer was accepted, even those before Carey began seriously to think about the matter, had a missionary tendency, and it is well known that Carey himself was strongly influenced by the spirit of the sermons preached by Sutcliff and Fuller on these occasions. All three had the same object at heart, the difference being that, whilst Carey was for instant action, the other two counselled deliberation and caution ; and it was well for the success of the Mission that his impetuosity was balanced by their wisdom.

For the furtherance of his motion of 1784 Sutcliff in 1789 republished Jonathan Edwards' work entitled "An humble attempt to promote explicit agreement and visible union of God's people in Extraordinary Prayer," which, according to the title-page, was "Printed at Boston in New England 1747, Reprinted at Northampton in Old England 1789." After stating that he does not consider himself answerable for every statement the book contains, Mr. Sutcliff concludes his preface in the following beautiful manner :—"In the present imperfect state we may reasonably expect a diversity of sentiments upon religious matters. Each ought to think for himself ; and every one has a right on proper occasions to show his opinion. Yet all should remember there are but two parties in the world, each engaged in opposite causes ; the cause of God and of Satan ; of holiness and sin ; of heaven and hell. The advancement of the one and the downfall of the other must appear exceedingly desirable to every real friend of God and man. If such, in some respects, entertain different sentiments and practise distinguishing modes of worship, surely they may unite in the above business. Oh for thousands upon thou-

---

[1] Mr. Sutcliff was still living at Mrs. Andrews's ; consequently it was in this house that Carey received instruction in the dead languages and other subjects.

sands divided into small bands of their respective cities, towns, villages, and neighbourhoods, all met at the same time and in pursuit of one end, offering up their united prayers like so many ascending clouds of incense before the Most High."

"This publication," says Fuller, "had a very considerable influence in originating that tone of feeling which in the end determined five or six individuals to venture, though with many fears and misgivings, on the mighty undertaking of founding the Baptist Missionary Society."

At first, as we have shown, Sutcliff and Fuller had counselled deliberation, but in April 1791, in their lectures at the Association at Clipstone, they expressed themselves as eager for instant action as was Carey. Both the lectures or sermons bore upon the meditated mission to the heathen, Sutcliff's subject being "Jealousy for God," from 1 Kings xix. 10; and both were printed at the request of those who heard them. At the next meeting of the Association, in the house of a widow lady, Mrs. Beeby Wallis, at Kettering, on the memorable 2d of October 1792, the Baptist Missionary Society was founded. Sutcliff was one of the five who formed the committee (a sixth, Mr. Samuel Pearce, was afterwards admitted), and from that day a very great portion of his work was in the interest of the Society.

III. THE SEMINARY AT OLNEY, 1792–1814 (TWENTY-TWO YEARS).

Of this famous committee of six the names of three are indissolubly associated : so tenaciously, to use an expression of Carey's, did they "hold the ropes" while the missionaries went down into the mine; so harmoniously and diligently did they labour together; and so important were the results of their combined efforts. "The intimate friendship," says Robert Hall, in his funeral sermon for Dr. Ryland, "which subsisted between that lovely triumvirate, Fuller, Ryland, and Sutcliff, which never suffered a moment's interruption or abatement, was cemented by their common attachment to that object" (the Mission). "Of congenial sentiments and taste, though of very different temperament and character, there was scarce a thought which they did not communicate to each other, while they united all their energies in supporting the same cause; nor is it easy to determine whether the success of our Mission is most to be ascribed to the vigour of Fuller, the prudence of Sutcliff, or the piety of Ryland."

The first missionaries, Carey and Thomas, embarked for India in June 1793.

Fuller and Pearce of Birmingham bear testimony that from the time when their people became interested in the Mission there was constant sunshine upon their congregations, that internal bickerings ceased, because people saw the folly of squabbling over minor differences of religion when whole continents were without the Word of God. At Olney it was just the same, and Sutcliff and his brother ministers found that the life they sought to impart to India came back in a double life from Heaven to themselves. People as well as pastors were fired with the new enthusiasm, and women as well as men were desirous of doing all they could to promote such a glorious undertaking.

In their preface to "The Memoirs of Miss Susanna Anthony" (published in 1803), Sutcliff, Ryland, and Fuller pay a warm and just tribute to the ardour evinced and the honourable part borne by the gentler sex in the great work, and make mention of the generosity with which they had contributed of their substance, their unwearied assiduity in assisting the missionaries, and the cheerfulness with which they left their country and kindred to encounter, with their husbands, the perils of distant lands.

In 1796 Mr. Sutcliff married Miss Jane Johnston, who had been a member of his church since November 29, 1781.

On May 7, 1799, four missionaries were designated for the mission field: Brunsdon and Grant, whose careers of usefulness were destined not a great while after their arrival in India to be cut short by early deaths; and Ward and Marshman, the missionary giants who subsequently with Carey formed such a distinguished trio. The meeting for the dismissal of Marshman and Grant was held at Bristol, and that for the dismissal of Ward and Brunsdon at Olney.

To Pearce of Birmingham, who had taken such an intense interest in the work of the Mission, and who, indeed, a short time previously, had himself offered to go to India, it was a severe trial that he was prevented by sickness from attending the services at Olney. He was present in spirit, however; and the following touching letter which he had written to Mr. Fuller was read at the close of the meeting:—

TAMERTON, *May* 2, 1799.

". . . Oh that the Lord, who is unconfined by place or condition, may copiously pour out upon you all the rich effusions of His Holy Spirit on the approaching day! My most hearty love to each missionary who may then encircle the throne of grace. Happy men! Happy women! You are going to be fellow-labourers with Christ Himself! I congratulate—I almost envy you; yet I love you, and can scarcely now forbear dropping a tear of love as each of your names passes across my mind. Oh what promises are yours; and what a reward! surely heaven is filled with double joy, and resounds with unusual acclamations, at the arrival of each missionary there. Oh be faithful, my dear brethren, my dear sisters, be faithful unto death, and all this joy is yours! Long as I live, my imagination will be hovering over you in Bengal; and should I die, if separate spirits be allowed a visit to the world they have left, methinks mine would soon be at Mudnabatty, watching your labours, your conflicts, and your pleasures, whilst you are always abounding in the work of the Lord."

For several years previous Mr. Sutcliff had educated students for the ministry, and now in his seminary at Olney he began to train for the mission field as well as for home labours. The houses he occupied were those in the High Street now numbered 21 and 23. The former, which was his private house, had belonged before his marriage to the family of Mrs. Sutcliff; the latter was for the students. Both have been considerably altered of late years.

Altogether there were thirty-seven students educated at Olney, twelve of whom were specially trained for and entered the mission field; and in connection with these labours we have the authority of Mr. Fuller for stating that in all that Mr. Sutcliff did "he saved nothing, but gave his time and talents for the public good."

The following is the list of those of the students whose names we have been able to obtain :—

Anderson, Christopher, of Edinburgh, born Feb. 1782, died Feb. 1852 ; at Olney in 1805 ; author of " Annals of the English Bible," &c.

Biss, John, Missionary, at Olney in 1802 and 1803.

Brown, W., laboured at Keysoe, Beds, where he died in 1818.

Brunsdon, Daniel, Missionary, at Olney in 1798 and 1799.

Burdett, E., ordained Pastor at Sutton-on-the-Elms in September 1811.

Carey, Dr. W., Missionary and Oriental scholar, at Olney 1785–87.

Carey, Eustace, Missionary, at Olney from 1809 to 1812.

Chamberlain, John, Missionary, at Olney in 1799.

Chown, ——, ordained at Burford, Oxon, in June 1811.

Coles, Thomas, at Olney in 1806, ordained at Gretton, Northants, in May 1808.

Compier, ——, at Olney in 1814.

Davies, ——, at Olney in 1806.

Dobney, ——, at Olney in 1806.

Franks, ——, left Olney in February 1814.

Gamby, William, of Southill, Beds, trained for the Mission ; was to have set out with Eustace Carey, but died at the early age of twenty-three, before finishing his course of study.

George, ——, at Olney in 1806.

Griffiths, ——, at Olney in 1814.

Harris, ——, at Olney in 1814.

Jarvis, Thomas, ordained at Newark-on-Trent in July 1810.

Knowles, William, ordained at Hackleton in 1815, where he died in 1866, aged eighty.

Lawson, ——.

Mardon, Richard, Missionary, at Olney in 1802 and 1803.

Medlock, Benjamin, at Olney in 1814, ordained Pastor at Pendle Hill, Lancashire, March 1817.

Moore, William, Missionary, at Olney in 1802 and 1803.

Peters, ——, at Olney about 1811.

Pope, ——, at Olney in 1814.

Richards, ——, at Olney in 1806.

Robinson, W., Missionary. Born at Olney, studied under Mr. Sutcliff in 1804 and 1805. Laboured in Bengal and Java.

Rowe, Joshua, Missionary, at Olney in 1802 and 1803.

Smith, J., at Olney in 1807 ; ordained Pastor at Burton-on-Trent May 1809.

Walsh, ——, elected Pastor at King's Lynn in November 1811.

Welsh, Thomas, ordained Pastor at Newbury in October 1813.

Worth, Sir Richard Moss, at Olney in 1810.

All Mr. Sutcliff's students felt the greatest affection for him, and ever looked back with great thankfulness that they had studied at Olney. "His piety," said one, "was not merely official and public, but personal and habitual. The spirit of devotion rested on him. He was the man of God in all his intercourse. He conducted the worship of his family with singular seriousness, ardour, and constancy, never allowing anything to interfere with it except great indisposition. He manifested a parental tenderness and solicitude for the welfare of his pupils, and took a lively interest in their joys or sorrows. He heard the sermons of his younger brethren with great candour, and if he saw them timid or embarrassed on public occasions, would take an opportunity of speaking a kind and encouraging word to them, and aim to inspire them with a proper degree of confidence."

His whole soul was with the missionaries, and on reading or hearing the communications from the East containing accounts of the success of the Gospel the tears would flow freely from his eyes. His counsel was sought on every occasion of difficulty by his friends Ryland and Fuller, and "his clear perception of the bearings of a case and his prompt and sound judgments seemed at once to dispose of a question." But though his thoughts were prompt he was generally slow in uttering them; and, if he saw others too hasty in coming to a decision, would pleasantly say, "Let us consult the town-clerk of Ephesus, and do nothing rashly."

IV. HIS LAST DAYS.

For several years Mr. Sutcliff had been in a declining state of health, but on the 3d of March 1814, whilst on a visit to London, he was seized with a violent pain across his breast and arms, attended with great difficulty of breathing. It took him two days to get home, and it was soon found that the illness was serious. He could not lie down without great pain, and consequently was pillowed up night after night in a large chair.

The last sermon he preached was on Sunday afternoon February 27, from Job xlii. 5, 6, "I have heard of Thee by the hearing of the ear," &c. Only once more was he seen in his accustomed place, and that was on one Sunday afternoon in May, when he rode up to the Meeting-house to administer the ordinance of the Lord's Supper. He stayed about half-an-hour. During his illness the pulpit was supplied by the students then at Olney, Messrs. Griffiths, Compier, Harris, Pope, and Medlock.

"The last time I visited him," says Mr. Fuller (who frequently during his friend's affliction had ridden over to see him), "was on my way to the annual meeting. Expecting to see his face no more, I said, on taking leave, 'I wish you, my dear brother, an abundant entrance into the everlasting kingdom of our Lord Jesus Christ!' At this he hesitated; not as doubting his entrance into the kingdom, but as questioning whether the term *abundant* were applicable to him. 'That,' said he, 'is more than I expect. I think I understand the connection and import of those words—"Add to your faith virtue—give diligence to make your calling and election sure—for *so* an entrance shall be ministered unto you *abundantly*." I think the idea is that of a ship coming into harbour with a fair gale and full tide. If I may but reach the heavenly shore, though it be on a board or broken piece of the ship, I shall be satisfied.'"

When something was mentioned of what he had done in promoting the cause of Christ he replied with emotion, "I look upon it all as nothing. I must enter heaven on the same footing as the converted thief, and shall be glad to take a seat by his side." Frequently during his illness he repeated the following verses :—

> " We walk a narrow path and rough,
>   And we are tired and weak,
> But soon we shall have rest enough
>   In the blest courts we seek.
>
> Soon in the chariot of a cloud,
>   By flaming angels borne ;
> I shall mount up the milky way,
>   And unto God return.
>
> My soul has tasted Canaan's grapes,
>   And now I long to go
> Where my dear Lord His vineyard keeps
>   And all His clusters grow."

"About three in the morning of the day on which he died," said Mr. Welsh, "like Israel he strengthened himself, and sat up on his bed. Calling me to him, he, in the most affectionate manner, took hold of my hand and expressed himself as follows :—'Preach as you will wish you had when you come to die. It is one thing to preach, and another to do it as a dying man.' Thinking of his people, whom he so dearly loved, and who on their part exhibited the greatest affection and veneration for him, he observed, 'If anything be said of me, let the last word be, "As I have loved you, see that ye love one another."' To Mrs. Sutcliff his parting words were, 'My love, I commit you to Jesus. I can trust you with Him. Our separation will not be long; and I think I shall often be with you. Read frequently the Book of Psalms and be much in prayer.'" On the 22d of June, about five in the afternoon, an alteration took place, and he began to sink. "It is all over," he said, "this cannot be borne long." "You are prepared for the issue," said Mr. Welsh, who stood by. "I think I am," he replied ; "go and pray for me." About half-an-hour before breathing his last he said, "Lord Jesus, receive my spirit—it is come—perhaps a few minutes more— heart and flesh fail—but God—that God is the strength of His people is a truth that I now see as I never saw it in my life." These were the last words he could be heard to speak. In this manner, and as the simple notice in the church-book puts it, "much lamented, having left a monument of great esteem in many hearts," died John Sutcliff, on the 22d of June 1814, in the sixty-third year of his age, after a ministry at Olney of thirty-nine years.

During the last few years of his life nothing had grieved him more than the dreadful conflict that was going on between England and France, and it had been his daily and fervent prayer that hostilities might be stopped and the spear turned into a pruning-hook. He lived just long enough to realise his fondest hope, for, Bonaparte having abdicated and retired to the island of Elba, peace was proclaimed between the allied sovereigns and France on May 30. As soon as tidings came to England, of course Olney was not behind other towns in hanging out flags, ringing bells, making feasts, and tapping barrels; a waggon too was hired, and the most celebrated musicians of the parish, commencing at the "Castle," paraded through the town with fifes, triangles, fiddles, and best of all with a big drum, whilst the tag-rag, not being able to get a seat in the waggon, followed behind, each with the best instrument of music he could procure. But it was well known that Mr. Sutcliff lay dying, and it is pleasing to be able to state that from so many yards before they came to his house to so many yards after they left it this joyous though somewhat unruly mob passed along with the quietness of a funeral.

Mr. Sutcliff was interred on Tuesday the 28th of June, the Rev. C. Stephenson, vicar of Olney, the Rev. Henry Gauntlett, then curate, and the Rev. T. Hillyard, Independent minister, being among the pall-bearers. The great respect in which Mr. Sutcliff had been held, not merely in Olney but in all the country round, and the knowledge that the funeral sermon was to be preached by his bosom friend the Rev. Andrew Fuller, caused great numbers to assemble.

It was hot weather, and Mr. Fuller, finding that the majority of the people could not be accommodated in the Meeting-house, took his stand in the graveyard, the windows being thrown open so that those within the building could hear. His subject was, "The principles and prospects of a servant of Christ," from the text Jude 20, 21 : "But ye, beloved, building up yourselves on your most holy faith, praying in the Holy Ghost, keep yourselves in the love of God, looking for the mercy of our Lord Jesus Christ unto eternal life." It was an occasion, we are told, never to be forgotten; many a tear that day stole from eyes that were but little given to weeping, and many a good resolve was made by those who had hitherto been indifferent to solemn subjects.

The great Robert Hall had been requested to write an account of Mr. Sutcliff's life, but after a few unsatisfactory trials relinquished the attempt, and wrote to Mr. Fuller the following letter, which curiously exhibits his characteristic diffidence :—

"MY DEAR BROTHER,—I am truly concerned to be obliged to tell you that I cannot succeed at all in my attempts to draw the character of our dear and venerable brother Sutcliff. I have made several efforts, and have sketched out as well as I could the outlines of what I conceive to be his character, but have failed in producing such a portrait as appears to me fit for the public eye. I am perfectly convinced that your intimacy with him, and your powers of discrimination, will enable you to present to posterity a much juster and more impressive idea of him than I can. I am heartily sorry I promised it. But promises I hold sacred; and therefore, if you insist upon it, and are not willing to release me from my engagement, I will accomplish the task as well as I can. But if you will let the matter pass without reproaching me, *sub silentio*, you will oblige me considerably. It appears to me that, if I ever possessed a faculty of character drawing, I have lost it, probably from want of use, as I am far from taking any delight in a minute criticism on character, to which, in my younger days, I was excessively addicted. Both our taste and talents change with the progress of years. The purport of these lines, however, is to request you to absolve me from my promise, in which light I shall interpret your silence; holding myself ready, however, to comply with your injunctions.—I am, my dear Sir, your affectionate brother,   R. HALL."

This unfinished portrait of Mr. Sutcliff's character may be found in most editions of Mr. Hall's works. A more perfect outline was given by Mr. Fuller in the funeral sermon already alluded to, from which in the foregoing account we have freely quoted. In his will Mr. Sutcliff bequeathed his library to Horton College, Bradford (now Rawdon College), and it was conveyed from Olney by a waggon and two horses.

Mrs. Sutcliff survived her husband only about two months, dying on the 3d of September of the same year.

Two persons still living in Olney remember hearing him preach and seeing him baptize in the part of the Ouse called "Ray Bawk." They remember, too, seeing Mr. Sutcliff, Mr. Stephenson, and Mr. Hillyard, that is to say, the Baptist minister, the vicar, and the Independent minister, walking arm in arm down the street. Sometimes the trio consisted of Mr. Gauntlett, Mr. Sutcliff, and Mr. Hillyard.

The following, so far as we know, is a complete list of his published writings :—

* 1779. On Providence.
  1783. The First Principles of the Oracles of God, represented in a plain and familiar Catechism for the Use of Children. It went through several editions.
* 1786. On the Authority and Sanctification of the Lord's Day.
  1788. An Address given at the Interment of the Rev. Joshua Symonds of the Old Meeting, Bedford, Nov. 27.
  1789. Recommendatory Preface to Jonathan Edwards's Book.
  1791. Sermon on "Jealousy for the Lord of Hosts," from 1 Kings xix. 10, delivered at Clipstone, April 27.
* 1797. On the Divinity of the Christian Religion.
* 1800. On the Qualification for Church Fellowship.
  1802. Introductory Discourse at the Ordination of Morgan of Birmingham.
* 1803. On the Lord's Supper.
  1803. Recommendatory Preface to the "Memoirs of Miss Susanna Anthony." (Possibly written by him.)
* 1805. On the Manner of Attending to Divine Ordinances.
* 1808. On Obedience to Positive Institutions.
* 1813. On reading the Word of God.

* Circular Letters of the Northamptonshire Association.

XIV

DR. CAREY AND THE BAPTIST MISSION.[1]

"I have brought myself by long meditation to the conviction that a human
being with a settled purpose must accomplish it, and that nothing can
resist a will that will stake even existence for its fulfilment."—LORD
BEACONSFIELD: *Endymion*.

I. HACKLETON AND OLNEY, 1775–1787 (TWELVE YEARS).

AMONG the famous men whose names are inseparably connected with Olney, one of the most remarkable was the
eminent missionary and Oriental scholar, William Carey. He
was born on the 17th of August 1761 at Paulerspury, a village
near Towcester, in Northamptonshire, where his father occupied the position of parish clerk and schoolmaster. At an
early age he evinced great love for reading. Books on natural
history and botany and records of voyages and travels were
his especial delight; and he used to explore the whole neighbourhood in search of what he had read about, coming home
loaded with spoil from the woods and spinnies. His extraordinary passion for flowers clung to him, as we shall see,
throughout life. Of insects, a literal menagerie, in every stage
of development, and confined in boxes of all shapes and
sizes, flourished in his own little room. His parents were too
poor to assist him in prosecuting his studies, and at the age of
fourteen, as he was unable to work in the fields on account
of a scorbutic disorder, he was bound apprentice to Charles
Nickolls, a shoemaker at Hackleton, in Northamptonshire,
a village about five miles from Olney. When he became
apprenticed his sister Polly took charge of his birds (whether
or not her protectorate extended over the insects we cannot
say); but so fond was she of her brother that she killed them
all with kindness.

[1] Compiled in part from "Carey, Marshman, and Ward," by J. C. Marshman.

At Hackleton he not only learned the gentle craft, but made some acquaintance with the Greek New Testament, being aided in his studies by a certain Thomas Jones, a journeyman weaver of the same village, who had formerly been well-to-do, but had become reduced in circumstances owing to his dissolute habits.   At the death of his master, which occurred about a year after his arrival in Hackleton, Carey transferred his apprenticeship to a neighbouring shoe-maker named Old.   It was here that he first met with the Rev. Thomas Scott, who at that time was residing at Raven-stone.   After delivering an address in the village Scott paid a visit to Mr. Old, whom he seems to have made a point of calling on whenever circumstances led him to Hackleton. Carey, "a sensible-looking lad, in his working apron," whose attention had been riveted on the address which had just been given, "exhibited tokens of great intelligence.   He said little, but occasionally asked questions so much to the point that Mr. Scott was led to remark that he would prove no ordinary character." [1]   In after days, when Carey had be-come distinguished, Scott used to speak of Mr. Old's house as "Carey's College."

He now began more and more to turn his attention to the study of the Scriptures, and, owing chiefly to the ministrations of Mr. Scott, whom he took every opportunity to hear, he made rapid advances in Christian knowledge.

His last doubts and difficulties having been removed by the perusal of the work of Mr. Hall, sen., "Help to Zion's Travellers," he realised the importance of true religion, and furthermore became eager to tell others of the Christ he had found for himself.   His first appearance in the pulpit was at the age of nineteen, and for about three years and a half he preached in the villages of Hackleton and Earl's Barton. He had previously been attached to the Established Church, but during this period his views on the subject of baptism changed, and accordingly he was rebaptized by Dr. John Ryland, on the 7th of October 1783, in the river Nen, a little beyond Dr. Doddridge's chapel in Northampton.

[1] "Carey, Marshman, and Ward," by J. C. Marshman.

At Mr. Old's death Carey, who was only twenty, took over his stock and business, and at the same time made what was perhaps the one great mistake of his life—he married Mr. Old's sister, an illiterate, weak-minded woman, who never had the slightest sympathy with his undertakings, and was utterly unsuited for his companionship.

After residing for about eighteen months at Hackleton, where he was reduced to great distress by reason of ill health and dulness of trade, he removed to Piddington, the next village, still continuing to make shoes and to preach, though several times brought low with ague and fever, which rendered him bald for the rest of his life.

The cottages in which he lived at Hackleton and Piddington are both standing, but have been much altered; and the room in which he preached his first sermon and the spot where stood his pulpit are still shown. The pulpit itself is now in the Hackleton Meeting-house.

Carey now joined the church at Olney, under the pastoral care of the Rev. John Sutcliff, his chief reason for doing so being because he could not see with the people of Hackleton, who were hyper-Calvinists. After his name in the Hackleton church-book are the words—

"Whent away without his dismission."

Mr. Sutcliff put a Latin Grammar into his hand, and through his help Carey began to read the Scriptures in Greek and Hebrew.

The following extracts from the church-book belonging to the Baptist church, Olney, are in Mr. Sutcliff's handwriting :—

"*June* 17, 1785. A request from William Carey of Moulton, in Northamptonshire, was taken into consideration. He has been, and still is, in connection with a society of people at Hackleton. He is occasionally engaged with acceptance in various places in speaking the Word. He bears a very good moral character. He is desirous of being sent out from some reputable and orderly church of Christ, into the work of the ministry. The principal question debated was, 'In what manner shall we receive him? by a letter from the people of Hackleton, or on a profession of faith, &c.' The final resolution was left to another church meeting.

"*July* 14, 1785. *Church Meeting.* W. Carey (see June 17) appeared before the church, and having given a satisfactory account of the work of God upon his soul, he was admitted a member. He had been formerly baptized by the Rev. Mr. Ryland, junr., of Northampton. He was invited by the church to preach once next Lord's day evening.

"*July* 17, 1785. *C. Meeting, Lord's Day Evening.* W. Carey, in consequence of a request from the church, preached this evening. After which it was resolved that he should be allowed to go on preaching at those places where he has been for some time employed ; and that he should engage again on suitable occasions for some time before us, in order that further trial may be made of his ministerial gifts."

"When the question," says Mr. Marshman, "of his receiving a call for the ministry came under discussion, the members expressed a doubt whether he possessed sufficient ability to make a useful minister, and the point was carried chiefly through the personal influence of Mr. Sutcliff." The sermon which he preached on this occasion he himself, some years afterwards, described "as having been as crude and weak as anything could be, which is called, or has been called, a sermon."

The other notices of Carey in the church-book at Olney are the following :—

"*June* 16, 1786. The case of Broʳ. Carey was considered, and an unanimous satisfaction with his ministerial abilities being expressed, a vote was passed to call him to the ministry at a proper time.

"*Augst.* 10, 1786. *Church Meeting.* This evening our brother William Carey was called to the work of the ministry, and sent out by the church to preach the Gospel wherever God in His providence might call him.

"*April* 29, 1787. *Ch. M.* After the ordinance our Broʳ. William Carey was dismissed to the church of Christ at Moulton, in Northamptonshire, with a view to his ordination there."

II. THE FOUNDING OF THE MISSIONARY SOCIETY, 1787–1793 (SIX YEARS).

At Moulton for a time he kept a school, but he had no notion of managing his boys, so it turned out a failure ; besides, his total income was only £16 a year. He therefore turned again to his former trade for a subsistence, and once a fortnight might have been seen walking to Northampton with his wallet full of shoes on his shoulder, and then returning home with a fresh supply of leather. The common impression that Carey made but poor work at his shoemaking is altogether wrong. His own words emphatically contradict the report. In one of his letters home he declares that he was accounted both "a skilful and an honest workman."[1] And as the most widely known anecdote concerning him attests, he was never ashamed of the conditions under which this and the previous part of his life had been passed. Some thirty years after, dining one day with the Governor-General, Lord Hastings, at Barrackpore, one of the guests made the inquiry of another whether Dr. Carey had not once been a shoemaker. He happened to overhear the conversation, and immediately stepped forward and said, "No, sir; only a cobbler."

It was whilst perusing "Cook's Voyages" and teaching his pupils geography that the great project of his life was formed, for no sooner had he become acquainted with the spiritual degradation of the heathen than he felt desirous of communicating the Gospel to them. As he sat in his little workshop he turned his eyes every now and then towards a large map suspended on the wall, on which he had rudely represented the spiritual condition of the various countries, and as much information as he had been able to gather regarding the national characteristics and the population. In this workshop, as Mr. Wilberforce afterwards said in the House of Commons, the poor cobbler formed the resolution to give to the millions of Hindoos the Bible in their own language.

Very few of his ministerial friends gave him any encouragement. Mr. Fuller himself was so startled by the novelty and magnitude of Carey's proposal that he described his feelings as resembling those of the infidel courtier in Israel, "If the Lord should make windows in heaven might such a thing be?" At a meeting of ministers held about this time at Northampton Carey suggested as a topic for discussion, the duty of Chris-

[1] "Life of Andrew Fuller," by T. E. Fuller,

L

tians to attempt the spread of the Gospel among the heathen;
when Mr. Ryland, senior, sprang to his feet exclaiming, "Young
man, sit down! When God pleases to convert the heathen,
He will do it without your help or mine!" Neither daunted
nor discouraged by repulses, Carey embodied his views in a
pamphlet, which he showed to Mr. Fuller, Dr. Ryland, Mr.
Sutcliff, and Mr. Pearce, and they advised him to prepare it
for publication. Meantime, in spite of his industry—for he
still worked at shoemaking—his family were almost starving;
for many weeks they had nothing but bread, and only a scanty
supply even of that. Now, in a greater degree than it had
ever been, his indomitable energy was in requisition; but difficulties seemed only to spur him onward, and he carried everything before him. Neither poverty nor disease, neither the
discouraging remarks of his friends nor the unsympathetic conduct of his wife, had any effect on his tenacity of purpose,
or if effective at all they only strengthened it. He was emphatically the man of one object.

In 1789 he accepted the pastorate of a church at Leicester.
At the meeting of ministers at Clipstone in 1791 the movement, as we have said, received a very great impulse. After
the meeting Carey, with almost agonising earnestness, pressed
immediate action, urging that something should be done that
very day towards the formation of a society to propagate the
Gospel among the heathen.

The ministers recommended him to publish his "Thoughts,"
and soon afterwards his pamphlet appeared, under the title of
"An Inquiry into the Obligations of Christians to send the
Gospel to the Heathen." The next Association was held
at Nottingham on the 30th of May 1792, and Carey was
appointed to preach. His sermon on this occasion has ever
since been remembered as having laid the foundation of the
Baptist Missionary Society. He took for his text, "Enlarge
the place of thy tent, and let them stretch forth the curtain
of thy habitations. Spare not; lengthen thy cords and
strengthen thy stakes; for thou shalt break forth on the right
hand and on the left; and thy seed shall inherit the Gentiles
and make the desolate cities to be inhabited." From this

text he deduced and enforced the two principles which were embodied in the motto of the Mission, "Expect great things; attempt great things." And such ardour did he put into his discourse, and so ably did he expound his views, that the ministers at length came to the resolution that "a plan should be prepared against the next ministers' meeting for the establishment of a society for propagating the Gospel among the heathen." "If," said Dr. Ryland, "all the people had lifted up their voice and wept as the children of Israel did at Bochim, I should not have wondered at the effect; it would only have seemed proportionate to the cause, so clearly did Mr. Carey prove the criminality of our supineness in the cause of God." At the next meeting, which was held at Kettering on the 2d of October 1792, in the house (which is still standing) of Mrs. Beeby Wallis, the question of establishing a Missionary Society was discussed; and all objections having been overruled by Mr. Carey's energy, a Society was constituted "to convey the message of salvation to some portion of the heathen world." In other words, the Baptist Missionary Society was formed, the first of our great Societies that have done so much towards spreading Christianity in foreign lands. The committee of five ministers which was appointed consisted of Andrew Fuller of Kettering, John Ryland of Northampton, John Sutcliff of Olney, Reynold Hogg of Thrapstone, and William Carey. The first subscription amounted to £13, 2s. 6d., a surprisingly small sum when we think of the thousands of pounds that have since been collected. And yet, trifling as were the incipient resources, no sooner was the subscription paper filled up than Mr. Carey offered to embark for any country the Society might select. His mind was fired with enthusiasm, but at the same time he was fully aware that great difficulties would have to be encountered.

Subscriptions now began to come in apace, and the committee soon found themselves in possession of a considerable sum. The London ministers, however, held aloof, the only one from whom Carey received any sympathy being a member of the Established Church, the now venerable John Newton, who "advised him with the fidelity and the tenderness of a father."

The connection with each other of the five great men whose
names are so intimately associated with Olney, and the connection of John Newton with each of the other four, is to us a
fact of extreme interest; and the following pentagon (which
reminds the reader perhaps of a chemical formula) will admirably illustrate it.

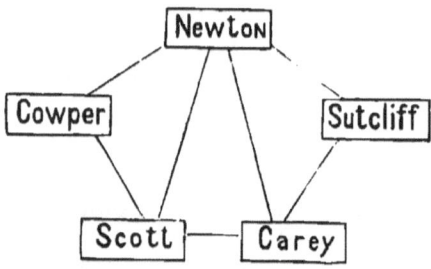

Newton was connected with each of the others; he was the
bosom friend of Cowper, the spiritual father and friend of
Scott, the adviser and warm admirer of Carey, and the kindest
relations existed between him and Sutcliff during the five years
they were contemporaries at Olney.

Cowper is linked not only with Newton but with Scott; he
rendered, as we have seen, kind assistance to him when "The
Force of Truth" was written, and the breach between them that
occurred afterwards was only trifling. Scott is linked with
Cowper, Newton, and Carey; Carey with Scott, Newton, and
Sutcliff; Sutcliff with Carey and Newton.

The question before the committee now was where the proposed mission should be established. Carey, who had drunk
deep draughts from "Cook's Voyages," thought of Otaheite;
Pearce, who had been reading about the recent kindness of
their king to the shipwrecked crew of the *Antelope*, suggested
the Pelew Islands. But just at this moment a gentleman
named Mr. Thomas returned from Bengal, who had repeatedly
written thence to the leading Baptist ministers in England
giving an account of his conferences with the natives.

"We found," says Dr. Ryland, "that he was now endeavouring to raise a fund for a mission to that country, and to engage
a companion to go out with him. It was, therefore, resolved

to make some further inquiry respecting him, and to invite him
to go back under the patronage of our Society." Although a
man of real piety, Mr. Thomas had been "guilty of many faults,
many weaknesses, and many failures;" but the result of the
inquiry proved on the whole satisfactory, and it was resolved
that Carey and Thomas should proceed to India together.

"It is clear," said Andrew Fuller to Carey, "that there is a
rich mine of gold in India." "And I will go down," returned
Carey, "if you will hold the ropes."

Many difficulties—too many even to enumerate here—now
arose. The first was, that Mrs. Carey, who had never moved
beyond the limits of her own county, refused to leave England.
Both Carey and Thomas went to Hackleton to try and persuade
her, but she so persistently refused to go that they left the
house. After they had walked half a mile an additional argu-
ment occurred to Mr. Thomas, and they went back. She
would go, she said, if her sister would go with her. Then they
pleaded with the sister, saying that it depended with her
whether the family should be separated or not. She hastened
upstairs to offer a few words of prayer, then came down and
said she was willing to go.

Carey's last sermon in Olney was preached on March 26th,
1793, the text being Rom. xii. 1—"I beseech you therefore,
brethren, by the mercies of God, that ye present your bodies
a living sacrifice," &c.; and after the sermon he gave out
the hymn commencing:—

"And must I part with all I have,
Jesus, my Lord, for Thee?
This is my joy, since Thou hast done
Much more than this for me"—

pronouncing with great emphasis the first four words of the
second verse—

"*Yes, let it go:*—one look from Thee
Will more than make amends
For all the losses I sustain,
Of credit, riches, friends."

Carey and his family and Mr. Thomas embarked in the *Kron
Princessa Maria*, a Danish Indiaman, on the 13th of June

1793, and arrived in Calcutta on the 11th of the following November. Those who are disposed to faint under difficulties should remember the trials, poverty, perseverance, and success of Carey. The race is not to the swift, but to the persistent. From his boyhood till about his twenty-sixth year an eager ambition to do good filled his mind, and he studied and preached; but, as he had no particular object in view, his efforts were not concentrated, and consequently their effect was comparatively trifling. Then came the missionary idea; he caught sight of a goal, made straight for it, and nothing could turn him aside, nothing divert his attention.

III. SERAMPORE AND CALCUTTA, 1793–1834 (FORTY-ONE YEARS).

At Calcutta Carey met with fresh difficulties and troubles: in the first place, Mr. Thomas, by his imprudence. dissipated their money as soon as it came in; again, the Government were hostile, and he was in constant fear lest he should be sent back to England; his wife, too, gave him additional trouble, and was constantly upbraiding him with their wretchedness; and, to crown all, his family were attacked by sickness. Driven almost to distraction by these accumulated troubles, he removed to the Sunderbunds, where he took a small house, and cultivated a piece of land for the support of his family. Amidst all his difficulties, however, he never lost sight of the great object which had taken him to India, but spent all the time he possibly could in preaching to the Hindoos and making himself proficient in their language.

At home the committee were doing their utmost to serve the Mission; Pearce, who used daily to gaze at Carey's portrait which hung in his study, since he could not join him in India, had resolved to do all he could for him in England; Fuller was traversing the country for funds, and Sutcliff at Olney was preparing students. Early in 1794 Carey's prospects brightened. He had an invitation to take charge of an indigo factory near Malda, which he reached on the 15th of June; and here he passed more than five years of his life, free from pecuniary anxieties, preparing himself for more extended labours, and devoting his whole income, after his family had obtained a bare subsistence, to the great cause that lay so near his heart. Had he not worked for his living he and his family would have starved, for the money sent from England, all put together, amounted thus far to only a small sum. Towards the close of 1799 he relinquished his appointment at Malda, where his principal attention had been devoted to the translation of the New Testament into Bengalee, and took up his residence in Serampore, which was in the possession of Denmark. In May 1799 he was joined by the new missionaries, Marshman, Ward, Brunsdon, and Grant. After a short time Grant, Brunsdon, and Thomas were cut off by death : Grant died on the 31st of October 1799, Brunsdon on the 3d of July 1801, Thomas on the 13th of October of the same year. Thus the number of the missionaries was reduced to three. At Serampore, where they purchased a piece of ground, built a house and established schools, they received the kindest possible treatment from the governor, Colonel Bie : indeed, had it not been that Serampore was at that time in the possession of Denmark, and had not the Colonel accorded them his protection, it is very doubtful whether the Mission could have stood its ground— so hostile, at first, were the East India Company and the English Government authorities. A boarding-school established by Mr. Marshman had great prosperity, and yielded an income of a thousand a year ; and the persistent study of the vernacular languages of India at length brought lucrative employment to Carey. The Governor-General, Marquis Wellesley, had taken upon himself the responsibility of founding a college in Fort William, in which the junior servants of the East India Company might undergo a regular course of training for the public service : and his choice fell upon Carey as the most fit person to fill the chair of Professor in the Sanscrit, Bengalee, and Mahratta languages. But it was not the object of the missionaries to make money for themselves ; each took for his personal expenses the smallest sum he could, and the rest was devoted to missionary purposes. Out of his income of £1000, Marshman took for the support of himself and family only £34 a year; Carey, out of his legitimate income of £600, was satisfied with £40 a year; whilst Ward, who did such important service by superintending the printing of the translations that were constantly being issued, would take only £20.

Of the further history of the Mission, and the great work performed by Carey and his celebrated colleagues, we can here give only a brief outline. On the 28th of December 1800 he had the privilege of baptizing his first Hindoo convert, Krishnu, who a few days previous had openly renounced his caste, by sitting down at the table of the missionaries. "Thus," says Mr. Ward, "the door of faith is open to the Hindoos, and who shall shut it?"

On the 7th of February 1801 Carey received from the press the last sheet of the Bengalee New Testament, the fruition of the "sublime thought which he had conceived fifteen years before." The work had been pressed on with such diligence that in spite of numerous difficulties it was printed within nine months.

The first convert of the kayust, or writer caste, which ranks immediately after that of the Brahmins, was Petumber Sing, baptized at Serampore on the first Sunday in 1802; the first Brahmin convert, the amiable and intelligent Krishnu-prisad, who before his baptism trampled on his poita, or sacred thread, to indicate his rejection of Hindooism.

"At the beginning of 1804," writes Mr. Marshman, "the missionaries laid before the committee the plans which they had been gradually maturing for the translation and publication of the Scriptures. They stated that there were at least seven languages current in India,—the Bengalee, the Hindoostanee, the Ooriya, the Teloogoo, the Kurnata, the Mahratta, and the Tamul, and they considered it practicable to make a translation of at least the New Testament into some, if not all, of these languages. This proposal exactly coincided with Mr. Fuller's large views, and he introduced it to the public notice by making a tour through the northern counties of England and through Scotland—travelling 1300 miles and preaching fifty sermons."

The principal portion of the translating was performed by Carey, who in 1805 published his grammar of the Mahratta language.

In 1806 ground for a mission chapel was purchased in the Lall bazaar in Calcutta, and a temporary bungalow, or thatched house, was erected on it. A chapel was afterwards built on the spot.

Among the kind friends who rendered most acceptable aid to the missionaries was Dr. Leyden, the renowned Orientalist, formerly the friend and literary associate of Sir Walter Scott; and Mr. Thomas Manning, the friend of Charles Lamb.

The chief work of Carey's life was the translation of the Scriptures into the languages of the East, and his philological labours were immense. His Mahratta Grammar was followed by a Sanscrit Grammar in 1806, a Mahratta Dictionary in 1810, a Punjabee Grammar in 1812, a Telinga Grammar in 1814, and a Bengalee Dictionary in 1818; these are only a few of the important products of his pen. Writing to a friend in June 1806 he says :—

"I give you a short view of my engagements for the present day, which is a specimen of the way of spending one half the week. I rose this morning at a quarter before six, read a chapter in the Hebrew Bible, and spent the time till seven in private addresses to God, and then attended family prayer with the servants, in Bengalee. While tea was getting ready I read a little in Persian with the Moonshi, who was waiting when I left my bedroom ; read also before breakfast a portion of the Scriptures in Hindoostance. The moment breakfast was over, sat down to the translation of Ramayun from the Sanscrit, with a pundit, who was also waiting, and continued this translation till ten o'clock, at which hour I went to college ; and attended the duties there till between one and two o'clock. When I returned home, I examined a proof-sheet of the Bengalee translation of Jeremiah, which took till dinner-time. After dinner, translated, with the assistance of the chief pundit of the college, the greatest part of the eighth chapter of Matthew into Sanscrit. This employed me till six o'clock. After six, sat down with a Telinga pundit to learn that language. At seven I began to collect a few previous thoughts into the form of a sermon, and preached in English at half-past seven. About forty persons present. After sermon, I sat down and translated the eleventh of Ezekiel into Bengalee, and this lasted till near eleven, and now I sit down to write to you. After this, I conclude the evening by reading a chapter in the

Greek Testament, and commending myself to God. I have never more time in a day than this, though the exercises vary."

His youthful passion for flowers clung to him throughout life. He was as anxious to increase his floral wealth when a venerable Oriental scholar and missionary as he had been sixty years previous when, a poor lad at Hackleton, he had waded for them into swamps and searched for them under the hedge-rows. Sometimes he would send to his friends in England Hindoo idols in exchange for tulips, daffodils, and lilies. On several occasions Mr. Sutcliff and others sent him quantities of flower seeds. The following extract from a letter to one of his friends will give an idea of his delight on receiving such presents :—

"That I might be sure not to lose any part of your valuable present, I shook the bag over a patch of earth in a shady place, on visiting which a few days afterwards I found springing up, to my inexpressible delight, a *bellis perennis* of our English pastures. I know not that I ever enjoyed, since leaving Europe, a simple pleasure so exquisite as the sight of this English daisy afforded me ; not having seen one for thirty years, and never expecting to see one again."

This incident gave origin to the well-known lines of James Montgomery :—

> "Thrice welcome, little English flower !
>   My mother country's white and red,
> In rose or lily, till this hour,
>   Never to me such beauty spread.
> Transplanted from thy island bed,
>   A treasure in a grain of earth,
> Strange as a spirit from the dead,
>   Thine embryo sprang to birth."

Dr. Carey was thrice married. His first wife died on the 7th of December 1807 ; his second, Miss Charlotte Rhumohr, a German lady, whom he married in 1808, died in 1821 ; his third wife, a widow named Mrs. Hughes, survived him. Both Miss Rhumohr and Mrs. Hughes were well educated and accomplished, and with them he lived very happily. He died on the 9th of June 1834, in the seventy-third year of his age, and was buried at Serampore.

A number of letters written by Carey to the Rev. John Williams of Fayette Street Chapel, New York, were published for the first time this year (1892) by Mr. Williams's grandsons, Leighton and Mornay Williams, with an Introduction by Thomas Wright.[1]

Dr. Carey, as we have seen, was a stern economist of time. His self-imposed tasks, indeed, were so numerous that we wonder how he managed to get exercise ; possibly, like Jeremy Bentham, he set apart for this purpose that portion of his time when friends happened to call on him, and invited them to take turns with him in the garden. His aptitude for the acquisition of languages has rarely been surpassed : the older he grew the more intense was his application : " to supply the Scriptures to the nations of the East in their own tongue became the ruling passion of his life, and he lived to see them, chiefly by his own instrumentality, translated into the vernacular dialects of more than forty different tribes, and thus made accessible to nearly 200,000,000 of human beings."

And this remarkable man lived for twelve years in the neighbourhood of Olney, and was for two years a member of the Baptist Church at Olney ; this remarkable man studied under Sutcliff, and owing to Sutcliff's influence was sent from Olney into the ministry ; and to Olney and Sutcliff owed a debt which he was ever willing to acknowledge. We would not on any account rob, or endeavour to rob, Paulerspury, Moulton, or Leicester of a tittle of the honour of being connected with William Carey, but at the same time we would infix it in our minds that he was one of us ; that he walked these streets, that he preached in yonder meeting-house, and that he heard the self-same church bells that we hear : and if at any time we should be tempted to bemoan our own puny trials and petty disappointments, may we the instant after be put in remembrance of the colossal trials and difficulties that Carey encountered, and the success that rewarded his efforts.

---

[1] "Serampore Letters," &c. G. P. Putnam's Sons, London & New York, 1892.

There appear to have existed at one time three different portraits of Dr. Carey :—

1. That referred to in Andrew Fuller's life of Pearce.
2. The portrait of Dr. Carey attended by his pundit, which was painted by Mr. R. Home of Calcutta. The one in our frontispiece is from this picture.
3. An oil painting presented to the Rev. John Sutcliff. After the death of Mrs. Sutcliff it passed into the hands of her nephew, Mr. Johnson, the first husband of Mrs. J. W. Soul of Olney, who died in 1885. Mrs. Soul bequeathed it to the Baptist Mission House, where it now hangs.

XV.

WESTON UNDERWOOD.

"I find myself here situated exactly to my mind. Weston is one of the prettiest villages in England, and the walks about it at all seasons of the year are delightful."—COWPER: *Letter to Joseph Hill, Esq., Dec. 9, 1786.*

I. WESTON HALL.

WESTON HALL, the ancient mansion of the Throckmortons, which stood on the left side of the road leading from Olney to Weston, just outside the village, was entirely demolished in 1827; and of its near appurtenances none are now standing except the iron gates with four stone piers, and a portion of the stabling and granary crowned by a cupola. It consisted of a quadrangle enclosing a court, or, as the villagers used to call it, "the jail-yard;" and drawings are in existence of each of its fronts. The north, principal, or Queen Anne front faced the park, and was built by Sir Robert Throckmorton about 1710. Projecting northwards and at right angles to it were the stables, the one on the west side, which occupied the site of the present Roman Catholic chapel, being for the coach-horses, the one on the other side for the hunters. The rest of the exterior was partly in the Queen Anne style and partly Elizabethan, the most irregular portion being the west front, which had a porch, and was a perfect medley of chimneys, gabled projections, and windows, the last dotted about in the oddest manner imaginable. From the general appearance of the interior it was judged that the house must have been commenced about the end of the fifteenth century; at the time of its demolition the southern portion was in ruins and had not been inhabited for two hundred years. Coats-of-arms which adorned some of the windows bore the date 1572, and over the door of one of the parlours were several ancient escutcheons of arms.

In taking the house down several interesting discoveries were made. In one place was a concealed door, which when bolted withinside could not be distinguished from the wainscot. Three of the garrets on the west side of the house had in days of persecution been thrown together to form a chapel; and in another garret next to the chapel was found a trap-door opening into a small secret room below, the situation of which was concealed from the outside by a large stack of chimneys. It contained a box sufficiently long for a person to lie in at ease; in which were two mattresses, a rough hewn ladder long enough to reach the trap-door, a candlestick, a crust of bread, some chicken bones, and a priest's breviary. Doubtless these hiding-places often had occupants in the troublous days of Elizabeth and James I., during which the Throckmortons suffered so much on account of their religion; but although it was a matter of history that hiding-places of some sort existed in the house they had not been known even to the family of late years.

In a portion of one of the walls, which at the sale of materials had been purchased by an inhabitant of Olney for eleven shillings, the workmen employed to take it down found a leathern purse containing twenty-eight guineas and four half guineas of the reigns of Charles II. and James II., as bright all of them, and in as good preservation, as if they had just come from the Mint. The library, the family portraits, and the coats-of-arms on painted glass with which the windows were adorned, were removed to Coughton, the principal residence of the family; the black marble and white flags which formed part of the pavement of the entrance-hall are now in the floor of the Roman Catholic chapel.

At the entrance of the village is still standing one of the gateways of the Park; the other, which was similar in appearance, and stood on the side nearest Olney, has disappeared. The road in front of the house, which ran through the park (from which it was not railed off), was formerly a private one, and consequently the gates were shut at night. The public road ran between the hall and the river, but with the exception of the portion abutting upon the village street, where stands the socket of the ancient cross, has since been done away with.

The fact that Cowper was connected with both Olney and Weston has ever since his day closely associated them together in the minds of the thousands to whom his works are dear, but it is worth noticing that from earliest times Olney has been more closely connected with Weston than with any of the other surrounding villages. In the first place, they once formed one parish; in the second, although ever since about 1400 parochially separate, they have frequently been united ecclesiastically, e.g., Scott was curate at the same time of both Olney and Weston; and again, the first mention we have of the wealthy family of Olney is as lords of the manor, not of Olney, but of Weston Underwood.

John de Olney, who is said to have built Weston Church, is buried in the chancel. Covering his grave is a very large blue flag with a Latin inscription in brass round its verge, and the symbols of the evangelists at the corners. He died in 1405.

In 1446 Margaret, daughter of Sir Robert Olney, married Sir Thomas Throckmorton of Warwickshire; and the Throckmorton family has owned the manor ever since.

The most famous of the early Throckmortons was Sir Nicholas, who rose to high dignities in the state in the reign of Henry VIII. In Mary's reign, however, he got into trouble for aiding and abetting the rebellion of Wyat; but at his trial he pleaded his cause so ably that, in spite of the strength of the evidence and the influence of the ministry, the jury acquitted him. The other prisoners, five in all, received judgment: one of them, Croft, obtained a pardon; the other four, the Duke of Suffolk, Wyat, Lord Thomas Grey, and William Thomas, private secretary to the late king, were executed. Throckmorton was detained a prisoner for some time and fined £2000. In the reign of Elizabeth he entered heartily into the intrigues of Court and became a principal in Leicester's faction, but the Earl's insincerity having involved him in trouble, he changed sides, made concessions to Cecil, and by betraying important secrets converted his late patron into a bitter enemy. To outward appearance, however, they still kept on good terms; but as far as Leicester was concerned it was only that the more easily he might carry out his sinister designs, for, a short time after, Throckmorton was attacked by a malignant distemper, caused, it is said, by a poisoned salad eaten at the Earl's; and the distemper proved fatal.

Sir Robert Throckmorton (knight), the next head of the family whom we can here notice, was the person who in 1578 rebuilt the greater part of Weston Hall. His wife, Elizabeth, is buried at the upper end of the south aisle of Weston Church, where there is a headless brass to her memory. At the feet of the figure are an inscription and a small brass representing her five daughters.

Sir Robert, the fourth baronet, died in 1791. Sir John Courteney Throckmorton, the fifth baronet, the friend of the poet Cowper and the Benevolus of "The Task," was born at Weston in 1753, and died and was buried at Coughton in 1819. He married Miss Giffard, the Maria of Cowper's poems. Sir George Courteney Throckmorton, the sixth baronet, succeeded his brother, Sir John. He married Miss Stapleton (Cowper's Catherina).

The poems addressed to "Maria" are the graceful lines entitled "The Poet's New Year's Gift," the lines "On the Death of Mrs. Throckmorton's Bullfinch," and those "To Mrs. Throckmorton on her beautiful transcript of Horace's Ode, 'Ad librum suum.'"

II. The Walks at Weston and Weston Lodge.

As we have already spoken of the eminence sometimes alluded to as "The Cliff," it will be more convenient in noticing Cowper's favourite walks to commence at the Ho-brook, a diminutive stream that crosses the road about half way from Olney[1] to Weston.

"This stream," says Mr. James Storer,[2] "according to tradition, was frequently so swelled, that it was dangerous to attempt a passage; and Weston being then a hamlet to Olney, the clergy made application to the Pope for leave to build a

[1] From the Weston Road, just outside the town, can be seen Goosey Bridge, near which occurred the incident that gave birth to Cowper's poem of "The Dog and the Water-Lily."

[2] "Rural Walks of Cowper," published in 1803.

church at Weston, alleging the danger of proceeding to Olney
for the purpose of worship, or of burying the dead. His
Holiness assenting to their request, Weston has ever since
been a separate parish. It is, however, worthy of remark,
whilst noticing the above tradition, that the building of a
bridge over the brook (which has lately been effected) would
have been attended with little expense compared with that of
erecting a church at Weston." Bounded on one side by the
Ho-brook is a long narrow plantation called, locally, the First
Spinnie, but better known to readers of Cowper as the Shrubbery. It is threaded by a winding path, and in its midst stood
the rustic hut or "moss-house," a favourite haunt of Cowper
(see p. 113), which had on one side of it a weeping willow,[1]
and in front a beautiful circular sheet of water. It was an
unpretending stone structure, with thatched roof, covered with
ivy and moss, and at a distance looked very like a great
mushroom.

The following lines on the Shrubbery, which were written
by Cowper in a time of affliction, were inserted in his first
volume of poems :—

> " Oh, happy shades—to me unblest !
>   Friendly to peace, but not to me !
> How ill the scene, that offers rest,
>   And heart, that cannot rest, agree.
>
> This glassy stream, that spreading pine,
>   Those alders quiv'ring to the breeze,
> Might soothe a soul less hurt than mine,
>   And please, if anything could please.
>
> The saint or moralist should tread
>   This moss-grown alley musing, slow :
> They seek, like me, the secret shade,
>   But not, like me, to nourish woe.
>
> Me, fruitful scenes, and prospects waste,
>   Alike admonish not to roam ;
> These tell me of enjoyments passed,
>   And those of sorrows yet to come."

---

[1] See letter to Newton, July 9, 1785.

In the Moss-house was placed a board upon which were inscribed the poet's lines :—

> " Here, free from riot's hated noise,
> Be mine, ye calmer, purer joys,
>   A book or friend bestows ;
> Far from the storms that shake the great,
> Contentment's gale shall fan my seat
>   And sweeten my repose."

But this board was stolen, so the poet put up another with the following lines, which are substantially the same as those in the sixth book of "The Task."

> " No noise is here, or none that hinders thought ;
> Stillness accompanied with sounds like these,
> Charms more than silence. Meditation here
> May think down hours to moments. Here the heart
> May give a useful lesson to the head,
> And learning wiser grow without his books."

Keeping to the windings of the streamlet, and passing many a pleasant nook, we enter the field in front of the "Peasant's Nest"—no longer, as formerly, a picturesque thatch-roofed cottage half-hidden in foliage. Its trees have been felled, and the building itself is transformed into a prim-looking farmhouse. Still keeping to our streamlet or "weedy ditch," into which the peasant used to dip his bowl, we are brought to another plantation, the Second Spinnie, crowded with firs, pines, and yews, from which we emerge into the Chestnut Avenue :—

> " Thanks to Benevolus, he spares me yet
> These chestnuts ranged in corresponding rows,
> And, though himself so polished, still reprieves
> The obsolete prolixity of shade."

An abrupt descent leads to the "Rustic Bridge," and the "gulf" where "the willows" used to "dip their pendent boughs, stooping as if to drink ;" and ascending the steep walk that borders the northern extremity of the Park we are brought to the Alcove. The walk from the Rustic Bridge to the Alcove is the one alluded to at the commencement of the sixth book of "The Task," where Cowper speaks of the sweet music of the Emberton bells :—

" How soft the music of those village bells,
Falling at intervals upon the ear
In cadence sweet, now dying all away.
Now pealing loud again, and louder still,
Clear and sonorous, as the gale comes on !

Again the harmony comes o'er the vale ;
And through the trees I view the embattled tower
Whence all the music.   I again perceive
The soothing influence of the wafted strains,
And settle in soft musings as I tread
The walk, still verdant, under oaks and elms,
Whose outspread branches over-arch the glade."

THE ALCOVE.

The Alcove, a hexagon in shape with three sides open, was
built by Mr. John Higgins in 1753 for Sir Robert Throckmorton; the grounds at Weston were laid out by Lancelot

Brown, a famous landscape gardener, or, as he was generally
called, from a phrase he was fond of using, "Capability
Brown."[1]   In speaking of this walk we do not wish to quote
more than necessary from Cowper's connective description,
our object being more particularly to point out those notices
of his loved haunts that are scattered in other portions of his
works; consequently, instead of dwelling on the Alcove, or
the Avenue of Lime trees, which next invites us, we would
refer the reader to the delightful description of them in the
first book of " The Task " (lines 278–350).

The Wilderness, with its ceaseless caw of rooks, whither we
are now wending, has still abundant charms; its walks, however, have not been "well rolled" for many a day, and the
monuments, adorned with bright green moss, and crept over
with ivy, are in a dilapidated state.   To some of the vanished
glories of this spot Cowper alludes in "Task," VI.   Laburnum
contributed its "streaming gold."   There were lilacs, syringas,
and Guelder roses.   He would have us notice the woodbine
also, and—

> " Hypericum all bloom, so thick a swarm
> Of flowers, like flies clothing her slender rods,
> That scarce a leaf appears : mezereon too,
> Though leafless, well attired, and thick beset
> With blushing wreaths, investing every spray :
> Althæa with the purple eye ; the broom,
> Yellow and bright, as bullion unalloy'd,
> Her blossoms ; and luxuriant above all
> The jasmine, throwing wide her elegant sweets,
> The deep dark green of whose unvarnish'd leaf
> Makes more conspicuous, and illumines more
> The bright profusion of her scatter'd stars."

The Wilderness is not now carpeted every spring, as it used
to be, with daffodils, snowflakes, and primroses; but snow-
drops are still numerous, and perhaps it was of those in the
Wilderness Cowper was thinking when he wrote :—

> " Winter has a joy for me,
>   While the Saviour's charms I read,
> Lowly, meek, from blemish free,
>   In the snowdrop's pensive head."

---

[1] See " Task," III. line 766.   He died in 1773.

The broad walk that borders the northern side of the Wilderness is ornamented with two monumental urns, and the statue of a lion in a recumbent posture.

Upon the pedestal of one of the urns is engraved the well-known epitaph on Sir John Throckmorton's pointer :—

> " Here lies one who never drew
> Blood himself, yet many slew :
> Gave the gun its aim, and figure
> Made in field, yet ne'er pulled trigger.
> Armed men have gladly made
> Him their guide, and him obeyed :
> At his signified desire,
> Would advance, present, and fire.
> Stout he was, and large of limb.
> Scores have fled at sight of him :
> And to all this fame he rose,
> By only following his nose.
> Neptune was he called ; not he
> Who controls the boist'rous sea,
> But of happier command,
> Neptune of the furrowed land :
> And your wonder, vain, to shorten,
> Pointer to Sir John Throckmorton."

On the pedestal of the other urn is an inscription written at the request of Mrs. Courtenay (Catharina) afterwards Lady Throckmorton. It was composed at Eartham in Sussex, at the time Cowper was visiting Hayley. The date of the letter containing it is August 25, 1792.

> " Though once a puppy, and though Fop by name,
> Here moulders one whose bones some honour claim ;
> No sycophant, although of spaniel race,
> And though no hound, a martyr to the chase.
> Ye squirrels, rabbits, leverets, rejoice,
> Your haunts no longer echo to his voice.
> This record of his late exulting view,
> He died, worn out with vain pursuit of you.
> Yes ; the indignant shade of Fop replies,
> And, worn with vain pursuits, man also dies."

The most conspicuous object in the Wilderness is the Gothic Temple, now in a sadly ruinous state, a frequent haunt of the Rev. John Newton as well as of Cowper. In front of it is a

large grass-plot surrounded by trees, and shrubs.   Another
interesting object is the bust of Homer, on the pedestal of
which is a Greek couplet from Cowper's pen, together with a
translation by Hayley :—

> " The sculptor ?   Nameless, though once dear to fame,
> But this man bears an everlasting name.".

Two of the monuments, as their dates show, were put up
long after Cowper left Weston : the recumbent lion already
alluded to, and the urn on the edge of the grass-plot in front
of the Temple.   The inscription on the pedestal of the
former is :—

> " Mortuo Leoni etiam Lepores insultant.
> 1815."

And on that of the latter :—

> " Adieu to destructive war,
> And mad Bellona, in her iron car,
> Welcome to our smiling fields again
> Sweet peace, attended by thy jovial train.
> 1815."

Weston Lodge, a large and comfortable house in the middle
of the village, was the residence of Cowper from November
1786 to July 1795.

In a letter to Mrs. Hill (November 5, 1793) he speaks of
some of the advantages of his situation :—

" The opposite object," to the Lodge, " and the only one, is
an orchard, so well planted, and with trees of such growth,
that we seem to look into a wood, or rather to be surrounded
by one.   Thus, placed as we are in the midst of a village, we
have none of those disagreeables that belong to such a position,
and the village itself is one of the prettiest I know ; terminated
at one end by the church tower, seen through the trees, and
at the other by a very handsome gateway, opening into a fine
grove of elms, belonging to our neighbour Courtenay."   The
front of the house was ornamented with vines and jessamines.
The shrubbery, which a later owner converted into an orchard,
was, according to Mr. Storer, " very generally admired, being a
delightful little labyrinth, composed of flowering shrubs, and

adorned with gravel walks, having convenient seats placed at
appropriate distances." Of the "lonely winding walk" in this
shrubbery Cowper speaks in his fragment "The Four Ages,"
and he gives the following amusing account of the erection of
an arbour in it [1] :—

"I said to my Sam—'Sam, build me a shed in the garden

WESTON LODGE.

with anything that you can find, and make it rude and rough
like one of those at Eartham.'—'Yes, sir,' says Sam, and
straightway laying his own noddle and the carpenter's noddle
together, has built me a thing fit for Stow Gardens. Is not
this vexatious? I threaten to inscribe it thus :—

[1] To Hayley, July 24, 1793.

' Beware of the building ! I intended
Rough logs and thatch, and thus it ended.'

But my Mary says I shall break Sam's heart, and the carpenter's too, and will not consent to it."

In this shrubbery stood the bust of Homer (now in the Wilderness) presented to Cowper by Dr. Johnson, which drew from the former the sonnet thus commencing :—

" Kinsman beloved, and as a son, by me !
When I behold the fruit of thy regard,
The sculptured form of my old favourite bard,
I reverence feel for him, and love for thee."

As the following letter will show, dated Weston, September 4, 1793, the bust was not the only appropriate present sent by Johnson to Cowper :—

"My dearest Johnny,—To do a kind thing, and in a kind manner, is a double kindness, and no man is more addicted to both than you, or more skilful in contriving them. Your plan to surprise me agreeably succeeded to admiration. It was only the day before yesterday that, while we walked after dinner in the orchard, Mrs. Unwin between Sam and me, hearing the Hall clock, I observed a great difference between that and ours, and began immediately to lament, as I had often done, that there was not a sun-dial in all Weston to ascertain the true time for us. My complaint was long, and lasted till, having turned into the grass-walk, we reached the new building at the end of it, where we sat awhile and reposed ourselves. In a few minutes we returned by the way we came, when what think you was my astonishment to see what I had not seen before, though I had passed close by it, a smart sun-dial mounted on a smart stone pedestal ! I assure you it seemed the effect of conjuration. I stopped short, and exclaimed—'Why, here is a sun-dial, and upon our ground ! How is this ? Tell me, Sam, how it came here ? Do you know anything about it ?' At first I really thought (that is to say, as soon as I could think at all) that this factotum of mine, Sam Roberts, having often heard me deplore the want of one, had given orders for the supply of that want himself, without my knowledge, and was half pleased and half offended. But he soon exculpated himself by imputing the fact to you."

This sun-dial after Cowper left Weston was removed by the Throckmortons to the Hall Garden, and in 1828 it was placed where it now stands, in the garden of the priest's house, and on or near the site of the porch that belonged to the west front of the mansion.

The only inscription on it is :—

"Walter Gough, No. 21 Middle Row, Holborn, London."

When Cowper left Weston for Norfolk neither he nor his friends intended anything further than a temporary absence ; but still he had a presentiment that he should never return, and it was with this feeling in his mind that he wrote the oft-quoted lines on a panel of the window-shutter in his bedroom :—

> " Farewell, dear scenes, for ever closed to me ;
> Oh, for what sorrows must I now exchange ye ! "

Below them are two dates written thus :—

> July 22
> —— 28, 1795.

In a letter to Southey the Rev. Josiah Bull gives several interesting particulars about these lines.

"That I might obtain an accurate copy of them, I rode over to Weston yesterday, and was fortunate enough to meet with a person who gave me some information which verifies their origin, and accounts for their preservation for forty years. This individual, whose name is Price, tells me that he assisted in packing Mr. Cowper's goods, and that he and others saw the lines after he left. He accounted for the second date by the circumstance that Mr. Cowper did not leave Weston on the day he expected, but not until nearly a week from that time. Price himself afterwards occupied the house, and says that for twenty years that very shutter was closed up to avoid the tax. It seems that it was afterwards opened ; but two years ago, when the present occupant came to the house, he found it again closed. This probably accounts for the preservation of the writing. It has been unfortunately retraced, but is evidently the fair and distinct hand of the poet. There is a word before the second date : but I am unable to read it."

In Weston Church are mural tablets to Bartholomew Higgins, the friend of Scott ; Charles Higgins, the friend of Scott and Cowper ; and Mary Higgins, Thomas Higgins, Dr. Gregson, and the Rev. John Buchanan, friends of Cowper.

The inscriptions to Mary and Thomas Higgins were written by the poet.

" In Memory of MARY HIGGINS,
The much-loved wife of
THOMAS HIGGINS, who died
On the fourth day of June,
MDCCXCI., aged fifty years.

" Laurels may flourish round the Conqu'ror's Tomb,
But happiest they who win the world to come :
Believers have a silent field to fight,
And their exploits are veil'd from human sight :
They in some nook, where little known they dwell,
Kneel, pray in faith, and rout the hosts of Hell.
Eternal triumphs crown their toils divine,
And all those triumphs, Mary ! now are thine."

" THOMAS HIGGINS Gent.
departed this life May 24th 1794, in
the 62nd year of his age.

" And on the blank, to Mary's join my name,
He said :—Too soon the stone assents his claim.
Snatch'd from those joys of life which Heav'n bestow'd
While in his bosom cares paternal glow'd !
This second loss he leaves us to deplore,
Yet the decree, as wise and good, adore.
Respected pair ! now safe in holy rest,
Whose nurture rear'd us, and whose guidance blest,
The filial thought and foot shall haunt this spot,
And your example never be forgot."

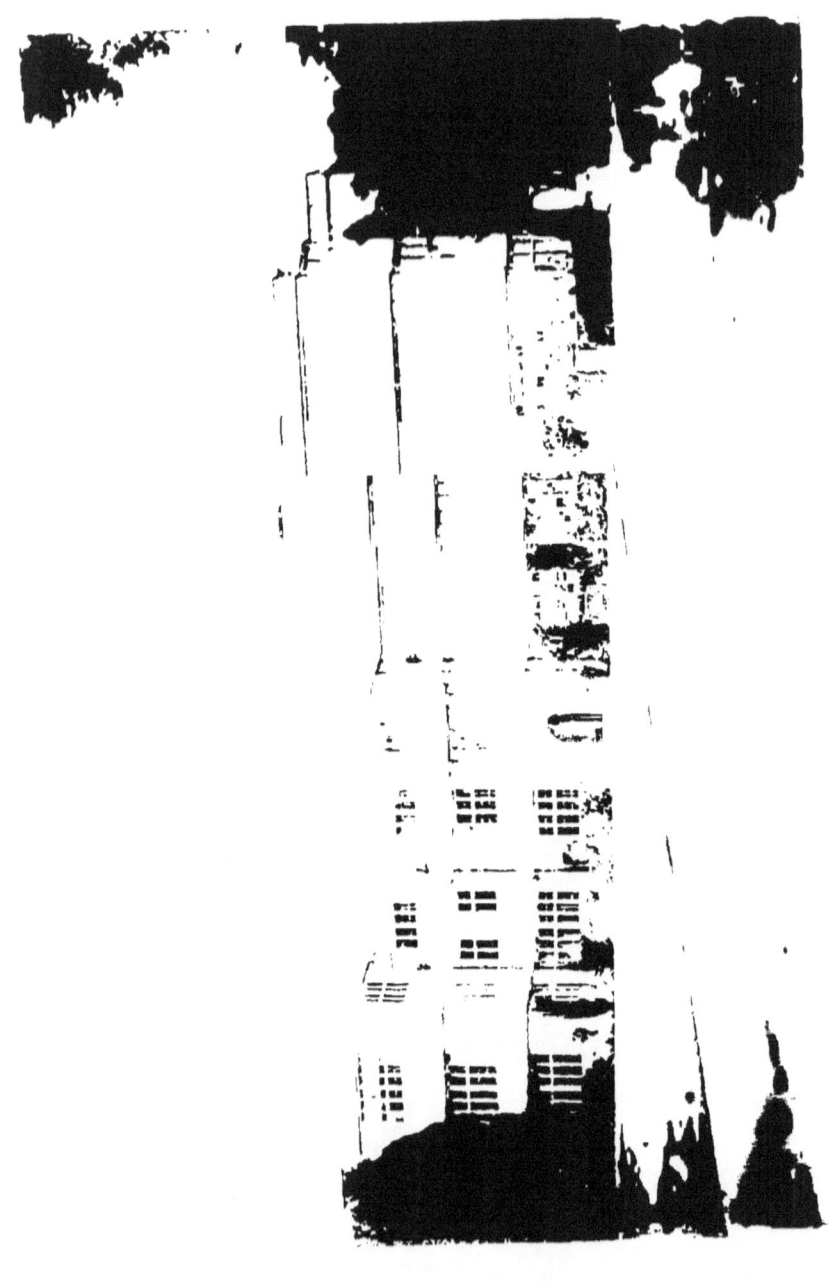

XVI

THE MANSION OF GOTEHURST.

" Parks with oak and chestnut shady,
  Parks and order'd gardens great ;
Ancient homes of lord and lady,
  Built for pleasure and for state."—TENNYSON.

" BEAUTIFUL exceedingly " are the surroundings of the handsome and stately old mansion of Gayhurst, or Gotehurst ; for
by the latter name in times gone by it was more usual to call
it.   The church, half hidden by its firs and yews, stands picturesquely at a short distance from the left wing ; the park
offers its fine old trees and sparkling sheets of water ; and the
gardens are ever pleasing with their terraces of smooth-shaven
grass, grey stonework, alleys of evergreen, and immemorial
yews.   On the east of the park a carriage-drive winds to the
Northampton and Newport Pagnell road, and ends at a lodge
of curious Tudor structure ; and on the west Digby's Walk,
overshadowed by yews, has for 300 years formed a shady
retreat—

  "Sweet Digby's Walk, cool shade in summer-time,
  Leads through an archway to the peaceful Ouse,
  Where boat and fishing-rod supply the taste
  Of those who seek the meditative charms
  To memory dear of sylvan river scene."

The high road itself, arched over with the foliage of magnificent beeches, is accompanied on both sides with so many
delights that one but instinctively feels that to scenes such as
these Gayhurst is indebted for its name.   The form of some
blue-eyed ancient Saxon rises before us, and we seem to hear
him say, as he gazes in ecstasy on his newly-gotten domain :
" It is Goddeshurst !— none other than the hurst or forest of

God." The mantle of this ancient Saxon descended to very
many of the lords of Gayhurst, for whether holding their
demesne by direct descent, marriage, or purchase, they seem
to have abundantly appreciated it, and to have taken pleasure
in adding to, or at least preserving, its numerous charms.   The
neighbourhood could formerly boast of several edifices, familiar and pleasing objects from Gayhurst, which have now quite
disappeared : Weston Hall, the seat of the Throckmortons,
no longer like a little town shows its numerous ends, peaks, and
gables above the woods and spinnies ; the ancient seat of the
Tyringhams, whose warlike sons had a hand in every quarrel
that distracted mediæval England, has given place to a modern
edifice ; whilst not a stone now stands of the ancient church of
Filgrave, the tower of which, as the antiquary Cole remarks, in
his account of its demolition, made a picturesque object from
Gayhurst.   But from various parts of the house and grounds
views are still obtained of the churches and villages of Emberton, Weston, and Tyringham, whilst the top of Olney spire,
peeping above the foliage, may also be descried.

The most interesting fact connected with Gayhurst in Saxon
times is the proximity to it of the once flourishing but now
entirely perished town of Bonstye, which gave its name to one
of the ancient Hundreds which have since been incorporated
into the Hundreds of Newport.

Newport Hundred, roughly speaking, consists of that part of
Bucks north of a line drawn from Bow Brickhill to Stony
Stratford.   It is divided naturally into three parts by the Ouse
and the Ouzel or Lovat, and each part formed a separate Hundred : Bonstow (deriving its name from Bonstye, its chief town),
lying to the north and west of the Ouse ; Molestow (so named
from Moulsoe), a long narrow strip lying east of the Ouse and
Lovat ; and Sigelai, the triangular Hundred to the south, which
possibly took its name from Chicheley.   These Hundreds after
a time ceased to be called by their distinctive names.   In the
despatches of the civil war between King Charles and the
Parliament they are denominated the Hundreds of Newport, a
name still retained,—the owner of Gayhurst being lord of the
manor of the three Hundreds of Newport.   The inhabitants

of Bonstye seem to have deserted it a little before the Conquest, migrating to the junction of the Ouse and Lovat, and
calling their new settlement Newport, in contrast to Bonstye,
their old port. The word port here merely = town, and has
nothing to do with the sea. Bunstay, as Bonstye is now called,
is in the parish of Lathbury, and lies between Gayhurst and
Stoke, which estates it cuts nearly in two. It contains no
ancient building, but is still a separate property.

When the first manor-house at Gotehurst was built, we have
no means of ascertaining. The first Norman owner of the
estate was Odo, Bishop of Bayeux, and after his treason (1087)
it fell to the lot of his tenant, Ralph de Nowers, in whose family
it remained 321 years.

The only event we need notice in this period is the marriage
of Sir William de Nowers in 1265 to Isabel de Stoke Goldington,
since which time the manors of Gayhurst and Stoke have been
united. The ancient manor-house of the Stoke Goldingtons
stood near Stoke Goldington Church, and some portions of it,
forming part of a farm-house, still exist.

In 1408 Joan Nowers, sole heiress, married Sir Robert
Nevill, son of Henry Nevill of Prestwold, County Leicester, and
the estate remained in the Nevill family for 173 years, towards
the end of which period the history of the present mansion of
Gayhurst commences.

Gayhurst house presents many of the principal characteristics of the finer mansions of the Elizabethan period, and its
extensive façade, noble, yet simple, is adorned with handsome
gables, large, finely proportioned, and many mullioned windows,
and a large ornamental porch. Gayhurst, however, although
largely, is by no means entirely Elizabethan : it was built in
three distinct periods, and we can best deal with its history by
taking these periods separately.

First Period : The Early Tudor House.

The oldest portion was probably erected about 1500 by one
of the Nevills, and we may style it the First or Early Tudor
house. It was oblong in plan, and although greatly altered

at various times, the position of its front door and entrance-hall can be easily pointed out. On each side of this Tudor house may still be seen rows of gigantic yews, which no doubt helped to enclose a small park or garden, much of which has since been built over. At the present day part of the old garden forms the kitchen-yard; and from this place the gables of the old mansion can still be traced, although they were hidden as much as possible by Mulso, a later owner, when he made this building the wing of a larger house. This old building abounds in narrow passages, thick walls, quaintly formed and unexpected roofs and gables, and curiously contrived gutters, the result of Mulso's alteration, down which the rain used to rattle and scamper, making its inmates believe the house was haunted with prancing horses and other ghosts, for the laying of which the nearest priest was often in requisition : at the present day the priest has given place to the layman, for it is found that a plumber with his pipes is more effectual than twenty paternosters.

Each of the many gables forms a room, and odd little rooms they are, with their small, strongly mullioned windows of the ordinary Tudor type, many corners, and doors and floors of oak ; but curious as this old house now is, it must have been more so in former times, for many of its irregularities have been cleared away. There were numerous and strange projections, and tall stacks of chimneys contrived to mask secret chambers and hiding-places ; there were trap-doors, narrow recesses, and ingenious cabinets and drawers for the deposit of papers. The old staircase occupied, as does the present one, the south-east corner. At the west end of the top of the house is a room partly in the roof, which is supposed to have been used as a chapel, up one side of which passes a huge chimney shaft that at one time probably contained a secret staircase.

SECOND PERIOD : THE ELIZABETHAN HOUSE.

In 1581 Mary Nevill, sole heiress, married Thomas Mulso of Thingdon, County Northants ; and it was their son William who built the second, or Elizabethan portion of Gayhurst, making

the new house, together with the old part, to form the letter
E, a common arrangement at that time with loyal gentlemen.
The old house corresponds with the lowest of the three limbs
of the letter; the porch is the short central limb. Thus
"Gotehurst changed its front," "the former Tudor house
became a wing," and the new façade exhibited its Gothic gables
and much admired beauties of Italian architecture. Like
Nevill's front each gable forms a room. In Mulso's building
the south wing (or old part) was retained by the family; the
north wing, which has a special porch and entrance, was for
entertaining great personages with retainers, or the yeomanry,
and for many years it was the custom to lodge visitors in this
part of the house, a custom that was kept up in Lord Carrington's time, when H.R.H. the present Prince of Wales was a
guest at Gayhurst. The first floor (now called the Guard-room,
the Prince's room, the Peacock room) was the quarters for the
officers, while the floor above was the barracks, and consisted
of one long empty gallery, since converted by the architect
Burgess into five bedrooms with a stone staircase. People
still living can remember it as one long gallery.

Directly in front of his porch, Mulso built a massive gateway.

In 1596 Mary Mulso, heiress, the daughter of William Mulso,
married the hapless Everard Digby, afterwards knighted, who
had the misfortune to be drawn into the Gunpowder Plot.

Joyous, doubtless, was that wedding-day, happy were the
youthful couple, and many, we can fancy, the guests that
assembled in the noble hall, or strolled along the beautiful
terraces, and through the alleys of topiary work; and yet in
how short a time did gloom and sorrow overshadow Gayhurst!
But no evil foreboding, we may be sure, troubled the Mulsos
and Digbys on that day: they were Catholics, it is true, but
as they belonged to the old-fashioned party, and had no
sympathy with the Jesuits and seminary priests, who at that
time were intriguing in England, they suffered but little if at all
from persecution.

Gayhurst is never so stately as when thronged with happy
guests—but it must have looked to its very best advantage on

that day—glittering with ladies and gallants in the picturesque
costumes of the period: the ladies with their farthingales and
ruffs, bangles and necklaces, and their looking-glass fans of
ostrich feathers; the gentlemen with their pointed beards and
trimmed moustaches, their stiffly starched ruffs, doublets of
quilted silk, short cloaks, and high plumed hats. We can
picture to ourselves the marriage-feast spread in the great hall,
the cumbrous tables groaning with the weight of flesh, fish, and
fowl, the well-fed ox roasting in the yard, the barrels of home-
brewed ale rolling from the capacious cellars, and the hearty
welcome accorded to both rich and poor.

A few happy years rolled by, and for a time, even after the
death of Queen Elizabeth, the laws against recusancy were
not enforced. Then came days of persecution, fiercer than
had burned against the Catholics even in the most bitter
period of Elizabeth: those who would worship according to
the old faith were obliged to do so in secret, their priests to
hide in holes and caves; and mass could not be celebrated
except at midnight, and in cellars, attics, or the depths of
forests. In the meantime a few desperate men, goaded to
madness most of them by persecution, were forming the
dreadful conspiracy known in history as the Gunpowder Plot.
Digby, who at the time resided mostly at Drystoke Park, in
Rutlandshire, was one of the last to join the conspiracy, and
thenceforward, both there and at Gayhurst, the daily life of his
family was shrouded in mystery.

The leading members of the conspiracy, and the priests
who are said to have abetted it, were frequent guests at
Gayhurst. The tall sinewy Father Greenway with his dark,
disagreeable countenance was often there, and you might
sometimes have seen Sir Everard in eager conversation with a
man who, to all appearance, was merely a poor pedlar anxious
only to sell his tawdry wares; but a more careful glance would
show that the keen blue eye and white hand were those of
the wily Jesuit Garnet, or Darcy, or Farmer, or Whalley, or
whatever other name he happened at the time to be styling
himself. Sometimes the sinister-looking, though handsome,
Catesby would appear—fierce, anxious, enthusiastic; though

more often, his servant, the luckless Bates, would hurry down the drive to deliver his letter or message, and after drinking a cup of wine, wiping the perspiration from his face, and pushing his shaggy red hair from his forehead, disappear as quickly as he had ventured thither. Sometimes you might have seen the coarse and ugly face of John Wright, or the huge form of Christopher, his equally guilty brother; the polished and accomplished Thomas Winter; the cold, cautious, and treacherous Tresham; and the tall, hook-nosed, white-headed Percy; Guy Fawkes too would occasionally grace, or, if you like, disgrace the board—dressed, not as we are wont to picture him, in slouched hat and military boots, but in the common garb of a serving-man—answering to the name of Johnson.

Many an exciting incident occurs to our mind when we think of those turbulent times; and we cannot help associating with Gayhurst scenes similar to those that were frequently enacted in other Catholic mansions at the time.

A midnight mass is being held in the attic already referred to in the old part of the house; a temporary altar has been rapidly fitted up and adorned with candles great and small, an ivory crucifix, the image of the Virgin, richly bound mass-book with elaborate clasps, and vases of flowers. Among the worshippers we notice members of the Gayhurst family and representatives of the great Catholic houses in the neighbourhood; of the Catesbys, the Throckmortons, the Mordaunts, and the Vauxes,—and perhaps two or three who afterwards died on the scaffold for participation in the plot. A priest ascends the richly carpeted steps that lead to the altar, his dress of flaming scarlet stiff with gold. It is the famous Father Garnet—for weeks he has been wandering in disguise in the counties of Northampton and Bucks. The voice of the droning serpent arises, mass is sung, and Garnet in earnest and eloquent tone appeals to his hearers, exhorting them to hold fast to the true faith, and exciting their passions by alluding to the broken promises of the King, and the troubles that menace them. Suddenly a tremendous hubbub is heard without—some of the worshippers turn pale, some draw their swords, and others clench their fists in defiance—then all hurry away, for well they

N

know what the tumult means, and that it would be ruin to be
discovered congregated thus. Two attendants alone remain behind. Lights are flitting about in the gardens. Shouts are
heard, and angry voices calling on the inmates to unbolt the
door unless they wish it burst in twain. "The priest! the
priest! where is the priest?" seems the one cry of the rude
mob that thus assails the mansion. "He shall not escape this
time, my masters," cries a burly smith from Weston to the pursuivant and his men-at-arms—and so saying the fellow lets fly
at the door with a heavy pickaxe. Suddenly a bright glare
shows that one of the ricks has been fired. The flames leap
to the sky, mingling their roar with the angry menaces of the
mob, and illuminating peak and finial of the mansion. They
lunge their sharp yellow blades among the trees, which stand
out black and sharply defined; roll their cruel tongues round
the fantastic turrets of the stabling; and singe the wings of the
doves as they flutter in consternation from the top of the great
square columbarium. Not a sound is heard from the inmates,
but the crashes at the doors and windows are increased. The
door, though of mighty oak and iron barred, at last gives way,
and with a ferocious shout the mob, armed as they are with
spades, rakes, and scythes, burst into the hall and through the
house. The pursuivant and his men rush about terrifying
the women and children, ripping up the beds, ransacking the
chests and wardrobes and littering their rich contents on the
floor, passing their swords through the handsome tapestry,
tapping the walls with mallets to discover whether they are
hollow, and shouting exultingly when they come upon a secret
chamber. The mob burst into the cellars and help themselves
without ceremony to the contents of the casks; their lanterns
flicker about on the roof; and their dark forms creep between
the counterfeit windows and the old gables—in short, they
wander in all directions, bent only on doing mischief and finding the priest. "Wrench down this window-seat," cries one;
"Creep into that cupboard, Dick Swivel," shouts another;
whilst a third calls to his comrade Hab Nokes to help him
tear up a hearthstone which he fancies may cover the entrance
to an underground retreat. But the most active and vindictive

of all the noisy throng is a certain Bob Carter, as his comrades
familiarly call him, dressed in the ordinary ploughman's habili-
ments of smock frock, rough worsted stockings, and cowhide
boots.   Cursing the papists and calling the vengeance of
Heaven on Jesuit and priest, he and five or six other stout
fellows are dragging in trusses of straw, and cramming them
into the fireplace in the hall; where they have just lighted a
fire as big as the great mouth of the chimney would hold, exclaiming that if the dog of a priest is hiding in its crooks and
corners he shall at least be roasted.   At length one man who
seems to know more about the house than the rest hurries his
companions up to the attic, lately the scene of the celebration
of the mass.   But the room is completely empty—for the
attendants had rapidly taken the altar to pieces, folded up
the carpet of crimson and blue, and carried away to some
secret closet candles, flowers, mass-book, and vestments.   And
where are the worshippers all this time?   Walking moodily
and sullenly about the house in twos and threes—knowing
resistance to be useless, and swallowing, as best they can, the
rude questions of the hinds and soldiery, to which they make
no answer.   And where is the priest?   In vain they search
every possible hiding-place—in vain they wander from chimney
to cellar, from cellar to chimney—in vain they crawl into
nooks, and descend the shaft of the huge chimney by the
secret steps they discover within it.   And no wonder they are
unsuccessful, for he himself is helping in the search!   Bob
Carter is merely Father Garnet in another suit.   The cunning
priest had slipped on the smock and boots of a ploughman—
one of the many disguises he was wont to assume, and taking
advantage of the darkness had glided from the house and
mingled with the mob, who, knowing him only as Bob Carter,
an occasional sojourner in their village, a hearty fellow, and a
fierce hater of the papists, had accorded him a noisy welcome.
At dawn of day Bob Carter would be far away from Gayhurst.
In many a mansion at this time throughout England were such
scenes enacted.[1]

[1] The preceding was suggested by the description of a similar scene in Mrs.
Marsh Caldwell's "Father Darcy."

In 1605 occurred the discovery of the Gunpowder Plot, for
participation in which Sir Everard Digby perished on the
scaffold. This was a dark time for Gayhurst, but brighter days
were at hand. Sir Everard left two sons, Kenelm and John,
both of whom were afterwards knighted—and the former, by
reason of his many talents, quite obliterated all memory of his
father's treason.

Third Period: The Queen Anne Portion.

We now come to the third period of Gayhurst. In 1704 two
daughters, heiresses of the Digby estates, sold their shares to
George Wrighte, son of Sir Nathan Wrighte, Lord Keeper to
Queen Anne. In 1725 George Wrighte made another addition
to the house, and he built it in the Queen Anne style. This
part, which consists of the dining-room below, the ball-room
above, and the grand staircase, is at the back of Mulso's main
building, filling up the space at the back of the ⊐⊏ between
the two large limbs. The ball-room, a very fine specimen of
Queen Anne, is corniced with most exquisitely carved hand-
work. George Wrighte was a faithful judge, who retired to the
country owing to the factions of the court, but was not less
diligent as a private gentleman than when in office. At Gayhurst we see him

> " Spending his leisure hours in active work,
> Enlarging house, and laying out the grounds."

Besides his additions to the mansion, Wrighte effected great
improvement in the park, but in order to a proper understanding of his alterations we must consult a curious old map (date
1711) still hanging at Gayhurst, which represents the estate as
it was when he bought it. In front of the mansion we notice
the massive gateway before mentioned, whilst here and there
are dotted the cottages of the village. The position of the two
rows of yews at the south wing is shown, as is also, though by
straight lines, Digby's Walk; and opposite the church we notice
the ancient parsonage. Wrighte pulled down the parsonage,

the old gateway, and the cottages, or mere hovels as they appear to have been at that time, and in 1738 built the present picturesque cottages near the lodge. We will now briefly relate the history of the house since the time of Wrighte. In 1830 Ann Barbara Wrighte dying unmarried, the estate passed to the Wyndhams of Cromer, Norfolk, a family unconnected with her by blood. In 1837 the estates came to two daughters ; Maria Anne Wyndham (Lady Macdonald) and Cecilia (Lady Alfred Paget). In 1842 the mansion, &c., was leased to the Honourable Robert Lord Carrington for five years. At the partition of the estates in 1854, Gayhurst and Stoke became the sole property of Lady Macdonald. In 1856 the whole estate was leased to Lord Carrington for twenty-one years. In 1882 Lady Macdonald, who during the five preceding years had resided at Gayhurst House, sold the estates of Gayhurst and Stoke Goldington to their present owner, James William Carlile, Esq., of Ponsbourne Park, Herts. For the sake of clearness the families in whose hands the estates have been longest may be tabulated thus :—

	Years.	
1087.—Nowers	321	
1408.—Nevill	173	
1581.—Mulso	15	617 years.
1596.—Digby	108	
1704.—Wrighte	126	
1830.—Wyndham	52	178 years.

Families who owned the estate by direct descent or marriage.

Numerous restorations and alterations were made by Lord Carrington under the able supervision of William Burgess, A.R.A., the architect—the large kitchen (adjoining the south wing), which he built in Tudor style, is peculiarly handsome and picturesque. Burgess also built the large fireplaces in the dining-room, which are ornamented with the sculptures "Paradise Lost" and "Paradise Regained;" and a number of other fireplaces in various parts of the house were ornamented by him—the most admired being one over which are, exquisitely carved, three monkeys pointing to and grimacing at one another.

The visit to Gayhurst for the purpose of gathering material

for the present sketch was made in June 1885. Leaving
the house, where we had passed from room to room admiring
the handiwork of famous architects and sculptors, and recalling
gay scenes and gallant forms of bygone days, we wandered
into the garden towards the gentle eminence called Digby's
Mound, along the terraces, and under the great and noble
trees. Everything seems peaceful and unmolested here; in a
fork of one fine old yew, which would take three men to stretch
round it, was a blackbird's nest, and as we peeped in at the
five dusky eggs we could not but feel thankful that there
are delightful retreats like Gayhurst, where the birds may rear
their young in safety, and schoolboys cannot break through
and steal. Thence we proceeded past the north wing to the
Dutch garden, startling on our way a leveret that scampered
off to join his comrades in Gayhurst Wood. A weather-stained
sun-dial next attracted our attention, bearing the motto "Nul
que une," the arms of Digby, the date 1670, and the inscription "Walter Hayes at the Cross Daggers in Moorfields
Londini fecit."

Of the labyrinth or maze that formerly existed between the
house and the church nothing now remains; nor is this to be
wondered at, for garden mazes, unless constantly attended to,
quickly fall into disrepair, and in consequence many famous
ones have been cleared away: its site, however, is indicated
by the different colouring of the grass.

Close to the Queen Anne front of the mansion is a monumental pedestal (which formerly stood in the shrubbery, near
the kitchen), with an inscription to a peacock [1] that belonged
to the last Miss Wrighte, or, as she was called by the tenantry,
"Madam Wrighte."

To y *Memory of a Beautifully Mottled Peacock.*

"Could tears avert or tend'rest cares assuage
The pangs of nature and decays of age,
The much lamented bird who sleeps beneath
Secure had triumphed over age and death.

---

[1] At the end of the last and at the commencement of the present century, it
was a frequent custom with the gentry to ornament their grounds with monu-

But fate has ravished from this widow'd wood
The spouse and parent of a numerous brood ;
Of all the feathered kind, where'er he roved,
The sprightliest, gentlest, loveliest, most beloved.

This humble tribute, this last mournful boon,
A weeping verse, a monumental stone,
His grateful mistress to his memory pays,
At once her grief recording, and his praise."

In the beautiful pleasure-ground by the river is a small build-ing called the Bath-house, and adjacent to it stood until recently, though in decay, a tasteful pleasure-house that was used by the Wrightes for picnics and afternoon tea. Nine years ago it was removed by the present owner, who placed it as a lodge (the one previously mentioned) at the commencement of the drive leading to the mansion, and it now bears the initials cut in stone, "G. W. 1751, J. W. C. 1882." In another part of this pleasaunce an urn on a pedestal (date 1751) stands over a chalybeate spring, which flows into a square trough, making it a deep saffron from the sediment that is continually falling.

COWPER AT GAYHURST.

The poet Cowper was a frequent visitor at Gayhurst, and speaks in raptures of what he saw there. "Your mother and I," he tells Mr. Unwin (September 21, 1779),

"last week made a trip in a postchaise to Gayhurst, the seat of Mr. Wrighte, about four miles off. He understood that I did not much affect strange faces, and sent over his servant on purpose to inform me that he was going into Leicestershire, and that if I chose to see the gardens I might gratify myself without danger of seeing the proprietor. I accepted the invitation, and was delighted with all I found there. The situation is happy, the gardens elegantly disposed, the hothouse in the most flourishing state, and the orange trees the most captivating creatures of the kind I ever saw. A man, in short, had need have the talents of Cox or Langford, the auctioneers, to do the whole scene justice."

ments to pet animals ; those in the Wilderness at Weston have already been spoken of. In the Wilderness at Chicheley Hall is a dilapidated monument to a horse.

Cowper's connection with Gayhurst, however, commences previous to this. In a letter to Mr. Unwin, dated December 3, 1778, he writes:—

"I made Mr. Wrighte's gardener a present of fifty sorts of stove plant seeds; in return, he has presented me with six fruiting pines, which I have put into a bark bed, where they thrive at present as well as I could wish. If they produce good fruit, you will stand some little chance to partake of them. But you must not expect giants, for being transplanted in December will certainly give them a check, and probably diminish their size. He has promised to supply me with still better plants in October, which is the proper season for moving them, and with a reinforcement every succeeding year. Mrs. Hill sent me the seeds; which perhaps could not have been purchased for less than three guineas. 'Tis thus we great gardeners establish a beneficial intercourse with each other, and furnish ourselves with valuable things that, therefore, cost us nothing."

Of these pines and Mrs. Hill's seeds we hear more at a later date. "The newspaper informs me," he writes to Mr. Joseph Hill (October 2, 1799),

"of the arrival of the Jamaica fleet. I hope it imports some pine-apple plants for me. I have a good frame, and a good bed prepared to receive them. I send you annexed a fable, in which the pine-apple makes a figure, and shall be glad if you like the taste of it."

Then follows Cowper's poem of "The Pine-apple and the Bee," which may be seen in most editions of his works.

"My affectionate respects attend Mrs. Hill. She has put Mr. Wrighte to the expense of building a new hothouse, the plants produced by the seeds she gave me having grown so large as to require an apartment to themselves."

To Lady Hesketh (December 7, 1785) he writes:—

"I have been repeatedly at Gayhurst, but we went only to amuse ourselves with a walk in the pleasure-grounds when the family were out. I was last year in company with Mrs. Wrighte. We met at Mr. Throckmorton's and were both highly pleased with her; but Mr. Wrighte himself is such a keen sportsman that he would doubtless find me an insipid animal, who have not the least relish for what he admires so much. For the same reason as well as for some others, I have never had a connection in the visiting way with any other of the gentlemen in the country."

In another letter to Lady Hesketh (May 1, 1786) Cowper speaks of the neighbouring gentry with whom he was intimate :—

"Gayhurst is five miles off. I have walked there, but have never walked thither. I have not these many years been such an extravagant tramper as I once was. I did myself no good, I believe, by such pilgrimages of such immoderate length. The Chesters, the Throckmortons, the Wrightes are all of them good-natured, agreeable people, and I rejoice for your sake that they lie all within your beat."

In the letter to Lady Hesketh dated November 3, 1787, mention is made of Mrs. Wrighte's serious illness and the accident that happened to her husband. Whilst fox-hunting in Yardley Chase, the hounds chose to follow the deer. Mr. Wrighte rode violently to whip them off, when, through his horse plunging into a slough, he was thrown and terribly injured. We quote one other letter (May 12, 1788) to Lady Hesketh :—

"Two days, _en suite_, I have walked to Gayhurst ; a longer journey than I have walked on foot these seventeen years. The first day I went alone, designing merely to make the experiment, and choosing to be at liberty to return at whatsoever point of my pilgrimage I should find myself fatigued. For I was not without suspicion that years and some other things no less injurious than years, viz., melancholy and distress of mind, might by this time have unfitted me for such achievements. But I found it otherwise. I reached the church which stands as you know in the garden, in fifty-five minutes, and returned in ditto time to Weston. The next day I took the same walk with Mr. Powley, having a desire to show him the prettiest place in the country. I not only performed these two excursions without injury to my health, but have by means of them gained indisputable proof that my ambulatory faculty is not yet impaired, a discovery which, considering that to my feet alone I am likely, as I have ever been, to be indebted always for my transportation from place to place, I find very delectable."

Such are the more interesting associations of Gayhurst with the poet Cowper; of the connection of Scott the commentator with Gayhurst we have already spoken.

GAYHURST CHURCH.

The ancient church of Gayhurst, within whose walls were buried the Nowerses, Nevills, Mulsoes and Digbys, was described just before its demolition as "very old, uncomely, and ruinous." "It consisted," says Cole, "of a body which was leaded and south aisle which ran the length of the church and chancel, which were tiled, and of a small chancel which was leaded; at the east end of which was a small oval circular building lower than the rest of the chancel, ceiled at top and tiled. At the west end was a low tower, covered with a rising tiled roof, in which hung three bells."

In 1712 all the inscriptions and coats-of-arms were gone, but there were several brasses in the pavement, and two or three old broken gravestones lay near the chancel, one of which was so much dilapidated that at the time the church was taken down, only the last word was legible. It was to John de Nowers, who lived at the time of Edward III., and the inscription, which was in French, formerly ran :—

> Jo : de : Nowers : gist : ici :
> Dieu : de : s'alme : eit : merci : Amen.

The present church, for the building of which George Wrighte (who had pulled down the old one) obtained a faculty in 1724, was opened for worship in 1728. It is in the Grecian style, with a square tower at the west end, surmounted by a cupola and four urns, one at each angle; and is historically interesting as being in all probability the last of the works of Sir Christopher Wren, which eminent architect, although he gave the plans for the church, never saw it finished, dying in 1723, in his ninety-second year.

It should here be mentioned that Wren was a friend of Dr. Busby, the famous schoolmaster of Westminster, who lived at Willen, and left an estate in Stoke Goldington for a charity.

Dr. Busby has always been represented by trustees from that school.

The architecture of Wrighte's Church everywhere expresses the Protestant feeling of Queen Anne's reign : the greater part exhibits striking simplicity, the only symbol in the church being the seven candlesticks above the reredos, indicating the Spirit's presence; and the cornice near the roof is decorated with bishops' mitres and open Bibles, indicating strongly the devotion of the family to the Protestant succession. The church, which is pewed with oak, is divided into four compartments; in the compartment at the south-east, which consists of one pew only, appropriated to the owner of the estate, is the indescribably beautiful monument in white marble of Sir Nathan and George Wrighte, each in an enormous Parian wig. There is no inscription; but this is explained by the fact that both father and son died before the completion of the church.

XVII

SIR EVERARD DIGBY AND THE GUNPOWDER PLOT.

WITHIN a few miles of Olney are several localities replete with memories of that famous conspiracy generally known as the Gunpowder Plot. At Turvey, four miles to the east, dwelt Lord Mordaunt, who, though probably innocent, was heavily fined for supposed complicity in it, and at whose mansion, Turvey Old Hall, Keyes, one of the conspirators, was a frequent visitor. Hardmead, four miles to the south-east, was one of the seats of the Catesbys; at Weston Underwood resided the Throckmortons (a family allied by marriage with the Catesbys and Treshams), at whose different mansions the conspirators frequently met; but the chief interest centres itself at Gayhurst, the principal residence of the gentle, gifted, misguided, and unhappy Sir Everard Digby.

Everard Digby was born in 1581 at his father's mansion of Drystoke in Rutlandshire; and, having been left a ward of the crown at an early age by the death of his father, had in consequence been educated in the Protestant faith. In 1596, when only about sixteen, he married Mary, daughter of Thomas Mulso, heiress of the magnificent estate of Gotehurst. Although greatly favoured by Queen Elizabeth, and seemingly on the road to high honours and distinction, for he was accounted one of the handsomest, most accomplished, and best informed men of his time, Digby retired at the age of twenty-one to Gayhurst, where he was converted to the ancient faith by the celebrated Garnet, the Provincial of the English Jesuits, a man who thenceforward exercised the greatest influence over him. In 1603 he was knighted at Belvoir Towers by King James I., who was journeying southward to take possession of the throne of England; and the same year was born his eldest son, afterwards the celebrated Sir Kenelm. After James had been on

the throne a short time, notwithstanding his previous fair promises, all the old and severe laws were enforced against the
Catholics, and in consequence many persons who previously
had been merely religious dissidents were converted into
political traitors. Sir Everard, who was of a mild and amiable
temper, was greatly touched at the sufferings of his co-
religionists, and deeply concerned at the fallen state of the
Catholic religion, upon the restoration of which his whole
thoughts were bent; but, for all that, it was with greatest difficulty he could be induced to join the Gunpowder Plot. The
main incidents of the conspiracy are familiar to almost every
one, but in these pages we shall tell the story more particularly
as it concerns Digby. The sufferings of the Roman Catholics
were terrible indeed. They were fined, imprisoned, mutilated,
many had been executed as recusants, and the persecution
increased rather than diminished. This treatment, together
with the double-dealing and deceit of King James, drove many
of them, who would otherwise have been peaceful subjects,
into the hands of the Jesuits and seminary priests, who for
some years previous had been travelling about the country
in disguise and intriguing against the Government. Bitter,
however, as was the persecution, the great body of the Catholics " chose rather to suffer in silence and hope for better days "
than to rise in rebellion. The originator of the plot, Robert
Catesby of Catesby Hall, Ashby St. Leger, near Daventry, a
brave though wild and dissolute man, had been engaged in
most of the plots against Elizabeth. He was at this time
about forty years of age. The idea of gunpowder being suggested to his mind he first unfolded his plans to his friend
Thomas Winter, who, though at first shocked at the idea, finally
fell in with it, and furthermore procured on the Continent the
services of Guy Fawkes.

The next to join the plot was John Wright, reckoned the
best swordsman of the day, who, unlike most of the other conspirators, seems never to have been troubled with any compunctions about the matter. These three, Catesby, Wright,
and Winter were the arch-traitors. In the words of Fawkes,
they " first devised the plot and were the chief directors of all

the particularities of it." It is a question, it must be observed, who was admitted first, Wright or Winter. The fifth conspirator was Thomas Percy. All five having previously sworn each other to secrecy in a house near London, adjourned to an upper room, and received, in confirmation of their oath, the sacrament from the hand of the Jesuit missionary, Father Gerard, who is said not to have known what they proposed to do. They are believed to have held their meetings in the room over the gateway of the Gatehouse of Catesby Hall, which apartment is still pointed out as the " plot-room." A house contiguous to the Parliament House was now hired by Percy under the pretence of convenience, because his office of gentleman pensioner compelled him to reside in the vicinity of the Court ; the real reason why this house was chosen being the fact that its back wall leaned against one of the walls of the Parliament House, into the cellars of which the conspirators hoped to break through. On the other side of the Thames, at Lambeth, which was then a scattered village, they had another house in which they secretly stored wood and gunpowder. Then, having laid in a stock of things that would keep, such as hard-boiled eggs, dried meat, and pasties, they at once commenced with their crowbars and pickaxes.

On December 24 (1604), after about a fortnight of uninterrupted labour, they discovered that Parliament was prorogued from the 7th of February to the 3d of October ; and, in consequence, stopped work and separated. Before their next meeting the secret had been imparted to two others, Christopher Wright and Robert Winter. We will not linger over the difficulties encountered in the cellar through the influx of water, and the hardness and thickness of the wall they were endeavouring to pierce ; their terror at the sound of the bell tolling beneath the ground, and the rumbling over their heads ; or their great joy on finding that the rumbling noise came from a cellar which lay under the House of Lords. The mine was abandoned, the new cellar hired, and into it, under the cover of night, were conveyed the barrels of gunpowder that had been collected in the house at Lambeth. The gunpowder having been concealed under stones and billets of wood, the conspirators again separated, to meet in September, a few days before the opening of Parliament.

In the meantime the persecutions of the Catholics increased in severity ; their priests were hunted down, their houses ransacked, and the most unprovoked hostility was excited against them all over the country. All this, however, pleased rather than irritated Catesby, who "considered his victims as running blindly to their own destruction, and argued that the more the Catholics suffered, the more readily they would join his standard after the explosion." Four new accomplices were now added : Bates (Catesby's servant), Keyes, a gentleman of decayed fortunes, the melancholy and taciturn John Grant of Northbrook in Warwickshire, and Ambrose Rookwood of Coldham Hall, Suffolk. In September Sir Edmund Baynham, a gentleman of Gloucestershire, was admitted, and sent to Rome, not to reveal the plot, but to gain the favour of the Pope and his Court when the blow should be struck.

To the alarm of the conspirators it was now announced that the Parliament would again be prorogued from October to the 5th of November. And they had reason to be alarmed, for their resources had run low, and they were at their wits' end to know how to get more money. They perceived, too, that their chances of discovery would be considerably increased. It was this second prorogation that caused them to think of Francis Tresham and Sir Everard Digby, both, on account of their great wealth, being desirable as accomplices. The difficult task of persuading Digby was performed by Garnet, who first of all insidiously laid bare to him a plan for glorifying God and the Church; but it is said that he was not made aware of the plot itself until a secret meeting between them, in the dead of night, in Gotehurst Church, where, after inducing him to swear a solemn oath before the altar, Garnet unfolded, to the horror of his victim, the plans for the destruction of the nobility. Other meetings ensued, Garnet also put a Jesuitical book into his hands, and, by degrees, the misgivings of the unfortunate gentleman were silenced ; he suffered himself to be persuaded to contribute a sum of £1500, and undertook to bring together, about the time of the opening of Parliament, most of his Catholic friends, under the pretence of hunting on Dunmore Heath in Warwickshire. The conspirators were now fourteen in number, and each, with the exception of Bates, was a gentleman by birth and education. Sir Everard's motives for joining the plot were afterwards declared by himself at his trial. The first was "not ambition, or discontentment of estate, neither malice to any in Parliament, but the friendship and love he bore to Mr. Catesby, which prevailed so much, and was so powerful with him, as that for his sake he was ever contented and ready to hazard himself and his estate. The next was the cause of religion, which alone seeing it lay at the stake, he entered into a resolution to neglect in that behalf his estate, his life, his name, his memory, his posterity, and all worldly and earthly felicity whatsoever, though he did utterly extirpate and extinguish all other hopes for the restoring of the Catholic religion in England, and the third motive was that promises were broken with Catholics, and lastly they generally feared harder laws from this Parliament against recusants; and that it was supposed that it should be a præmunire only to be a Catholic."

Before, however, he would consent to the gunpowder policy Sir Everard wished to try milder plans, and among other expedients he and Tresham presented a memorial to Bancroft, the Archbishop of Canterbury. But the mission to Lambeth was of no avail—for the only rejoinder they could obtain from this "pretensed archbishop," as the Catholics called him, was "that the measures of Elizabeth which these gentlemen were pleased to deem severe, would be found mild in comparison with those which were soon to be passed and executed in earnest!"—a rejoinder no less cruel and impolitic than the similar one that Rehoboam of old made to his discontented subjects, and one which had like to have been followed by a far greater disaster.

By this time the plan of operations was completed: Guy Fawkes was to fire the mine; Percy, who as one of the gentlemen pensioners could enter the palace without suspicion, was to obtain possession of Prince Charles; Digby, Tresham, and Grant were to proceed to the house of Lord Harrington, near

Coventry, and possess themselves of the infant Princess Elizabeth.   Everything being now fully arranged, the conspirators
again separated: Rookwood departed for Clopton, Percy and
the two Wrights set out for Gotehurst ; the two Winters repaired
to their mansion of Huddington ; Fawkes and Catesby remained at White Webbs, a house in Enfield Chase, which had
of late been used for their meetings.   Keyes went to visit
Lord Mordaunt at Turvey Old Hall, a mansion that occupied
the site upon which Turvey Hall farm now stands.   The farm-
house is on the right of the railway going from Olney to Turvey,
and a short distance from " Woodside," which is on the opposite
side of the line.   It can be seen from the railway in passing.
There is nothing left to show what this old mansion was like ;
but the moat, the bowling-green, and the gardens are clearly
indicated by the configuration of the ground.   At White Webbs
some of the conspirators received an unexpected visit from
Tresham, and there was an embarrassment in his manner and
a visible effort at concealment that alarmed his associates.
He earnestly pleaded that warning should be given to Lord
Mounteagle, his brother-in-law, and in addition suggested
further delay.   These proposals confirmed the suspicions of
Catesby, but he thought it advisable to dissemble, especially as
several of the other conspirators had friends whom they desired
to save : Percy, for example, wished to warn his relative Northumberland, and Keyes his friend and patron, Lord Mordaunt.
The story of the delivery of the letter at Lord Mounteagle's
house by the tall man whose features the page could not
recognise in the dark is familiar to the reader.   It counselled
Lord Mounteagle to absent himself from Parliament.   " Though
there be no appearance of any stir," it ran, "yet I say they
shall receive a terrible blow this Parliament, and yet they shall
not see who hurts them."   The mysterious letter was laid by
his lordship before the Secretary of State.   Who wrote it cannot be ascertained.   Some consider it to have been written by
Mrs. Abbington, a lady to whom we shall again refer, but most
probably, and as the other conspirators believed, it was the
work of Tresham ; "at any rate there was evidently a secret
understanding between this miserable man and Lord Mount-

eagle. The facts of the case appear to be that no sooner had
Tresham given his consent to become a conspirator, than he
repented of it, and sought to break up the plot without betraying his associates, and his first expedients failing he wrote this
letter. taking care to inform them on the following evening that
it had been carried to the Secretary, in hope that the danger
of discovery would induce them to make use of the opportunity
to escape." [1] Although the conspirators were informed of the
delivery of the letter, they concluded from the fact that the
cellars had not been searched that it had led to no discovery.
They charged Tresham, however, with perfidy, and could they
have found proof of his treachery would certainly have killed
him ; but he repelled the charge, and satisfied them with his
asseverations. Meanwhile Sir Everard Digby had removed with
his family to Coughton Hall, the residence of Mr. Thomas
Throckmorton, in order to be in readiness for the grand hunting-
party to be held on the 5th of November on Dunmore Heath.
It was now the 30th of October, and Guy Fawkes engaged to
revisit the cellar every day till the 5th, in order to assure himself
that no search had been made. The next few days were a time
of great anxiety to the conspirators : it was thought by some
that the plot had been revealed, and these counselled flight, but
the counter-arguments of Percy prevailed : so they made new
arrangements, resolving to wait one day, and then come to a
final resolution. Towards evening the cellars of the house were
visited by the Lord Chamberlain, who merely made a few
casual remarks to Fawkes, asked one or two questions, and
then withdrew. " In spite of this warning Fawkes persisted in
the idea that the plot was not known, and a little after midnight
(the reader will observe that it was now the 5th of November)
again visited the vault ; but at the very moment he opened the
door he was seized by Sir Thomas Knevett and a party of
soldiers." On the removal of the fuel were discovered two
hogsheads and about thirty barrels of gunpowder. His associates, as soon as they heard of his apprehension, mounted their
horses, and on the same evening reached the hunting-party at
Dunmore, where, after a long conversation with Sir Everard

[1] Lingard.

Digby, they endeavoured, though unsuccessfully, to induce the guests to share their desperate fortunes. The conspirators, nevertheless, resolved to hold together and proceed to the houses of their friends in the neighbourhood, persuading themselves that the standard of rebellion being once raised all the Catholics of the adjacent counties would flock around them. After passing through Leamington Priors, where they supplied themselves with provisions at the first farmyard, they proceeded to Warwick, and there defeated a well-armed body of men under the Sheriff of Warwickshire, who was shot dead. But the inhabitants of Warwick beginning to assemble at the sound of the alarm-bell, the conspirators, desirous at present of avoiding an engagement, took to their horses again. They now rode off to Grant's house at Norbrook, whence they proceeded to Huddington in Worcestershire, the residence of Robert Winter. What with losses in fight and numerous desertions their numbers had seriously diminished, whilst they found to their bitter disappointment that the Roman Catholics, instead of rallying round them, held aloof, and would have nothing at all to do with the conspiracy. From Huddington they proceeded to Hewel Grange, near Stoke Prior, which they attacked, and having driven out Topcliffe, the pursuivant, and a determined body of men, possessed themselves of a great quantity of arms and provisions, and strengthened their numbers by about twenty recruits. Quitting Hewel Grange they marched towards Stourbridge, where they defeated a large body of men under Sir Richard Walsh, Sheriff of Worcestershire, and finally reached Holbeach, a large and strongly built mansion belonging to Stephen Littleton, a gentleman who had recently joined them. After the house had been put in a state of defence, Digby quitted them in the hope of getting succours. In crossing the Stour their powder got wetted, and whilst they were drying it a blazing coal shot from the fire, causing an explosion, and seriously injuring several of the conspirators. Still undaunted, however, they strengthened their defences, and awaited the attack of the enemy. A new misfortune was now announced. An engagement had taken place in a wood about five miles from thence between Sir Everard Digby and Sir Richard Walsh, and the former, unable to cope with superior numbers, had been taken prisoner. This destroyed Catesby's last hope, but he resolved to die sword in hand. Attacked on the following day by the troops under Walsh and Topcliffe, the conspirators after a short and furious fight were surrounded and completely beaten: Catesby, Percy, and the two Wrights were shot dead, the two former by the same bullet; all the others surrendered, and those who had previously deserted were captured a few days after. The trial did not take place until about two months after their apprehension, the Government being desirous, before taking further measures, of capturing the three Jesuits, Gerard, Garnet, and Greenway.

Gerard and Greenway escaped to the Continent, but Garnet was discovered on January 28 at Hendlip House. Mrs. Abbington, the wife of the owner of the mansion, the lady who some think wrote the mysterious letter, was sister to Lord Mounteagle, and had it not been for Lord Mounteagle's intercession Mr. Abbington would have been executed. At their trial the prisoners, although they pleaded not guilty to the whole of the indictment, acknowledged that they had entertained the design they were charged with, but denied that the Jesuits had been the authors of the conspiracy, or had ever held consultation with them on the subject: asserting that as far as had come to their knowledge all three were innocent.

Very bitter were the last few days of Sir Everard's life. The verses that he wrote in the Tower, entitled "Jesus Maria," brim over with grief. In these sad lines he speaks of the knocking he seems to hear, and the call which he knows, and has known ever since it made him know himself. "O stay," he cries, "my Lord, I come—

> "Come in, my Lord, whose presence most I crave,
>   And show Thy will unto my longing mind;
> From punishment of sin thy servant save,
>   Though he hath been to thy deserts unkind."

And what punishment did he wish to avert? Was it the gallows and death? No: he was tortured with a greater sorrow than these. He was thinking of his innocent and beautiful wife at Gayhurst, of his young children, and the other members of his family, who he feared would suffer on account of his crime.

> " But to undo desert and innocence
> Is to my mind grief's chiefest pestilence."

The poems and letters sent furtively by Sir Everard from the Tower were discovered by accident some seventy years after his death. The executors for the estate, who were about to sell it, having inquired for writings to make out the titles, were directed by an old servant to a secret cupboard, in which some papers lay hid that she had observed Sir Kenelm used often to read. They were laid together in a velvet bag, but proved to be not title-deeds, but the original letters and poems of Sir Everard, written with juice of lemon.

When sentence of death was passed upon him he seemed much affected, and, making a low bow to those on the bench, he said : " If I could hear any of your Lordships say you forgive me, I should go more cheerfully to the gallows." Whereupon the Lords answered : " God forgive you, and we do."

After acknowledging his guilt, he petitioned " That since the offence was confined and contained within himself, the punishment might extend only to himself, and not be transferred to his wife, children, sisters, or others; and therefore he humbly craved that his wife might enjoy her jointure ; his son the benefit of the entail made long before this action was thought of ; his sisters their just and due portions which were in his hands ; his creditors their rightful debts. . . . For himself he had only one petition, he entreated to be beheaded, desiring all men to forgive him ; and that his death might satisfy them for his trespass." [1] His request that his punishment might be commuted to beheading was disregarded, but the other parts of his petition seem to have been attended to.

Four of the prisoners, Sir Everard Digby, Robert Winter, Grant, and Bates were executed on Thursday, January 30, at the West End of St. Paul's in London ; and the other four, Rookwood, Thomas Winter, Keyes, and Guy Fawkes, the next day, in the Old Palace Yard at Westminster.

[1] Jardine.

Sir Everard was the first to receive the fatal summons. Mounting the scaffold with a firm step, his youth (for he was only twenty-six), his noble aspect, and undaunted demeanour, awakened—as they had done throughout the trial—the sympathy of the beholders. Looking round, he thus addressed the assemblage: "Good people, I am here about to die, ye well know for what cause. Throughout the matter I have acted according to the dictates of my conscience. They have led me to undertake this enterprise, which in respect to my religion I hold to be no offence, but in respect of the law a heinous offence, and I therefore ask forgiveness of God, of the king, and of the whole realm."

Crossing himself devoutly he then knelt down, and repeated his prayers in Latin; after which he arose, and again looking round, said in an earnest voice—"I desire the prayers of all good Catholics and none other."

Stephen Littleton was executed at Worcester. Garnet's execution was deferred till May 3, when it took place in St. Paul's Churchyard. The fate of Tresham, who was not apprehended until November 12, is shrouded in mystery. He died in the Tower on the 23rd of December, and it is generally thought he was poisoned.

Notwithstanding the revelations that had taken place, King James still believed that many ramifications of the plot had not yet been discovered, and in consequence, on no other ground than that of mere suspicion, severely punished several other gentlemen. The Earl of Northumberland, chiefly on account of the crime of being related to Percy, was fined £30,000, and ordered to be imprisoned for life; whilst Lord Mordaunt, and others, although they appear to have been entirely innocent, were condemned to fines of £10,000, and imprisonment during royal pleasure.

According to Lipscomb, in one of the apartments at Gayhurst "was formerly shown a movable floor, which to ordinary observers offered nothing remarkable in its appearance, but was made to revolve on a pivot, which, by a secret bolt, disclosed underneath it another room (receiving light from the lower part of a mullioned window, not discoverable

exteriorly unless at a very great distance), in which the conspirators were said to have holden their meetings." That
some of the conspirators held meetings in this room, which
for many years was called "Digby's Hole," is very possible ;
but the tradition that it was the hiding-place of Sir Everard is
utterly without foundation, for the north wing, in which was
this room, at the time of the conspiracy had been built only a
few years, and no one would dream of hiding in a place
almost fresh from the architect's hands, every cranny of which
must have been well known ; neither is it likely that he hid in
any other part of the house, for previous to the panic at
Dunmore he had no occasion to hide, and after the panic he
fled with the other conspirators to Holbeach.   It is possible,
however, that Garnet found shelter at Gayhurst during part of
the two months he was dodging about the midland counties
after Sir Everard's apprehension ; but if so his hiding-place
must have been one of those in the south wing, or oldest
portion of the mansion.

If the tradition is true which Lipscomb quotes that the
conspirators met in " Digby's Hole," their reason for choosing
this place would be the desire to conceal their affairs not
so much from their enemies as from their friends ; for they
wished all knowledge of the plot to be kept from Digby's
wife and family.   And so closely, it should be observed, was
Sir Everard's secret kept that the discovery of the plot was
the first intimation that Lady Digby had of its existence.

Sir Kenelm Digby, the celebrated son of Sir Everard, and
author of the well-known " Private Memoirs " (written to please
his beautiful wife Lady Anastasia), and other works, also spent
most of his life at Gayhurst.

XVIII

CLIFTON REYNES.

ON the brow of Clifton Hill, in the time of Cowper, stood three structures of interest—the Church, the Rectory, and the Hall ; but the last, called also the Manor House, the "Mr. Small's house" of Cowper's letters, has now quite disappeared.

Clifton Hall was a large, square, and strongly built mansion of stone, with a large porch at the front that faced the river. It was of no great antiquity, having been built by Alexander Small, Esq., about 1750 (his bust in a large wig by Scheemaker can be seen in the church), but it stood doubtless on or near the site of the ancient castellated mansion of the Borards and Reyneses, lords of Clifton, whose effigies lie in the church.

The mansion built by Mr. Small stood at a distance of about eighty yards to the north-west of the church : the fishpond, the orchard, a portion of the avenue, and the wall round the garden still remain, and as the gate between the Hall garden and the churchyard was removed only recently, its position is indicated by the new appearance of the added portion of the wall.

The only appurtenance to Clifton Hall now standing is the remarkable circular dove-house, built of local cornbrash, which stands in the middle of the village. Its circumference at the base is 63 feet. The other ancient dove-house of the parish, that of the Wake Manor, which was square in plan, has disappeared.

The Rectory is a building of considerable antiquity, portions of it being about 300 years old. In a terrier (Nov. 11, 1639) of Thomas Webb (a rector who, by the bye, is said to have been suspended for sheep-stealing) it is described as "The Parsonage, consisting of five bays, built of stone, and covered with thatch."

It is an interesting fact that the next rector to Mr. Webb

was named Samuel Pepys, and that he died in 1703, the same
year that his namesake (possibly his cousin), Samuel Pepys, the
celebrated diarist, died. The Rev. Samuel Pepys was instituted
July 23, 1661, on the King's presentation by lapse, the living
having remained vacant since the death of Mr. Webb. He

THE DOVEHOUSE, CLIFTON REYNES.
(*It now belongs to the author.*)

was buried in Clifton Chancel, April 15, 1703. Pepys the
diarist died in May, and was buried in Crutched Friars Church,
London. The chief interest of Clifton Rectory arises from its
having been for some time the residence of Lady Austen, of

her sister, and her sister's husband, the Rev. Thomas Jones; and the frequent resort of the poet Cowper during the earlier period of his residence in Olney. The chief attraction for Cowper at Clifton was of course Lady Austen, who first came there in the summer of 1781; but long before that date Cowper had been intimate with Mr. and Mrs. Jones, with whom he had doubtless become acquainted through their common friend, the Rev. John Newton. Mr. Jones was one of the six students who on March 11, 1768, had been expelled from St. Edmund's Hall for holding Methodistical tenets. It was in vain that the principal of the college, Mr. Dixon, had defended their doctrines from the Thirty-nine Articles of the Established Church, and spoke in the highest terms of the piety and exemplariness of their lives; his motion was overruled, and sentence was pronounced against them. It was a matter of accusation, too, against all six students, that they had previously been tradesmen, and Mr. Jones, who had originally been in business as a hairdresser, was charged with the heinous offence of having made "a good periwig" only two years before. As a matter of fact, however, Mr. Jones had left business four years before he entered the University, part of which time he had spent in studying the Greek and Hebrew Scriptures under Newton. After their expulsion Mr. Dixon recommended the students to Lady Huntingdon, who obtained ordination for Mr. Jones, and befriended him on many occasions. He was curate at Clifton from about 1772 to 1792 (the rector, a pluralist, lived elsewhere), and was married to Martha Green, the sister of Lady Austen, on the 15th of May 1778, at Clifton Church, by John Newton. Mr. Jones was Martha Green's second husband; her maiden name and that of Lady Austen was Richardson. Five of the letters in Newton's Cardiphonia are addressed to Mr. Jones.

Clifton Church is an exceedingly picturesque little edifice, and by reason of its elevated site may be seen for miles around rising from the masses of the surrounding trees. It is mostly of the Early Decorated style of architecture, but some portions are Perpendicular.

Above the chancel arch a portion of ancient fresco painting

is still dimly discernible. At the beginning of the last century the windows were profusely ornamented with the coats-of-arms of the family of Reynes and their alliances, in stained glass, but all have disappeared except a few fragments in one of the clerestory windows.

Two years ago the church was restored with great judgment and taste. The ugly plaster ceiling of the chancel gave place to a handsome oak roof, which is covered with lead and surrounded by a stone parapet agreeing with the parapet of the aisles of the nave; and a stained-glass window representing in rich colours " The Three Maries," the gift of T. Revis, Esq., took the place of its plain predecessor. The hagioscope in the wall southward of the chancel arch, the small window above the chancel arch, and the leper window in the south wall of the chancel, all of which had formerly been blocked up, were opened out.

The easternmost part of the south aisle, which has a piscina (there is another piscina in the chancel), was probably in ancient times a chapel or chantry railed off from the rest of the church.

In the north aisle of the chancel, or sepulchral chapel of the ancient lords of Clifton, which opens into the chancel by two pointed arches of the Decorated Period, are six effigies and three memorial brasses, the former forming by far the most interesting group of sculptured monuments in the county. It appears that as early as the Saxon period there were two separate manors at Clifton. At the Conquest the principal one (afterwards called Reynes's Manor, was given to Robert de Todeni; the other, afterwards called Wake's Manor (because it subsequently came into possession of the Wake family) to the Bishop of Constance. "The Reynes's Manor," after being for many years in the family of Todeni, passed, in the reign of Henry III., into the hands of Simon de Borard, who had formerly been their feudatory tenant. The last Simon de Borard (for there were four persons of the same name in regular descent) died about 1260. It was in all probability this person and his wife Margaret that the most ancient monument in the sepulchral chapel was designed to commemorate.

Sir Simon left, besides three sons, a daughter named Joan, who married Thomas Reynes of Statherne, Co. Leicester. The sons were successively lords of Clifton; each died without issue, and the youngest conveyed his lands to his nephew, Thomas Reynes, the son of his sister Joan.

At his death Thomas Reynes was succeeded by his son Ralph, who died about 1310.

Ralph de Reynes married twice—first, Amabel, daughter of Sir Henry Green of Boughton; and next, another Amabel, daughter of Sir Richard Chamberlain of Petsoe Manor. To Ralph de Reynes and his second wife is assigned the second monument in the chapel.

Thomas, the son of Ralph de Reynes, a minor, married the daughter of his guardian Sir John de Tyringham, and probably before his father's tomb was completed, for the arms of Tyringham are found upon it. Sir John de Reynes, the grandson of this Thomas Reynes, married three wives—1. Catherine Scudamore; 2. Joane Betler; 3. Alice Hartwell.

He died in 1428, and was buried in the sepulchral chapel at Clifton, where his effigy in brass yet remains; he is represented in the armour of the time in which he lived, and at his feet is a brass on which is inscribed:

> Hic iacet Johēs Reynes Miles qui obiit xxv' die Marcii Anno
> dni Millimo ccccº xxviii' cuius aïe ppicietur deus.   Amen.

On a large marble slab next to that to which Sir John's brass is affixed are two brasses of women in shrouds, supposed to represent his wives, Joane Betler and Alice Hartwell. To this same Sir John, and his first wife, Catherine Scudamore, must be assigned the third monument, which consists of an altar tomb, on which rests the effigies of a man and woman in white stone —not alabaster as usually stated. It was erected probably by himself, in his lifetime, and soon after her death; for many of the arms on this tomb are the armorial bearings which she quartered, and which no other person of the family of Reynes, except this John, could with propriety have affixed to his tomb.

APPENDIX.

(1.) *Chicheley Hall* (the residence of the Chesters), which Cowper sometimes visited, is a handsome mansion of red brick with stone dressings, situated about four miles south-east of Olney. It was erected in 1715. One of its rooms is wainscoted with oak panelling of a date antecedent to the rest of the house, and over the fireplace is a beam, on which is the following inscription :—" Cave ne Deum offendas, cave ne proximum lœdas, cave ne tua negligentia familiam deseras, 1550."

(2.) At *Horton House*, about five miles from Olney, was born, in 1661, Charles Montague, first Earl of Halifax, author of "The Country Mouse and the City Mouse."

At *Easton Maudit*, about six miles from Olney, resided for many years (1753–1782) Dr. Percy, and it was from Easton Maudit Vicarage that his famous "Reliques of Ancient Poetry" was given to the world.

At *Yardley Hastings*, Edward Lye, who was for thirty years rector of the parish, compiled his great work, the Anglo-Saxon and Gothic Dictionary. He died in 1767.

At *Turvey* laboured the Rev. Legh Richmond (author of "The Dairyman's Daughter"), who was rector of the parish from 1805 till his death in 1827.

(3.) *Cooper or Cowper?*—How ought the poet's name to be pronounced? As Cowper himself pronounced it, decidedly. How did he pronounce it? The answer is as simple as the question : we are told by the Rev. William Bull, Cowper's friend, that the poet pronounced his name *Cooper*. It was actually *spelt* Cooper by the Rev. John Newton in several of his first letters to Huntingdon. This is an additional proof, for it is evident that Mr. Newton was misled by the pronunciation.

INDEX.

www.ingramcontent.com/pod-product-compliance
Lightning Source LLC
Chambersburg PA
CBHW030805020726
47499CB00006B/1779